To PHIL —

GOOD TO MEET YOU AT
LAKESIDE...

ENJOY THE BOOK!

MARC JOENZ

The Terminal's Redemption

Marc Joenz

ISBN: 978-1-4834-0183-6 (sc)
ISBN: 978-1-4834-0185-0 (hc)
ISBN: 978-1-4834-0184-3 (e)

Library of Congress Control Number: 2013914563

Lulu Publishing Services rev. date: 9/30/2013

I dedicate this book to my beautiful muse, which, without your siren song beckoning, would not have been possible.

Foreword

Watching the news on TV, browsing the Internet, or scanning the tabloid headlines in the supermarket checkout aisle provide ample fodder for works of fiction.

The use of real situations, people, or places to add credibility or relevance to a plot is frequently desired, occasionally unavoidable. There are several such elements mentioned in the following pages, however, the events contained within are purely fictional.

Remember, reality is often stranger than fiction.

Distant Shore

Alone I gaze from a distant shore.
But will I stand alone no more?

Another shore, waits ghostly silent for me;
white capped waters, and bristling trees.

Wind swept surf, beckons my soul;
for unfilled love, my heart does toll.

Will I find myself, on far flung misty sand;
no angst of heart, with intact pride of man?

Will the silvery mist, yet unfold;
reveal new hopes, not yet told?

Recurring dreams, no nightmares have I,
of not reaching that shore; heavily, I sigh.

These horrific nightmares that I share;
of rock tossed visions, my heart does tear.

I feel the aberrations, coming true,
my spirit becoming darkly blue.

With ravaged mind, and body aches;
the journey there, so long can take.

Uncertainty, doubt, my mind does race;
that never again will I caress her face.

And wicked time, it doesn't creep;
engulfing souls, in forever sleep.

But 'til then my mind's eye will soar;
to be upon, that distant shore.

Prologue

"Halloran and Associates."

"Michael Halloran, please."

"May I tell him who's calling?"

"Samuel Tagaki from UCLA. It's urgent."

"One moment please."

"Hi, Boss. Sorry to bother you, but a Samuel Tagaki from UCLA is on the line. Says it's urgent."

Michael was reviewing the scale model of the museum's new annex—getting it ready for the opening ceremony that evening and didn't want to be interrupted. This had better be urgent. He didn't have time for any distractions.

"Thank you, I'll take it."

Michael knew about Sammy, and was curious to know why Keith's friend was calling. He pressed the line button.

"Michael Halloran here. What can I do for you Mr. Tagaki? Keith told me quite a lot about you."

Sammy responded formally, in kind.

"Mr. Halloran. Keith shared a lot about you as well. He told me all about his plan with you, Rita, and the ring. Which is why I'm calling. I promised Keith I would make sure the ring was given to Rita. Keith told me you already had it in your possession. Is that true?"

"Actually, it's at my jewelers being modified. I thought the ring by itself was too...conspicuous. Someone somewhere might recognize it, and then our whole charade would be exposed. So, I decided to have it disassembled, by a professional of course, and the components designed as parts of an ensemble, then give it to her a piece at a time. I'm not poor, but I could never afford to purchase the whole ensemble at once. Rita would pick up some weird vibe. I know she would. Keith agreed."

"That's a good plan…but I've got bad news."

"What bad news?"

"The reason I'm calling is I received a call from the Spanish government. It seems that they're going to exhibit the contents of the treasure chest we found on that sunken Spanish galleon. They told me that during their inventory of the chest's contents, the Queen's ring, the piece of jewelry currently in *your* possession, turned up missing. They concluded that the ring must have been stolen. They were all in a tither but I explained to them that the ring was the one item we, S and K Enterprises, decided to maintain possession of. We explicitly stated this in our press release all those years ago. They didn't like that response. They're actually pretty pissed off despite the fact that we had graciously returned the bulk of the treasure to Spain as a gesture of goodwill. Even though legally they don't have a say in the matter, they've already reported it as stolen to their insurance company, and now they need verify its existence. Some sort of bureaucratic snafu"

"That is bad news. Any idea how soon they need to see it?"

"They'll be here in California next week."

1

The Beginning of the End

His perception of reality was still somewhat blurred. The visions rendered his perception of reality into a disjointed blur. He blamed this on the combination of chemotherapy treatments and painkillers. The effects of all those chemicals had caused his life to become ethereal—out-of-body—a twisted separation of physical certainty and the irrational juxtapositions in his head. Throughout the day, he had the sensation he was on the outside looking in, as if he was watching a movie, with him and everyone around him as the characters.

"Shakespeare got it right," he mused. "'All the world's a stage'."

At night, dreams straight from a Bosch painting clouded his visions, fitfully creating a state of horrific ether—somewhere in the micro-fine gap connecting lucidity and fantasy.

The scars on his face were wretched testament to his surgeon's knife. While quite adept with state-of-the-art technologies, his surgeon simply could not repair his countenance without it looking ghastly—cartoonish. To rid him of the scourge devouring his body, his cheeks were deformed into a horrible grimace. His new look: Black Dahlia. His surgeon was naturally reluctant to perform these procedures on him—the results were disturbing, humiliating, and permanent. He concluded that additional surgeries would be feckless gesture.

After formal greetings and a motion for him to sit in a huge, overstuffed, maroon, leather, wingback chair, Ezekiel, 'Zeke', Tarkanian, Keith's psychiatrist, spoke gently, calmly, and with measure. "I've read your file Dr. Vintner, and if you don't mind me cutting to the chase...bad choice of words....getting to the point...damn. What I mean to say is that I want to find out what's going on inside that head of yours. Your physicians are taking care of the remedial aspects of your condition. My job is to help your psyche. If I'm going to help you...and I do want to help...*you* need to help *me*."

Zeke had read the file on his newest patient, Dr. Keith Anthony Vintner, twice: entrepreneur, treasure hunter, engineering visionary, intellectual eco-geek with a meteoric career. Dr. Vintner *had* led an incredibly full life that was now unexpectedly being cut short.

Zeke was very concerned about Keith's mental health. Aware of his patient's initial reluctance to seek psychiatric assistance as he struggled—physically and emotionally—to survive.

"Start from anywhere," Zeke suggested. "Recent events, your childhood, anytime...but Keith, we need to start peeling back the layers."

Zeke paused and then continued. "You're a smart guy. You know why I'm asking you what makes you tick."

Keith indeed knew the score—*why* he was there. He had experienced a severe psychological breakdown after enduring the vigorous chemotherapy treatments—heavy doses of the latest clinically trialed drugs. He had had a severe reaction with one of the known possible side effects—his doctor's called it an 'oops' reaction. 'Cracking up' is what Keith called it—a feeble attempt at humor to make the situation less traumatic than it was. According to his doctors, the cocktail of miracle drugs that he violently reacted to was his last hope for survival.

As part of Keith's recovery process, his doctors insisted he regularly see a psychiatrist to monitor his mental state, while he tried to cope with the side effects of his chemically induced mental malaise. And the fact that he would soon be dead.

Keith finally agreed to his physicians' demands. Even though he was strong, he realized he couldn't get through this ordeal without professional assistance.

So there he sat. His aching legs gingerly draped over one of the large wings of the leather chair, resting his weary frame, dreading this act of disclosure, even to someone who was ethically bound to silence and came as highly regarded as Dr. Tarkanian.

A background check on Dr. Tarkanian wasn't necessary, since one of Keith's good friends, as well as one of his physicians, made a recommendation.

Keith noticed the decor of Zeke's elegant office. A hodgepodge of international figurines, masks, books, and paraphernalia—representing all seven continents—lined the mahogany shelves. They were clearly not some knock-offs purchased from the local import boutique. Keith had seen enough of the real artifacts during his own travels to know the difference.

"Nice office. Although the wall festooned with diplomas is a bit much," Keith thought. Keith guessed it must be comforting for some of the doctor's patients to see that he was well schooled *and* well traveled. And this *was* Malibu, so he concluded that it made perfect sense.

He thought he might as well make the best of things, so he settled in and gathered his thoughts. Whichever way he looked at it, it wasn't going to be easy or enjoyable.

"We might as well get this started," he stated, suddenly. "Pre-incident...or post?" Keith asked. He wanted to make Zeke's job as easy as possible. Didn't want to bore him with unnecessary details.

"Any time, really," Zeke empathetically replied. "I can glean some information from your background as we go along. I'll ask you questions if necessary to help me fill in the blanks. If you prefer, we can certainly start out by talking about what's happened to you recently." He looked over the top of his glasses and added, "You've been through a lot."

"I know I need to help you...help me," Keith said. "When you net it out, the copious amounts of medical input from my doctors doesn't say much about my mental health, does it?" he asked.

Zeke didn't give him an answer. He patiently waited for the floodgates to open.

Keith shifted in the big comfortable chair, sifting through memories, trying to determine exactly what to say and where to start.

"Well, Doc," Keith began, resolve intact, "since we've only got fifty minutes." He glanced at his Rolex Mariner. "Make that forty-seven. I'll have to give you the condensed version for starters."

Keith's face broke into what Zeke supposed was a smile. A dollop of drool began to slide from the corner of Keith's mouth, down his scarred, transplanted jowl, toward what would normally be considered a chin. Zeke wasn't sure if Keith couldn't feel the drool's decent or if he just didn't care about it. Keith did nothing to stop the cascading spittle from falling to his chest.

"We may not get through everything today," Keith finally said. "But I'll give it a shot. You caught me at a good moment. I'm lucid and, uh, in a cooperative mood. Get your pen ready. Here comes the life story of Keith Anthony Vintner."

—>◦<—

Any person would, at the very least, be a *little* jealous of Keith's early life, which was a flamboyant journey full of twists and turns and a great deal of fame and fortune. The archetypal everyman's man: intelligent, diligent, resilient, affable, stable, charismatic, and ecologically- and community-minded.

Keith graduated at the top of his class at California Polytechnic University at San Luis Obispo, with bachelor degrees in Marine Sciences and Mechanical Engineering. Then he continued his educational endeavors with a Masters in Mechanical Engineering at USC, while he worked full-time to pay for his tuition.

When he finished at the top of his class at the University of Southern California, they offered him a full scholarship to obtain a Masters, then Doctorate, in Marine Environmental Biology.

4

Always on the go, he was an extreme overachiever—a 'type A' personality on steroids. Keith's hard work, perseverance, and resolve paid off—he graduated Summa Cum Laude from USC. Afterward, the Scripps Institute in San Diego, where he had interned during college, offered him a job.

During his time at Scripps—nurtured by some of the finest minds on the planet—he realized that he had an intense interest for, and understanding of, the theoretical and practical applications used by public aquariums and theme-park water attractions.

Keith applied his knowledge of the ocean and its inhabitants, along with crude yet brilliant engineering prowess, and developed some particularly innovative designs that transformed the marine entertainment industry. There *were* other enormous aquarium and wave-machine designs—but none like his.

Keith masterfully drafted a business plan for a new division for Scripps, similar to the model used by MBARI, the Monterey Bay Area Research Institute, in Moss Landing, California. MBARI had a separate division that consulted with international companies to solve *their* business needs.

Keith spent a great deal of time researching the secretion of barnacles that binds them to the hulls of ships, reefs, or piers. These secretions are remarkably stable and impervious to, among other things, incredible amounts of environmental abuse, and can withstand thousands of pounds of pressure and retain their powerful adhesive properties. Nature's super glue. That type of adhesive strength and durability changed the world in innumerable ways. The patent on that technology was literally invaluable.

Keith proposed many of his revolutionary concepts to the appropriate channels at Scripps and was rewarded with a position developing commercial applications of his concepts for public aquariums, water theme parks, as well as for other research institutions.

Keith set out to prove that thriving reefs could be *created*. Tides and natural currents could be designed to replicate nature herself. He envisioned perfectly formed waves and beaches built in

San Antonio, Texas that could rival any Hawaiian shoreline. The only thing missing would be the trade winds. Keith felt that, given enough time, even those could be replicated.

———⟫●⟪———

Keith's unique concepts were cutting-edge, but technically and economically feasible. His common sense approach to copycatting nature quickly transformed into big money—but not for him. After all, he was a Scripps associate, so all his concepts and related patents belonged to them.

For obvious reasons, Scripps couldn't have been more pleased with his success.

———⟫●⟪———

Globetrotting with his best friend Samuel—'Sammy'—Tagaki was a big part of Keith's life. After graduation, the duo spent a great deal of time treasure hunting and filming nature documentaries around the world.

Keith and Sammy's initial exploration was funded by Sammy's father, 'Pop', who had made his money the hard way—running a multi-national electronics business he had started in his garage. Wozniak and Jobs weren't the only ones who achieved enormous success back in those days.

Pop Tagaki thought the two young men were 'chasing windmills' crazy, but believed enough in them to fund their 'hair-brained scheme'.

Keith and Sammy's maiden exploration was to search for—and maybe find—a ship that was *allegedly* lost off the Azorean coast, *allegedly* filled with a king's treasure. They also intended to record—without protective cages—the mating habits of hammerhead sharks that they knew would be there, just in case the treasure didn't show up.

The venture ended up paying off in a big way.

Compensated for his investment—and his elevated blood pressure—with fifty percent of the take, netting him $400,000,000, Pop was happy.

Sammy and Keith quickly adapted to fame and fortune—the two amigos scoured the seven seas in search of aquatic creatures and pirates' plunder or kings' riches from sunken ships. Sammy was the chief cameraman and Keith led the expeditions. They were a formidable team. Sammy received several Academy Awards for his documentaries.

After a handful of their 'hair-brained schemes', they both had nearly a billion dollars in their bank accounts.

Along with his intellect, Keith's self-deprecating charm brought him swift industry- and social-recognition. Over the years, his weathered countenance had graced the covers of renowned publications: National Geographic, People, Popular Mechanics, Scientific American, Time, Newsweek. His treasure-hunting escapades as well as his astonishing aquatic designs garnered fevered interest by the media.

Raised in a middle-class, cost-conscious household, Keith learned frugality early on, and like everything he undertook, he enthusiastically applied the concepts of money management: investing his money wisely, foregoing wasteful spending, significantly increasing his net-worth. His off-the-grid home—paid in full with cash—was modest by the standards of his egregiously wealthy neighbors in the chic coastal town of Malibu Beach, California.

Keith's house was located in an isolated, pristine location— the natural curves of the landscape and the dense foliage of its surroundings shielded the house from the prying eyes of his neighbors. The house had breathtaking views from every room, and an infinity pool that overlooked the Pacific Ocean. It was Keith's private paradise.

Keith's six-feet, two-inch, one-hundred and eighty pound athletic frame—bronzed since youth—caught the eye of every woman in Malibu. His dishwater blonde hair, bleached from constant exposure to the sun, added to his rugged west-coast looks. Growing up in Malibu, he had easy access to the Golden State's wealth of outdoor recreation. Ocean, streams, lakes, mountains, coast, and desert, were his playgrounds.

Like the rest of his siblings, Keith had gladly 'suffered' the mandates of his parents. All the Vintner children, regardless of gender, were regularly exposed to the splendors of the great outdoors. Keith's parents, Ralph and Wanda, were second-generation California natives and were well aware of the massive population growth in California. They wanted their offspring to experience the natural wonders of the state's vast array of climates, terrains, flora, and fauna—all within a few hours' drive from their home—before it was all gone.

Family camping trips were routine in Keith's youth. Watching the Vintner brood preparing for a camping trip was not unlike watching a well-seasoned circus troupe. It was at least as colorful. Each family member was assigned a designated task: loading the truck, packing the camping and fishing gear, filling the coolers with food and beverages, grabbing the dog, leash, dog food and bowls.

The final act of departure: corralling everyone, each child and creature, into the car and in their assigned location. 'All systems go', the vehicle loaded with every known, or needed, camping item, was a truly a remarkable sight. An outsider might get the impression they were embarking on a month-long excursion, not merely a weekend jaunt into the Sierra Nevadas.

About the time Ralph and Wanda's offspring were entering puberty, Fred, Ralph's older brother, gave Ralph his 'old' fishing boat as a present. Fred had recently purchased a larger boat on which he and his wife Emily planned to retire. Fred and Emily emptied their bank accounts, rented their home, sold some technology stocks, and set off for open seas. Fred loved his little brother's family as if it was his own, and he couldn't think of a better home for the 'old hull'. Besides, Fred figured he would need access to a smaller fishing boat from time to time and he might as well keep it in the family. That was the justification he gave Emily. When Emily heard Fred's rationalization, she smiled knowingly, stood on the tip of her toes, and gave Fred a warm kiss. "That's the thing I love about you sweetheart, big and masculine on the outside, soft and squishy on the inside," she whispered.

'Big' Fred—six-foot, four-inches two-hundred and fifty pounds—and his very lovely, petite wife, did not have children of their own, and Ralph and Wanda's family, extended, incorporated, or whatever one called it, filled the void nicely. Fred and Emily had often taken Ralph and Wanda's kids out and about the countryside, giving the younger couple a little alone-time now and then without the kids hanging on their shirttails. For this, Ralph and Wanda were eternally grateful.

Ralph was flabbergasted, completely taken off guard at his brother's generosity. This offering—the boat—was more than a little over the top. Fred's' old hull' was pristine—with all of the amenities. It was perfect for his blossoming family. It would be ideal for the kids to learn the ways of the water, learn to ski, and to generally just blow off some steam. Ralph and Wanda's children were overwhelmed with joy—they had a new toy!

Keith, more so than the other Vintner children, took to outdoor sports with his characteristic zeal. Hiking, backpacking, snow skiing and snowboarding, he truly loved, but it was water sports—swimming, surfing, and scuba diving—that really got his adrenaline pumping. *This* was California. The good life. Diverse, abundant, scenic. It could be enjoyed twelve months a year. Once Keith's mobility had escalated to four wheels, on weekends he would drive to Big Bear or Mammoth for snow skiing/boarding on Saturdays. On Sundays, with permission to use the boat, he would visit Lake Casitas for water skiing or take a group of divers out to Catalina Island. The perfect weekend only California could provide.

Keith's involvement in community service started at a young age. Ralph and Wanda had insisted that their kids get involved in some form of community service. It didn't matter what it was: help the local food bank, clean a local park, beach, or camp site, volunteer at the local animal shelter. As far as Ralph and Wanda were concerned, whatever their children's philanthropic interests were could be their community service contribution—it didn't matter. Ralph and Wanda frequently took the kids with them when they performed their own methods of community service, convinced there was no better way to teach than by example.

Keith eagerly grasped ecological issues. He participated in every event and organization that protected or preserved the planet. He happily volunteered much of his time for worthy causes, despite his normally busy schedule.

Keith's community service activities varied greatly. He might assist with campground restoration with the Sierra Club or pick up trash on the beaches with the Surfrider Foundation—of course, only after taking time to catch a series of 'gnarly' waves at sunrise. Alternatively, he might perform marine-sanctuary research with the Cousteau Society and the Save Our Shores organizations. Keith also found it rewarding to make time for photography dives with his friends from school. Keith's middle name Anthony, could more appropriately have been 'Passion'.

⟶⟫●⟪⟵

Dr. Keith Anthony Vintner was not a typical, bleeding-heart, tree-hugging liberal, even though he was often accused as such. The root of his discontent was the planet's rapid deterioration. He wanted future generations to enjoy it as much as *he* did.

Attuned to the overwhelming evidence put forth by leading eco-scientists—if human beings continued on the current path of global abuse the earth would someday soon be inhabitable—he decided he was not going to sit on the sidelines and do nothing. The serious consequences notwithstanding, Keith quickly realized the added benefits of his efforts—they kept him busy, in shape, and outdoors. Exactly where he wanted to be.

Keith never felt the need to take a bride—bachelorhood suited him fine. As far as he was concerned, he had never met a woman who snagged his attention long enough for matrimonial bliss. Not that there were not any that tried—most women considered him to be a fine catch. He didn't believe that they had what it took to capture his heart hook, line, and sinker. The infrequent 'serious' relationships had not advanced even close to the point of engagement, let alone cohabitation. When either he or the woman du-jour acknowledged that the relationship was not going in the desired direction, an amiable separation inevitably transpired. Keith remained friends with all his former lovers. It was not uncommon for him to invite them to dinner, a movie or the theater, then back to his or her place for sex—another activity he approached with characteristic fervor.

⎯⎯⎯⎯⊰●⊱⎯⎯⎯⎯

Keith shifted his weight in the chair once more, repeated his grimaced smile, and expelled more drool. Again, Zeke noticed no attempt to stop the cascade of saliva.

"Then my freewheeling attitude about women was elegantly shattered. It was a beautiful spring day in Boston. I was at the New England Aquarium on a business trip," he recalled. "A perfect day that I'll never forget. The Boston Marathon had taken place in the morning, and the Red Sox played a home game that night. Two of my favorite signs that spring had finally, truly arrived. The flowers were in full bloom and their bright colors attracted bees, butterflies, and hummingbirds in great numbers. The translucent sky was robin egg blue dappled with an occasional ambling cotton ball cloud. Couples strolled around the lake, hand in hand, sometimes pausing to kiss, sometimes observing other couples and families cheerfully piloting their pedal boats. Artists were everywhere painting or sketching the lake, boaters, and lovers—whose short sleeves and pants exposed milky white skin yearning for the sun's rays from months of nothing but grey skies and biting-cold temperatures. Wielding their brush or charcoals, the artists captured the sunlight

11

on that gorgeous eastern-seaboard day. What a magnificent day it was."

I was there to demonstrate my latest aquatic-design concept, with high-hopes that the aquarium would approve it for their latest exhibit. I was at the reception desk inquiring about my business meeting, when I met the woman who would change my life in ways I never thought possible."

Zeke, I immediately thought to myself, 'she's something special'," Keith fondly reminisced.

Checking his watch and looking up, Keith remarked, "You really should meet her someday, Doc."

2

Rita

Rita Clarisse Haley was Patrick and Sheila Haley's fourth child—their second of three daughters in a brood of six. Good, wholesome, Irish-Catholic kids, all raised near Clark and Addison in the community known as Wrigleyville by locals because of its proximity to the famous ballpark located in the middle of the northside suburbs.

The Haleys lived in a typical Chicago neighborhood. Brownstones, prairie styles, two-flats, and multi-use buildings, with local shops or taverns on the ground floor and residences atop. For generations, the city's politicians, real-estate agents, and inhabitants, named and added new neighborhoods, modified areas, gesticulated and gerrymandered the boundaries and nomenclature of its urban-scape—some for logical reasons, others not so logical. No one quite knows for sure. Ask ten locals and they will give ten different explanations.

Patrick Haley's income as a mailman never afforded him the luxury of providing his family with weekly outings to the bustling city's ubiquitous swanky restaurants, or excursions to foreign countries, or anything that required a significant amount of money. But he did provide his loving family with a sturdy roof over their heads, plenty of food in their bellies, holiday weekends at Aunt Maddie's cabin in Lake Geneva, Wisconsin, or the rare treat of seeing the Cubs in the 'friendly confines'.

Born and raised in Chicago, Patrick was a first-generation American citizen, highly patriotic, and an unabashed, die-hard,

Cubs fan. Patrick never missed a game, faithfully listened to WGN radio broadcasts during his daily mail-delivery rounds. Cubs baseball was as much a religion for Patrick as his devout Catholicism. He considered himself truly fortunate that the United States Postal Service allowed him take his radio on his route so he could hear his beloved Cubs' afternoon games on WGN.

Patrick, along with countless other Chicagoans, thought Harry Caray was the best damn baseball announcer on radio, ever. After Caray's demise, he held status in the heavens right next to all the Popes, no disrespect intended to the Pontiffs. In Patrick's idea of heaven, there was baseball every night, the Cubs would win a World Series, and he knew the bespectacled Harry would be announcing the games. Once a Cubs fan, always a Cubs fan, regardless of the misfortunes and foibles of the allegedly 'cursed' team. As far as Patrick was concerned, all the hooey over a goat, or a cat, or the fan-interference, was just that, hooey. There was always next year—just ask any true believer.

This modest existence was just fine by Patrick. He knew that things of importance or real value couldn't be bought, and he believed he was the richest man on the planet. He had a lovely wife, a beautiful family—all healthy, happy, and loving. What else did a man really need?

Rita, Patrick's most endeared offspring, was not named after one of his favorite actresses—Rita Hayworth—rather after his great aunt Rita. Ironically, Patrick's daughter turned out to be as charismatic and beautiful as the wildly popular movie star. The ambiance became electrified everywhere Rita went. Her personality and heart were as big, bubbly, and beautiful as Buckingham Fountain.

Urban life for a child in the Windy City—so-named for the proliferation of hot air expelled from its blustering politicians, not from the omnipresent winds—was at best tumultuous and often malevolent. Nature was harsh and mankind cruel, but Rita, part of the Haley clan, was unwavering. Family always came first and all Haleys fervently subscribed to the belief in an 'honest day's work for an honest day's wages'. This was, after all, the land of opportunity—anything could be achieved if one applied one's self and pulled their own weight.

In contrast to the Haley's modest existence, there were starving children in any number of third-world countries to compare lifestyles to if a complaint was ever uttered. It didn't matter what the other children in school had. They, the Haley kids, were raised to feel blessed to have a loving family unit, clean clothes to wear, a roof over their head, and a full stomach. There were so many children who didn't have these luxuries—and the Haley kids knew it.

As time went by, she had no desire to stop it, only to help it along. Rita had many friends from all walks of life. She trusted everyone to a fault, to the extent it became her biggest imperfection. Forever seeing the good in others while ignoring their flaws. To Rita, no one was a stranger, at least not for long. She and her friends would be waiting for a bus on Clark Street, and she would start a conversation with anyone: old, young, white, black, blind. It didn't matter. Rita had no prejudices. Rita felt that as humans we had a common bond—each person endured the same bitter winters and muggy summers as the next. "There's only one planet, you might as well try to get along," was her mantra.

Although she was quite tall, athletically built, and excelled at each of the school sports she played—softball, field hockey, and soccer—Rita chose to dedicate most of her time to her studies. She firmly believed that a good education was critical to her future. She loved school, applied herself, and achieved a GPA worthy of a full-scholarship to Northwestern University in Evanston, Illinois.

It was while at Northwestern, in her junior year, that she met Northwestern Wildcats football-star and big-man-on-campus, Simon Cathcart.

Patty, a WildPride Spirit Squad cheerleader, thought Simon was dreamy, but she was already dating the 'center' for the Wildcats football team, Bob 'Ski' Smudowski. Ski and Simon were like brothers, on and off the gridiron.

The young studs devoured Italian beef sandwiches and washed them down with Old Style beer—two notable Chicago institutions—when Ski noticed Patty and Rita approaching them. He wanted to get Simon's attention as quickly as possible—which wasn't going to be easy because Simon had his head lowered as he busied himself with his gigantic beef sandwich. Not-so-subtly Ski jabbed an elbow into his Simon's rib cage and slightly jerked his head in the direction of the two young women coming toward them. Ski had told Simon about Rita earlier, said she was worth a look, but heard she was picky. She had turned down a couple of dates with other jocks—rumor had it that she liked nerdy types and she wouldn't be easy pickings. But she was obviously worth a try—a natural beauty.

Simon flinched and growled from Ski's elbow to his gut. He had been *disturbed*. And was pissed off. He was ready to let loose a verbal barrage of blue-tinged expletives when he realized why his friend was desperately trying to get his attention.

"Ski was right! Rita *was* hot," Simon thought. He swallowed hard, snatched his beer, downed several massive gulps, and tried not to belch. He was unsuccessful.

"What shitty timing," he thought. He wiped his face with his sleeve, the copious amounts of residue surrounding his mouth from the last bite now an impervious stain on his shirt. He turned to Ski, grimaced, and mouthed, *"Asshole!"*

"Hey ladies, ready for a night to remember?" Simon asked. His arrogant bravado sounding more like a suggestion than a question.

"Patty was right. Simon *was* cute," Rita thought. On first impression, he seemed a little rough around the edges, but he was certainly everything Patty said he was. It was all Rita could hope for that he actually had a brain. This 'blind' date might not be as dreadful as she had feared.

———◦———

It didn't take long for Rita to fall in love with the side of Simon that *he* wanted her to see: popular, the fast car, all night parties, the wads of cash pulled from his fat wallet, the nice toys, rich people in plush estates that called him 'friend'. What was there not to love?

———————

Simon's dark side soon revealed itself. Still naïve—Dante's eternal optimist at heart—Rita would patiently forgive Simon when he would lose his temper. She unwittingly bought into his warped, psychopathic logic, and fell into a pattern of blaming herself for his outbreaks, periods of mental instability, and tirades. She tolerated his nights out with the boys, kept herself busy with homework, and focused on her degree and future. Despite his bad side, Rita thought Simon had potential if he could change just a *little*, and not drink so *much*. And he was *so* good looking. She truly felt she could do a lot worse.

She was already the talk of the campus. "Who was the new girl dating Cathcart?" was one of the big gossip questions on campus. Everyone in the in-crowd suddenly took notice of her. Maybe she *could* live with Simon's numerous faults. So, she went along for the bumpy ride. "What relationship was perfect anyway? Right?"

Sadly, Simon's lack of motivation was—despite the glamorous lifestyle he enjoyed as a hometown football star—tenuous at best. He dedicated little time to education, and erroneously believed that just by being on campus, knowledge would magically manifest in his cranial matter.

By the end of his junior year, his lack of scholastic dedication and some of his not-so-harmless extra-curricular activities finally caught up with him. Simon lost his football scholarship and the team gave him the boot.

In typical Simon Cathcart fashion, he fabricated a lie that he told friends, family, and Rita, as to why he abruptly left the team. Simon thought that, for the most part, they seemed to buy it.

He was almost right.

———————

Simon had no desire to pay for, or even continue his education, so he had a heart-to-heart talk with his uncle Joe in Boston, who was a dock foreman in the harbor. Simon talked his way into a job hoisting freight. He had a strong back and the labor didn't require any mental brilliance. It was decent money, and most important, he didn't need a degree.

Joe was well aware of Simon's less-than-squeaky-clean past, nonetheless he felt sorry for his nephew, and gave him a chance. Joe told Simon that he had to show some mettle, otherwise, as his uncle, and dock foreman, *he* would catch hell. And he reminded Simon that shit rolls downhill. Simon agreed to the strict working conditions. It would be the perfect alibi. After Simon told his cohorts of his plan to move to Boston, they went on a two-day farewell binge. Several bottles of hard stuff, four cases of beer, and an ounce of Humboldt's-finest later, the topic turned once again to girls. And sex. In the communal haze in the back of his van, Ski asked Simon what he was going to do about Rita now that he was moving to Boston. Half-jokingly, he suggested that, since Simon hadn't even gotten to third base with Rita yet, he should propose to her and maybe that would do the trick. So, on a whim and advice from his drunken advisors, desperately wanting—mostly for bragging rights—to score with Rita before he left Chicago, Simon decided to propose to Rita.

Ski, after hearing Simon's declaration, yanked Simon's White Sox cap from his head and waved it in front of Simon's face and said, "You should shower and brush your teeth before you try anything. You reek."

⤜➢●◄⤛

"So do you want to go with me, or what?" was the way Simon proffered his proposal. He sloppily munched on a dry hamburger in the university's cafeteria, which would be operating under summer hours by the end of the week. Finals were almost over, and aside from the small number of summer- and evening-class, it would soon be cavernously devoid of humans.

Hardly romantic, he admitted, but he had to report for work in two weeks, clean out his stuff at the frat house, and drive to Boston. It was going to take him a couple of days to get there. Then he would have to get an apartment.

"Well, do you? It's now or never." With those words, Simon pushed a simple gold-plated band across the table—hastily purchased at the local pawnshop for $50—and waited for Rita's answer.

Stunned, Rita had hoped for a fairytale marriage proposal, but life *was* full of little surprises. She realized that his was one of those life moments to be quickly grabbed or rejected. Rita gleefully accepted the band as if it were a Princess Cut diamond ring and put it on her ring finger. She leaned over the small linoleum table—etched with various promises of lasting love—and kissed him affectionately.

"Yes, on both accounts," she said. "I'll marry you *and* move to Boston. I'm sure I'll be able to transfer my credits to some school there in time for next semester. I'll call my family and tell them the good news!"

Rita Haley became a June-bride at the courthouse in the Richard J. Daley Center on 50 West Washington Street. Frannie, Rita's older sister, was Rita's bridesmaid. Ski was Simon's best man.

The entire Haley clan attended the civil ceremony and packed the entire left side of the gallery. The women's murmurs of joy mingled with infants' cries, the buzz from the men and boys swapping lies, and the hushed gossip of the young girls.

The Haleys came from all over the country to be here, even at the drop of a hat. This was one of their own, and they were there to support her. If Rita thought Simon was the one for her, then so be it.

On the groom's side of the gallery—sparsely occupied—were Simon's mother and a few of Simon's former football team members.

Simon's father left when he was eight years old,—moved to New York City with a waitress from the corner tavern. Neither Simon, nor his mother, had seen him since. They didn't know how to contact him. Didn't care.

Uncle Joe, Simon's mother's only living relative, was waiting in Boston for the newlyweds to arrive.

The rest of the football team, and Simon's other friends, were either passed out, or nursing Bloody Mary hangovers at Simon's old fraternity house, deciding to attend the reception at the Knights of Columbus Hall later that afternoon instead of the ceremony itself. Wedding ceremonies were always so boring, and, besides, it wasn't a real wedding—it was a simple civil service at the courthouse.

How memorable could *that* be?

3

oston, with all its splendor and being one of the world's finest cultural cities, was not her beloved Chicago. She had no support system in 'Beantown', no friends, and no family, with the exception of her new Uncle Joe. Luckily, Northeastern University in Boston accepted her transferred units so she could continue her education. However, they didn't transfer her scholarship, so Rita took out a student loan to pay for her senior year. Rita figured she could pay it off after she graduated and became gainfully employed. Her final classes were challenging, but she enjoyed the marketing-, sales-, and business-models they studied and created. She seemed to possess an innate knack for understanding how marketing campaigns and media programs affected potential customers in certain ways, made them react like a company or organization wanted them to react—to unwittingly purchase their products or visit their websites or places of business.

Now that she had earned her degree she thought she could apply these talents in the corporate world, but for now her life was limited to searching for a job and the occasional night out.

Once they were married, as the breadwinner of the family, Simon not-so-subtly seized control of the household finances and essentially dominated Rita's life. He would cash his paychecks and give her the amount *he thought* would cover the rent, bills, and groceries. And beer. "Never run out of beer," was his stern, unambiguous directive. Of course, Simon being Simon, he never gave Rita any money to spend on herself, or to help pay off her student loan. As far as Simon was concerned, that was *her* problem, not *his*. It didn't matter so much to Rita in the beginning, when Simon actually brought most of his earnings home—she truly believed they could make ends meet.

But as time went by, he developed a routine of stopping off at a local bar, 'The Tin Horn', cashing his paycheck there, and spending most of it on rounds of drinks for him and the rest of the regular barflies. Buying popularity was part of Simon's psyche, because he was well aware that it didn't take long for people to see the real Simon—especially after he had drank a few boilermakers.

―――❖―――

Watching their tenuous marriage unwind was like witnessing a high-speed train wreck in slow motion. There was nothing anyone could do to stop it—all one could do was watch the disaster and hope they didn't become collateral damage. Short of winning the lottery, Rita felt their only option out of their financial mess was to declare bankruptcy and start over. They could not borrow any more money from family—Rita was too embarrassed to even ask. In six short months, they had been evicted from three apartments. Rita figured that had to be some kind of record.

Their latest nest was a squalid studio with tobacco-stained walls, carpets that reeked of animal feces and urine, appliances from the '50s, and triple dead-bolt locks on the doors. It was barely big enough for their sofa bed, a nightstand converted to an end table—upon which stood a gifted antique table lamp—and a tiny coffee table, which they had to move when folding out their sofa bed. A small kitchenette table, two chairs, and their television, which sat on a milk crate, completed their suite of furniture. One singlewide closet held their clothes, which was fine with Rita, because between the two of them, to say their wardrobes were sparse would be a gigantic understatement.

As each day passed, it became more and more obvious to Rita that they were falling deeper into the abyss of financial ruin. Their arguments, no matter how- or why-initiated, invariably ended up about money. The couple's finances and his excessive drinking were the reasons they argued frequently, and why they were in such dire straits in the first place.

One particular inglorious hung-over morning, Simon staggered outside their apartment, late for work as usual to find that his car—his baby—was *gone*. His first thought—if a foggy, alcohol induced realization could be considered a thought—was that it had been stolen. It was a decent shape late-model Mustang—worth a pretty penny, even parted out. Simon puzzled over the facts that he didn't see any broken glass and the car alarm had not gone off—he would have heard *that* no matter how drunk he was. He stormed back into the apartment and called the police to report his stolen vehicle. During the call, he ranted and complained about the apparent, to him, indifference and incompetence of the police, when reality—instigated by the desk-captain's harsh explanation of his vehicle's status—crashed down on him.

"Calm down young man, I'm trying to tell you we know where your vehicle is."

"Where the hell is it?" Simon demanded.

"This punk is an asshole," thought Desk-Captain Wayne Collier. So, with authority and intentional sarcasm, Captain Collier replied a little harsher. "I said *calm down* young man. Ace Recovery Services has dutifully informed the Boston Police Department that they impounded your vehicle for delinquent payments, and it is presently at their facility on 14th Street where it will remain until you catch up on your payments, and, of course, pay the impound fees. Then and *only* then can you reclaim your vehicle. You can call them at 617-555-1212. So don't worry. It's not stolen. We know *exactly* where it is."

Captain Collier saved his best jab for last. "Have a nice day," he quipped. A wide grin appeared on his face and he quite happily disconnected the call.

"What the hell am I gonna' do now?" Simon thought. His blood pressure and frustration rising.

The newlyweds clearly didn't have the money to catch up on the payments, not to mention the impound fee, to get Simon's beloved vehicle from Ace Recovery Services. As far as Simon could foresee, his baby was gone. For good.

Simon would have to swallow his pride and bum a ride to the docks with a co-worker until he and Rita scrapped together enough cash to put a down payment on another car. They eventually purchased a ten-year-old, two-door, Honda Civic with a loan co-signed by Frannie, Rita's sister. "How fuckin' humiliating," Simon thought.

Simon asserted his authority over her constantly. He literally deprived Rita of any social activities outside those *he* could not control, and automatically dismissed any activity Rita wished to partake in as too expensive or just plain stupid. Even worse, he accused her of having an affair—insinuating that she had been cheating on him.

Simon had always been jealous or hurt whenever Rita wanted to spend time with others. At first, Rita thought it was adorable that Simon always wanted to know where she was, what she was doing—that he truly cared about her—but she learned the hard way that his intentions were not cute at all. Far from it.

Rita yearned for more from her existence. Her social life could hardly be considered such—sadly, there was little or nothing social about it. Beyond cooking, cleaning, and washing, her life was limited to the occasional Friday night at The Tin Horn with Simon, where she had opportunities to chat with the girlfriends or wives of the other dockworkers. Rarer still were nights out at the movies to see an action film—Simon's choice—then inevitably a visit to The Tin Horn. Over time, Rita started to feel guilty about doing anything outside the home. She feared the consequences.

Rita felt extremely isolated living in Boston, and only once travelled to her beloved hometown, Chicago. She had rarely talked to her family since that visit, and none of her family members had come to Boston to see her, because even though no one in her family talked about it openly, she *knew* they all hated Simon. There was that, and the fact that her family member's *own* lives were getting fuller by the day, with the day-to-day activities and problems of their own growing families, which always made for a good excuse not to go anywhere, let alone go to Boston. If it wasn't their kid's soccer games, it was baseball. If it wasn't baseball games, it was basketball or hockey. Rita's nieces and nephews, or her brothers and sisters were constantly struck by the latest malady spreading around, making travel 'unadvisable'.

To add more stress to their marriage, Simon and Rita's phone had been disconnected the previous month, and they simply couldn't afford a mobile phone. Even a pay-as-you-go plan would be difficult to justify. At least in Simon's twisted mind.

During times when Simon was at work, Rita would sneak down to the corner market, whose owner, unbeknownst to Simon, she had befriended. It was at the market where Rita could call her sister Frannie, collect, of course. Sometimes, when she had a few extra quarters left over from doing laundry, and absolutely *had* to talk to *someone* about how terrible things had become, she would toss the clothes in the dryer, run down to the phone booth three blocks away and drop the spare change in the slot, and called one of her lifelines.

One day, talking to no one in particular, she thought, "Come on! What was so wrong with going out with the girls to window shop, or to see a movie?"

Simon never wanted to go to see chick flicks, let alone take her shopping. Rita felt like she lived in a cocoon.

Frannie answered one of Rita's lifeline calls, and got on her soapbox again—and rightfully so. "Get a job, for Christ's sake. Get out and find something productive to do, make somethin' outta yourself. Don't let that scumbag take you down any more. You're better than what you've let him do to you. Where's the old Rita we all know an' love, huh? Where is she?" Frannie prodded relentlessly.

For Rita, the loneliness and dread was overwhelming. It was a given that she needed to get her self-esteem back—a certain self-fulfillment that a good job could provide. She and Simon urgently needed more income, Simon spent over half of his apprentice salary at the bar, pouring their life down his throat, and the throats of others.

Her life had somehow gotten off track. It was time to make a change for the better. Damn the circumstances. Soon after her talk with Frannie, Rita started to apply for jobs around the neighborhood.

She had not gotten any nibbles from her job applications. It was obviously tough not having a telephone to call potential employers, or on which a prospective employer could call her.

In desperation, Rita asked a neighbor—not one of Simon's cronies, but a new resident—Diana Swain, a single gal whom Rita met while in the elevator of their building, if she could use her telephone number on job applications. Rita politely requested of Diana, that if anyone happened to call for her, to *please* take a message, and then to discretely tell her, so she could return the call.

"I know it's a pain, but I'd really appreciate it…I'm…I'm in a world of hurt right now, and I don't know who else to turn to," Rita, practically in tears, explained to her neighbor.

Diana obligingly acquiesced. She was a waitress—worked two shifts but barely made ends meet. She had been in the same situation as Rita not long ago, and sadly, understood Rita's situation all too well.

Diana genuinely wanted to ease poor Rita's concern. She said, as jovially as possible, "I only have my telephone number recorded on my greeting anyway, so no one would possibly know it wasn't your phone number. I'd love to help out any way I can. Oh! And how about coming over for coffee or tea sometime? We can girl talk."

The New England Aquarium had a free day for locals and Rita decided that since the apartment and laundry were cleaned she would visit the aquarium. Rita told a meddlesome neighbor—one of Simon's spies—that she was going grocery shopping. Rita *knew* Simon had people watching her to see if she left the apartment or had anyone over while he was gone. His paranoia had taken on a life of its own.

Rita checked in at the front desk at the New England Aquarium, noticed a flyer announcing that they were hiring, and decided to apply for a Member Services position. Rita thought she was under qualified, but after all, she did have a business degree, worked well with others, applied herself, and was a hard worker. She figured she might as well give it a go.

<hr />

Much to the chagrin of Simon, who wanted to keep her at home, under his thumb, under his or his crony's watchful eyes, Rita landed the job.

The pay wasn't great, but it was enough to pay off her student loan, and maybe stash a couple of bucks out of Simon's reach. She smiled at the thought of buying a new bra.

Her new job revitalized her and opened possibilities of the outside world. She buried herself in her work to escape Simon's tirades and abuse, but the more she worked, showed her old spunk, the more his outrage manifested. Rita became frightened to go back to her own house after work. Simon typically came home stinking drunk, threw her on the couch, and demanded sex. He thought it was *manly* to come home and ravage his woman. How wrong he was but Rita didn't want to think about what would happen if she didn't succumb to his horrid wishes.

<hr />

Frannie was on one of her soapboxes again, a tall one this time. "Sis, you need to leave that rat bastard. Now. Not next week or next month. He's going to hurt you. It's just a matter of time. I knew he was good for nothin', and I knew it from the moment I laid eyes on him. And frankly, I feel horrible that I didn't utter a peep at your wedding! I'm so pissed off at myself for keeping my trap shut I wish I could kick my own ass. Now my baby sister is gonna' be killed by her deranged husband because I didn't stop the marriage when I had the chance. I should have stood up in that courthouse and shouted, 'Stop! Don't marry that bastard! You deserve better!'"

Frannie was on a roll and she let it all out. "Besides being damn good looking, which I have to admit he is, and having some talent on the football field, he's nothin' but a piece of white trash and you know it.

"I wish I could tell you different, but we both know it's true. You got a good job, makin' ok money. Get a good divorce lawyer. You'll need one. He's nothin' but a lowlife snake. I'm tellin' you! Stay in a hotel 'til you can get a place of your own. Or better yet, get your skinny ass back here to Chicago and get away from that abusive prick. You can find a job out here."

Rita knew her sister's assessment was spot on. "You're right Frannie, he is a prick, and I should have seen it right off the bat...I was such as fool. I was star struck. He seemed like every girl's dream. Rich, popular, and handsome. At least *I* thought he was. But it was all a sham. Big sister, you're right again. I'll do it. I'm getting a divorce!"

Frannie didn't hold back her elation. "Hallelujah! I got the name of a lawyer for you. He's a damn fine one. Remember Eva Berkowitz who moved to Cambridge a few years ago? This lawyer got Eva a bundle. Not that you'll get a bundle, but you should get somethin' for putting up with Simon's shit. And best of all, this guy's office is right there in Boston!"

———⟫●⟪———

Rita made an appointment with her new lawyer, went to his office on her lunch break, and asked him to draw up divorce papers. Two long, agonizing weeks later, she paid the lawyer out of her 'spare' money. The lawyer cautioned Rita that the divorce could get nasty—that many of them do.

Rita waited for Simon. She anxiously rubbed her sweaty palms on her pants as she anticipated Simon's reaction. She fretfully kneaded the envelope that contained the divorce documents between her fingers.

Her new colleague Colleen offered to be there when she gave Simon the news. Rita wished she had taken her up on the offer.

Rita knew Simon had arrived when she heard a loud crash outside. He had plowed right into the apartment complex's trashcans and recycle bins after he recklessly turned the Honda into the parking lot. Trash, bottles, and aluminum cans scattered across the parking lot. Rita pulled the curtains back to see what caused the commotion. She felt her stomach tighten as she watched Simon get out of the car, curse and wave his arms at the nefarious receptacles like they able to understand what he said to them.

"What the fuck were you doin' there?" he reprimanded the trashcans.

"Damn it; he's wasted again," Rita groaned. She hoped the car was still operational. She could live with dings—but they were not able to pay for repair work.

Rita feared for her safety as she prepared to hand Simon their divorce papers. She was terrified because she knew precisely how Simon would take the news. She began to have second thoughts. Should she wait and serve him the divorce papers when he was in a better mood—and sober? She decided this had to be done now.

Nothing Simon could do could change their marriage for the better. Not now. It was only going to get worse. Rita's innate Irish-resolve bubbled to the surface and she was absolutely determined to put an end to their marriage. Simon's rage had reared its ugly head one too many times. In the past, she had docilely endured his psychotic outbursts, due to her misguided romantic ideology, but not tonight. She knew she had to dump him.

Deception, domination, and fear were truly the foundations of their farcical marriage. "Tonight," she reaffirmed to herself.

She watched as he yelled at the displaced bins for several minutes until he realized they were not listening. Simon gave one of the trashcans a powerful kick and sent it careening across the pavement of the half-filled parking lot. Determined to get in a final word, he yelled at it again. Simon didn't bother to clean up the mess he had made, instead, he stumbled into the apartment complex lobby and got into the elevator.

Rita waited on the sofa for him to come up to their apartment and got more perturbed with each passing second. Simon meandered down the hall in a drunken stupor.

Dinner was ready hours ago—she had come to expect him to be late for dinner. The ugly truth, that alcohol was more alluring to him than she, got her even more riled up. Simon never was, and never would be, the kind of man who would call to tell her he was going to be late. He showed up whenever he pleased and expected dinner to be waiting for him. Then he usually watched some TV and demanded she engage in dispassionate sex with him before he passed out on the sofa bed.

"What was I thinking when I got into this relationship?" was the thought racing through her mind. Her heart pounded as Simon staggered through the doorway.

Terrified of what was to come, Rita raised herself off the sofa, calmly put the envelope containing the divorce papers on the coffee table, and braced herself for the hurricane of outrage that was about to hit her full-force.

Simon stumbled past her without so much as a greeting, but noticed what she had just done. "Wha's that, another late notice? The rat bastards can wait 'nother week. I had a tab at The Horn to take care of. Wha's their fuckin' problem anyway?"

Rita was awestruck—Simon was actually mocking the fact that they were spiraling into poverty, and seemed to be proud of the fact that it was because of *his* selfish behavior and stupidity. His vitriolic words were the final shot across her bow. Her ire had been raised. She would no longer bite her tongue and capitulate. Rita would no longer remain silent out of fear of retribution. Her anxiety had transformed into livid resentment, angry for being sucked in and dragged down into his powerful vortex of self-destruction.

"How could I be so gullible?" she thought.

Without a second glance in her direction, Simon threw his soiled, rancid coat on the couch, flopped down next to it, and loudly plopped his muddy boots on the coffee table.

"Grab me a cold beer. And dinner. I'm fuckin' hungry." He reached for the remote control and turned on a sports channel, ignoring her all the while, as if she was only there to satisfy his every whim—his eyes, and attention, glued to the screen.

Rita's learned civilized behavior dissolved like sugar in water. Her genteel-filter disengaged. "No Simon, it is *not* another late payment, we got one of those yesterday!" Rita picked up the divorce papers and boldly shook them in his face. "This envelope contains divorce papers, Simon. *Our* divorce papers. I'm leaving you. As for dinner, if you can focus long enough, you'll find your precious beer and cold cuts for sandwiches in the refrigerator. You *do* know where the refrigerator is don't you?"

Simon couldn't believe what he was hearing. Did she just say she was leaving him? No one left Simon Cathcart! *He* did the leaving. *He* was the one in control. "What? What the fuck are you talkin' about, bitch? Divorce papers? You...you're leaving me? Oh, that's fuckin' brilliant! Jus' 'cuz a guy likes to stop off at the bar for a drink after a long day's work, you get all pissy. You get to sit around all day and talk. How fucking hard can *that* be?"

Simon's face began to contort. "You wanna leave me...then do what? You think you can live on your own? Answerin' phones at the 'quarium? *Do you?* You think you can make enough money to live on with your skills? You better listen to me and listen good, miss high-and-mighty, 'look at me I have a degree'. So you have a degree. So what? A degree doesn' mean shit anymore."

Simon felt his face begin to flush as rage consumed him. His eyes bulged—red veins on his forehead prominently exposed themselves. Rita thought he was literally about to explode.

"What do you want, huh? You want nice things like this lamp?" he shouted as he snatched the antique lamp off the tiny coffee table, given to the newlyweds for the traditional 'something old'. Simon had wanted to pawn it for beer money several times, but Rita held her ground even back then. "No, this is a family heirloom. Besides, it's not worth much money anyway, only sentimental value," she lied to divert his attention. Truth be told, it was worth a pretty penny.

Simon ripped the precious lamp's cord from the wall-socket and hurled it against the wall, sending glass and ceramic missiles across the room in all directions. Rita ducked as one of the shards of glass flew past her head. "There. You can have the damned lamp," he spat.

She knew this was exactly how Simon would react to the divorce papers. The now demolished lamp was proof that her husband's violent behavior had no limits. Rita knew she had to stop this madness—but how? She was furious that Simon had broken something of such value to her, but wasn't sure how to stop his outburst. Rita was certain this hurricane of violent behavior was not going to reverse its course.

Simon continued his childish, dangerous rant. He railed, "how about this cute little thing?" He suddenly grabbed the small Lladro figurine from its place on a lace doily on the bookshelf. It was one of Rita's favorite keepsakes—another special gift—from her father. She cringed as he screamed, "You like *this* too? Here, you can have it." He viciously threw the fine Valencia porcelain piece—an homage to humanity's nobility—against the wall. It smashed into a framed photo of him as a high school football star, demolishing both in an frightful blend of shattered porcelain and glass on the floor.

"Stop it!" Rita screamed. The irony of the destruction of an object so beautiful and virtuous infuriated her. Her anger erupted to the dome of her consciousness. "Stop it right now!" she screamed.

"What the fuck are you doing?" she asked, in verbiage he was not accustomed to hearing from her. "What are you trying to prove by destroying my things? How *big* a man you are?"

Simon suddenly froze—dumbfounded.

"Well it doesn't. It just shows how *small* a man you really are."

Simon's eyes betrayed him—a mix of confusion and fury. Rita could see his mind trying to wrap around the concept of not having her around anymore to manipulate. Suddenly Simon stopped, as if a rational thought had blossomed in his malevolent mind.

"Oh...oh yeah. I know wha's going on," he seethed. "You got a boyfriend don'ya you now? Tha's why you wanna divorce. You don't need me anymore, you gotta sugar daddy. Going out and gettin' a little on the side, are we? Tha's it, isn' it? I knew it…get the fuck outta here slut. You disgus' me. Get out!" he barked like the figurative dog he was. "Get the hell out! I can' believe this shit. Pack your bags, hit the streets… be on your own, see wha' it's like out there bitch. Go fuck your boyfriend for all I care. I'll give ya' an hour to pack up your crap and get out. The locks will be changed by morning. And don' bother coming back, there won' be anything left, it'd be a waste of your time." He snatched his coat, headed for the door, turned, and added, "I'm goin' to The Horn. I'll be back in an hour.

"Don't be here when I get back or you'll regret it."

Simon was not getting off that easily. Rita's own fury had suddenly eclipsed his as she listened to his illogical discourse. No longer afraid of consequences, she raised herself up, glared at him and screamed. "Stop right there Cathcart! An hour? That's what you're giving me to clear out my belongings, an hour? Ok Simon, if that's the way you want to play it, so be it."

She saw the confusion in his expression again. He had never seen her empowered side before. More of the same was about to steamroll him.

"You know what I wanted from *you* Simon? I wanted *you* to get your shit together and be a decent husband, but I finally saw that wasn't ever going to happen. At one point I thought you were mature and charming, even caring, but I was wrong. So very wrong," she said, fighting back tears.

"You know what *I* want? *I* want to live a happy life, and not have to put up with all the bullshit you dish out every single day! I want to get away from all of your drunken, manipulative, dishonest passion. Your cowardly bullshit. *I* want a *normal* life. Hell, at this point, I'd even settle for a boring life."

"No sense stopping now," Rita thought.

"Do I think I can make it on my own? *Damn* right I do! Better than I can with you! Do I have a boyfriend? No, you delusional, pathetic miscreant. You want me out of here in an hour? Ok, I'll be out of here in an hour. Sign the papers. Now. Get me out of your hair once and for all. I'll pack all my clothes, a few pots, pans, and dishes that you haven't the faintest idea how to use anyway, and I'll go find a place to live. I'll do fine by myself. I can't do any worse than *this*. And by the way, I'll be taking the car to get the hell out of here. If you're lucky I'll even drop it off in the morning before you need it to go to work. *If* you're lucky," she seethed.

"Now, get out of my way. I'm going to move the car closer so I can get my things out of here faster." Snarling, she continued, "And do you think you could calm down enough to not break anything *else* before I get back? Do you?"

Simon could only stare at her in stunned disbelief. Eyes wide open. Jaw agape.

Rita snatched her purse, grabbed the keys, flashed a scowl that would freeze Hades, and brushed past him.

Simon was too drunk to make a one of his typical snappy insults. And bewildered. He had never seen Rita behave like this before. "What the hell was happening?"

As Rita marched down the hallway, she spun around and saw Simon staring at her, hands on hips, still trying to come up with a witty retort to take back the upper hand.

However, *she* was determined to get the last word. "I was *so* stupid to fall for such a loser." Then she turned away quickly. She didn't want him to see the tears start to stream down her cheeks. She didn't even try to wipe the tears away. As the door to the elevator closed, she heard him yell, "You *bitch*!" as he slammed the door.

⸻⟫●⟨⸻

Rita returned to find nothing else had been taken while she was away, with the exception, not surprisingly, being the alcohol. As were the divorce papers. Rita quickly packed her things into the Honda. She was going to find a cheap hotel for a couple of days until she found a place she could call home. She knocked on her neighbor Diana's door to tell her she was leaving Simon, and that she would miss her terribly, but that she had to leave.

With a drawn, fretful face, Diana said she understood. "Take care out there. I'll stop by the aquarium and say 'hi'."

—————————

The next morning Rita told her friend and co-worker Colleen about what happened the night before. Colleen insisted that Rita stay with her until she found a place. Colleen assured her it was no problem—that she had a second room she used for company and her place was plenty big enough for two single gals.

—————————

Through sheer luck, or fate, Rita found a nice studio on a monthly lease, four blocks from the aquarium. She could walk to work even in the harsh Boston winters. Since she didn't need it and couldn't afford it at this point anyway, she yielded the car to Simon, who promptly traded it in for an beat up old muscle car. Some things never changed.

—————————

Simon reluctantly signed the divorce papers, with some modifications and stipulations about alimony penciled in. He didn't want to have to pay her each and every month forever. So, after a bitter and lengthy legal battle, Rita was finally and completely rid of her husband, who according to sister Frannie, 'was a good for nothin' piece of white trash.' After what she had just endured with Typhoon Simon, she thoroughly concurred with that sentiment.

—————————

The alimony payments came more and more infrequently. Simon had fallen deeper into the pit of self-denial. And booze. Simon being Simon, he childishly and vehemently blamed others for his failures. He was well and truly deranged. This most certainly could be confirmed by a medical or psychological test.

———⇒⊷●⊶⇐———

A thought snaked its way into her head one day—she feared Simon was stalking her. She would be walking home from work and see a car that looked like his parked down the street. Not in front of her place, but just close enough for her to believe it was Simon. A motionless silhouette could be seen in the driver's seat. The car would be there in the morning and when she got home in the evening.

Panic crept in like fog on the Chicago River. She told Frannie how frequently the phenomenon had occurred. "Holy shit bat girl," Frannie exclaimed after hearing Rita's suspicions.

Being subtle was not part of Frannie's fabric. Her ensuing interrogation began with rapid-fire questions. "What the hell is going on? Why are you letting him control you like this?" Then she escalated her interrogation. "Wake up little sister. The rat bastard doesn't own you! Oh god, I'm so pissed off I could spit tacks. He's dangerous…I'm so afraid for you I'm about ready to pee my pants. Would you please get a restraining order?"

Frannie continued her earnest histrionics, and used another deific invocation for emphasis. "Jesus, Mary, and Joseph, I'm worried about you, Rita," Frannie said. She quickly made the sign of the cross on her chest—a ingrained routine whenever she mentioned those sacred names.

"I wish you weren't so damn stubborn. Please! I'm begging you, be careful and protect yourself. Move back to Chicago!"

Rita knew her sister had valid points and rationale. She knew Frannie cared very much for her safety. She admitted her sister was right. "Damn it Frannie, you're right. Again. Shit, I hate when that happens. I am worried about Simon's real or imagined deeds. It's scaring the hell out of me, even worse than we were living together. It's like he's possessed or something. Or I am.

"All right. I'll get a restraining order placed against him, but I'm not going to move to Chicago. I don't mean to sound pig-headed, but I'm not going to let Simon control my life. That's what you said, right? I'm back on track. I love my job and I'm not going to be forced to move by anyone."

⸺⟫●⟪⸺

She was determined to make it on her own. On her own terms. Rita energetically embraced her work, used her finely polished social-skills and business-acumen to catapult her career to new heights. It didn't take long until everyone at the aquarium knew who she was—the entire board, membership holders, and most of the frequent visitors.

She became known as the *go-to* girl. If there was a tough job that needed to be done, Rita could and would get it done. Her knack for customer service was incomparable. She was cherished by everyone—even the curmudgeons loved her charismatic persona. Her work had become her obsession. Her life.

Her innate passion for communicating with and helping people had surfaced at quite the opportune time.

4

Back in Chicago

Eduardo, 'Eddie', Ramirez—waiter extraordinaire—was well known for attending to the needs of his patrons. This evening proved no exception as he constantly eyed each of his tables and their occupants, quickly provided water or fresh table settings as warranted. Eddie was always right there to provide whatever was needed whenever it was needed.

At the counter, he checked the status of his orders. The next plates coming up should be his and ready any minute.

———⟹●⟸———

Prior to his shift, Eddie spent extra time primping himself to look as professional as possible. His hair was neatly combed, moustache neatly trimmed, button-down, long-sleeve, white shirt, black tie, and pants, were freshly cleaned and pressed. His black shoes were so shiny one could easily imagine Eddie as a boot camp recruit meticulously spit shining his boots. To Eddie 'the perfectionist', these shoes were showing their age. He needed to get another pair— and he would, just as soon as he brought in enough money. With a final glance in the mirror, he confirmed that he was looking good, and was certain he had been making a good impression with customers and staff alike. Eddie was smart—and smart enough to know he was lucky to be working in today's dreary employment situation—especially to be working in a place like *this*.

The extra time grooming himself paid off handsomely.

Eddie knew he got this job because his roommate, Steve, had worked there for years. Steve had recently graduated and had just landed a job in New York. As a favor between college roommates, he gave Eddie first shot as his replacement. Steve assured Eddie that some serious money could be made there, a lot more than the dump where Eddie had been working.

———◦◦◦———

Louis 'Lou' Santorini, had just heard that Steve was quitting and moving east, and was extremely relieved to find that Steve already had his replacement picked out. Steve's college roommate Eddie, had plenty of experience, good references, worked hard, and was reliable. Were it not for all of these qualities, Steve would not have considered recommending Eddie to his soon-to-be former boss Lou. Steve said he could bring Eddie around for an interview with Lou the following day.

———◦◦◦———

"Mr. Santorini," Steve said respectfully, as he introduced Eddie, "This is Eddie Ramirez, the man I think should replace me."

———◦◦◦———

Eddie's interview with Lou was relatively informal, as interviews go. Afterward, Lou, firmly extended his big hand, shook Eddie's vigorously, and looked him directly in the eyes. "Eddie, welcome aboard, ya got da' job. You're workin' somewhere else right? Ok, give 'em two weeks' notice. It's only fair. I know they'll miss you. Stevie, have Eddie here sign all the paperwork, ok?" he addressed them both, in a raspy, old-school voice.

The two young men bobbed their heads in unison, as if they had practiced the routine countless times.

"Good." Lou continued, "Stevie, show 'im the ropes. I assume you informed Eddie of the pay, and how hard ol' Lou' pushes you.

You said you're leavin' in a month, right Stevie? That means ya' got two weeks to train Eddie."

Lou shook Eddie's hand again. "Eddie, welcome to my restaurant. I mean it. Stevie here has been apart'a the missus and my family for almos' five years now. He's a good kid, and he knows he better keep in touch. He already tol' me all about ya' Eddie, and ya' look like another good kid. So what I'm sayin' is, if Stevie here says ya' can do the job, that's good enough for ol' Lou'. See you in'a coupl'a week's Eddie. I gotta' run ta' the kitchen now."

Lou spun around and hit the two-way doors to the main kitchen like a bull.

Eddie and Steve turned to each other and grinned. Eddie couldn't think of anything to say. This job was, as they say, an opportunity knocking. It was obvious to Eddie that he would have a chance to make something out of himself, and the icing on the cake was a chance to pay for college.

Steve said, beaming. "Welcome to 'Lou's On Clark', Eddie. Wait until you meet Mrs. Santorini." Steve rubbed his belly and his eyes gazed upwards. "My friend, you'll never go hungry again."

Employees were family to Lou. He worked side-by-side with each one of them, day in, day out, no matter the task. No one worked harder than Lou did and he expected everyone to pull his or her fair share. For doing so, he paid a very fair wage and fed everyone well.

Lou's On Clark—a fixture on North Clark Street—was one of the hottest spots in Chicago to work, and Eddie Ramirez was not going to screw up this chance to make some good cash. Lou's On Clark had been around for as long as anyone could remember, serving countless savory dishes, each carefully handmade from scratch from recipes passed down by Lou's parents, and their parents. And *their* parents. The Santorini family tree was replete with fun-loving people who enjoyed food and good wine and especially, preparing delectable dishes.

The décor at Lou's On Clark was simple, yet elegant. The menu-selection was diverse, with enormous portions. No one ever walked away from Lou's On Clark feeling hungry or without a personal visit from Lou himself.

The vast majority of the patrons of Lou's On Clark were regulars. Some were famous, most were not—but all were well aware of the reputation of Lou's On Clark as one of the finest eateries in Chicago. Generations of happy Chicagoans had left Lou's On Clark with their bellies and spirits full. When Eddie began working at Lou's On Clark, many of the employees, told Eddie tongue-in-cheek, that Lou knew half the city on a first name basis and was related to the other half. The way the place was constantly packed—it followed logic. There was always a long wait for a table, even after Lou expanded the restaurant with a full bar, added a robust appetizer menu, and provided live music five nights a week.

Eddie was beginning to believe all the stories he had heard. Lou, the old geezer—Lou had to be at least one-hundred years-old—was a human 'Energizer Bunny', always fresh, running around the place, doing this and that. Every day except Sunday. "Hey, even God took'a breatha'," Lou was frequently heard to chortle.

Lou's practically inexhaustible energy—day in and day out, bustling about the kitchen to see that each dish smelled and looked perfect, stopped at every table, inquired about the service and the food—was mentally incomprehensible. Lou's ceaseless bustle was seemingly age defiant.

Eddie's dark brown eyes were focused on the couple seated at Table 26. As soon as they were seated, Lou, seated the couple himself, walked over to Eddie, stopped. "After ya' get Table 25's order served, make sure ta' take good care of Table 26, they're very good friends a' mine."

"Oh man; I've been here two weeks and now the boss wants me to wait on some good friends of his," Eddie thought, uneasily. "This is a test. Shit. Ok, pull yourself together Ramirez, you're good. Why else would the boss have thrown this at you?"

Lou's friends at Table 26 looked rich. *Really* rich. The gentleman was middle aged, impeccably dressed in a designer suit and tie.

His date was a '10' on anyone's scale—a striking young woman much younger than her gentleman companion, with a couple of noticeable piercings, but professionally attired, with long blonde flowing hair, and bewitching eyes. A natural beauty.

"Well look who I get to impress tonight," Eddie thought as he straightened his shirt and his wait-cloth, then grabbed his note pad, and headed toward the table, his confidence rock-solid.

———————

"Michael, you really should try one of those professional dating services, do a video, check out the profiles of the available women. The whole enchilada. Most of them are legit, I swear. How do you think I found Chuck? They have all kind of filters to weed out freaks who only want who-knows-what. C'mon Michael, jump into the twenty-first century. Take the plunge. I'm quite sure you haven't been active at anything other than work for far too long. I thought I was a workaholic. But no, compared to you, I'm unworthy of the title. You inspire me! Type A all the way. All day. All night. Michael, you've gotta get out there and *live*!"

"Sarah, I'm not into that whole dating scene. I'm not sure I'm ready to get serious with someone yet."

"Are you kidding me? You're a damn good looking man Michael. You're as rich as a Rockefeller and have an absolutely wonderful personality. Seriously, come on, you've got that big fancy home all to yourself, and no one to enjoy it with. You know you love to travel, and haven't done so since Liz died. You need someone…so you can do things like that again. And *other* things."

After taking a large bite out a piece of fresh, steaming-hot Palermo bread, Sarah doused the remainder in a plate of extra virgin olive oil with imported, aged balsamic vinegar, and continued. "Take it from me, one who has had many moments of angst finding that certain someone. You need to hook up, Michael, really bad. As your friend, I'm telling you. Believe me when I say you need someone in your life. All work and no play is making Michael a dull boy."

Having her first hunk of carbohydrates, Sarah dipped her next morsel into some of the complimentary garlic infused butter. She was starving, but that didn't stop her from jabbering on one iota. "I love you Michael. Damn it, you're more like family than a boss. Elizabeth was like a sister to me. I miss her. Without her I wouldn't have made it through these last few years. You...and her were always there for me. She meant the world to me, but so do you, more than you know. I've never told you this, but during one of my visits, when you would let us girls chat for a while, she took my hands in hers, and made me promise to introduce you to someone that I thought would be a, um, good match. She loved you so much that she wanted you to be happy, and the only way you can be happy is to share your life with someone else. Some people can live life in solitude. You shouldn't. You are way too cool of a guy not to latch on to some solid babe and be happy for the rest of your life."

Sarah needed to share these thoughts with Michael—wished she would have said something sooner. "Look, if someone as weird as I am can hook up with a hottie like Chuck, imagine what kind of babe you could get hooked up with. That day, I promised Elizabeth that I would find you someone, and I intend to keep my promise. I haven't found her yet, but until I do, I don't want you to disappear into obscurity and become a recluse. Go on a date would you! You need it, boss. Bad."

Without missing a beat of her mastication cadence, Sarah changed the subject like a pro. "You're buying, right? Good, let's order, I'm famished. You worked my ass hard all day, my friend."

"Good Evening. Welcome to Lou's On Clark. My name is Eduardo. I'll be your waiter for the evening. Let me tell you about this evening's specials."

5

The Heart of the Matter

Keith Vintner took another deep breath. Exhaled. "Whew. So, that's my life story. And then I met Rita. I was bowled over the moment I saw her." Keith stared out of the floor-to-ceiling windows overlooking the Pacific Ocean, waves pounding relentlessly against the shore. He thought about the awkward, yet wonderful moment he met Rita. "You should have seen me then, Doc," he chirped.

Keith's eyebrows involuntarily raised in approval as Rita caught his eye. The heavenly vision—short, tussled, cinnamon hair, big hazel eyes, tall, firm body, and bright grin—crashed into his cranium like a velvet covered wrecking ball. As his dad would say, "She's a looker."

Keith noticed she was not wearing a ring, and decided to put on the charm. Love was in the air, he could feel it fill his lungs. Or was it *lust*? *Who cared*? Boston had some very attractive residents, and he wanted to get to know at least one of them intimately.

Keith's heart thumped in anticipation of his first words and suddenly found himself starting to over analyze the situation. Should he come on to her before he got the contract at the aquarium, maybe let her know, subtly, how attracted he was to her? That seemed too primal but did have potential for the desired outcome. He decided it was best that he keep it professional. For now. Besides, they had not approved the project yet. But, lunch or dinner, maybe a nightcap back at his hotel? They all sounded like good ideas to him. Who knows what could happen?

When his turn came, he stepped up to the information counter with as much aplomb as he could possibly muster. "Good morning, do you know where I might find Dr. Peter Sneed? I was told to track him down, and I have no idea where to start." Keith flashed a smile.

Her Svengali's gaze was at that very moment setting the hook—her infectiousness already reeling him in. He might as well give in right then and there—the gaff and net were out and ready.

Rita smiled back at him, replied professionally, but in a slightly playful manner. She could tell by his posture that he was flirting with her, but she still wanted to maintain propriety. It felt nice to be noticed, especially by a such a good-looking man. "Right here is a good place to start, and I certainly can track down him for you. May I tell Dr. Sneed who's looking for him?" she asked with a impish smile on her pretty face.

Klaxon horns and flashing red lights went off in Keith's head. "Uh oh! No push over here," he realized. He wanted to impress her, but not seem full of himself, so he cranked up his 'impress-o-tron's' sincerity and enthusiasm levels. "Keith Vintner, of the Scripps Institute in San Diego. I'm here to demonstrate a new tank for the aquarium's new exhibit. This is my first time to the New England Aquarium, the only major aquarium in North America I haven't seen yet, and I'm really excited to be here," he rambled in one breath, convinced it was a succinct explanation for his request.

"Rita Haley, at your service, Mr. Vintner. Welcome. We're very proud of our facilities. Let me get Dr. Sneed for you," she remarked courteously.

Rita walked back to her desk and dialed Dr. Sneed's extension. She could tell by the number of rings that the call was being transferred to his mobile phone. After several moments he finally answered. "Pete Sneed."

"Hi Pete, Rita. There's a Mr. Vintner here at the front desk. Says he has a meeting with you this morning. Would you like me to show him to your office?"

Static, boisterous human-voices and strange echolocation noises emanated from his mobile phone. "Thanks Rita, but no. I'm tied up at the dolphin tank right now, then I need to check up on the sea lions. Seems like we have an issue over there that needs some attention."

Pete's phone crackled noisily. Rita imagined Pete up to his elbows in something odorously foul. Her nose crinkled at the thought of the repulsive smells she had occasionally encountered in the back of the aquarium. The public was lucky they rarely found out how utterly disgusting a sea lion's flatulence could be.

"Have Mr. Vintner wait for me in the boardroom, give him a quick tour, burn some time, make him feel at home, offer him a cup of coffee or something. You know the drill. I'll be a few minutes. I've got to get cleaned up. Thanks Rita, you're the best, I owe you."

Rita hung up the phone and turned to Keith. "Dr. Sneed will be a few minutes. Since you've never been here, I'd be delighted to give you a little tour, and then take you to the boardroom. Dr. Sneed will meet you there. Would you like some coffee...tea...water? We have some organic fair-trade coffee that I'm told tastes absolutely wonderful, if you like coffee. I'm a tea drinker myself."

"Coffee would be great, thank you, Rita.

"Damn." Keith thought. "Too bad she didn't say coffee, tea, or *me?*"

She exuded sensuality. She was drop-dead gorgeous. All her parts fit together nicely. But, beyond the obvious, there was something else about Rita that Keith couldn't quite put his finger on. He would have to work on *that.*

"Excellent, follow me please." Rita led Keith through the facility, and since he had not been there before, she pointed out some of the popular exhibits as they weaved their way to the boardroom.

Keith was thinking that, by all outward appearances, this was a world-class organization. Keith could tell Rita believed this to be the case by the way she prattled on about the exhibits and how beautiful they were—raved about the interactive displays, the way children would play- and learn-with them.

They stopped in the staff lounge. Rita gave Keith's his coffee and then they continued to the boardroom. When he could, Keith slowed his pace slightly, and nonchalantly checked out Rita's body as she walked in front of him. Even in khaki slacks and a New England Aquarium polo shirt, it was a nice view. She had a sexy voice. It purred, even when being professional. Her voice was that of a siren calling to maneuver his ship toward her, and his ship was steering willingly towards the rocks, mesmerized.

Rita could tell Keith was checking out her ass—staying just far enough behind her to get a good look. "Typical male," she thought, though she didn't mind. Not now. She had recently shed a few pounds, got her hair coiffed in a new look, and was newly single. She decided it felt good to be noticed again.

"Here you are, Mr. Vintner, the boardroom. Please make yourself comfortable." Rita reached over to a stack of folders in a stand-up display, and held one out for him. "This is the latest Annual Report that shows more of who we are and what we do. This should keep you busy until Dr. Sneed arrives."

"Thank you Rita, and please, call me Keith."

He sat in one of the comfortable chairs and watched Rita shut the door behind her, sneaking one last glance as she exited. "I take that back, it's a *very* nice view," he thought as he opened the folder.

Rita enjoyed the attention she was getting from Keith. It had been a long time since someone had taken notice of her. She wondered if she would see him again. "Oh well, back to work." She said to herself.

6

A New Project

"Dr. Vintner, damn good to meet you," Dr. Sneed, world-renowned marine curator, proclaimed as he barged into the boardroom and threw out his paw. "Pete Sneed. Sorry for the smell. We had a little...mess to clean up...you know...sometimes you can't wash all the stink off. Anyway...welcome! So, you're the new wunderkind of aquarium design and you're here to show us the latest and greatest. I've got to tell you, I'm impressed by your work. I flew down to check out Scripps' new tank down in Florida and have to say, it was stunning. Helluva' design. You want to do the same kind of thing for us?"

Pete continued impatiently. "Show me your idea. I can't wait to see it. Did you bring your mockup with you?"

Keith blushed slightly. Although accustomed to praise, he was *not* used to it coming from someone so highly respected. "I did. It's down in the receiving dock. Once I unpack it, setup is simple. It won't take long at all."

Keith was very excited to show off his latest concept. It was the largest, most ingenious tank system he had ever conceived—it was able to hold more than twenty million gallons and would mimic a natural flow of every fluid ounce.

When completed, the exhibit would include a winding plexiglass tube corridor, literally through the center of the exhibit, stimulating the visitors' senses—the surge of the waves as they crashed could be felt, seen, heard, and even smelled! Visitors would feel like a fish and the fish would feel right at home. Because of the curvature of the tubular corridor, a visitor could reach out, and almost touch the exhibit inhabitants. It would be an impressive exhibit and habitat. The New England Aquarium would be the perfect showcase for it.

"Splendid," Pete replied. "The board members and committee should be here in about an hour. I hope that will give you enough time."

"Plenty," Keith shot back.

<hr />

Pete Sneed, after seeing the mockup demonstration, looked around at the reactions of the board members. The Secretary, Willimina 'Willi' Tedeski, chimed in, catching Pete's attention. "Chairman, board, committee, I motion that we vote on Keith's design right now. We have seen all the others, and for the sake of expediency in completing the project on time, I suggest we vote," said Willi. "Pronto."

Pete seconded the motion, which meant it was time for the board of directors to vote. "Keith, I'm afraid you don't get to be privy to this part of the meeting. We'll take a vote and get back to you. I'll call you at your hotel as soon as we've tallied all of the votes."

"Of course," Keith replied. He hoped no one in the room had notice the few beads of sweat that suddenly appeared on his slightly furrowed brow.

Keith was about to get up from his chair, but was stopped by an overzealous Willi. "*Poppycock!* Come on Pete, you know this is the best damn design we've ever seen. It beats all the others hands down...and I'm not forgetting protocol. Keith is going to find out soon enough anyway. My motion and your second stands. Let's vote. Have a seat Keith."

"All right, Willi," Pete replied, intrigued by her aggressive proclamation.

With a barely audible sigh, Keith sat back down.

"By a show of hands, who is in favor of adopting Keith's design for our new exhibit?" The vote was unequivocally unanimous by the show of all hands in the room rising in unison.

The meeting with the board of directors was an overwhelming success. The meeting quickly concluded. Keith bid adieux to everyone, assuring them all that the project would be started as soon as possible, and that he would return to Boston in a few weeks to get the ball rolling.

"It looks like I'm going to be in Boston for a while," Keith mused.

7

Filled with poise, bolstered with self-assurance, Keith shifted his focus toward a different kind of prize. The meeting with the New England Aquarium board of directors finished a tick before noon and his new goal, if at all feasible, was invite Rita to lunch. Truth be told, Keith wanted to do more than lunch with her, but he had to start somewhere. "What the heck, she's good looking, a little sassy, seems like she might be fun to know. What better way to start a relationship than by going to lunch," he thought. He confidently, and, with not-so-innocent intentions in mind—or evident—strode to the aquarium's reception desk.

As he approached the desk, he could see Rita multi-tasking on her computer—typing and having a conversation on her wireless headset. Luckily for Keith, she was alone and no one else was at the counter vying for her attention. He patiently waited but felt his confidence start to evaporate. Self-doubt—not a natural emotion for Keith—steadily chipped away his psyche. Keith could not shake the idea that something about Rita made him feel *different*. Rita didn't seem to be in a hurry to get off the phone when she saw him standing there. She just kept on talking and typing. Maybe she already had a boyfriend and he was barking up the wrong tree. Maybe she was just being kind to him earlier. Maybe he was losing his touch. She was just *too* attractive not to have a boyfriend, lover, or partner. Maybe Keith's unexpected newfound agenda was a just waste of time. But deep down, he knew it was too late to shed his feelings of excitement and anticipation of being with Rita.

"Damn these human emotions! Keep up the appearance of cool, bucko, it's just lunch. Ok, so she's beautiful. Don't let that throw you off your game. You won't know if you don't ask," he thought. As he stood there, he attempted to look as calm as possible, his physical attraction to her had obviously, to him, taken over his train of thought. She had gotten into his *head*. He tried to imagine what she looked like without the champagne-colored polo style blouse.

Rita's eyes briefly diverted from the screen. She noticed Keith waiting. Was it her imagination or did he look nervous? She finished the call, turned and looked at him, a hint of amusement in her big, beautiful eyes. "You've been here a while," Rita said to Keith in a playful manner. How'd your meeting with Dr. Sneed and the board go?" Keith didn't respond. She paused and asked, "Is there something I can do for you Keith?"

"Damn headsets, you can never tell when someone is talking to you or not! She was talking to *him*," Keith scolded himself. Keith snapped back to reality and tried to vanquish his last thought from his head, which had nothing whatsoever to do with his business meeting, and everything to do with what Rita might look like sans clothing.

He nervously and unintentionally blurted out a response, "Oh...hi Rita. The meeting went very well, thank you for asking. It looks like I'll be in Boston for a while. The project is set to begin in two weeks."

Still feeling a bit off-kilter, Keith struggled to get his mind back on business instead of Rita's body. "I was wondering...do you know where Cheers is? I know the original bar is on Beacon Street, but I'd heard there's a replica bar in the Faneuil Hall Market? I know it's become a tourist trap and everything, since the TV series made the original bar so popular, but I can't resist the temptation. I might as well check this off my bucket list while I'm here right now. Should I go to the original bar...or the one in Faneuil? One of them is close enough to walk to from here, correct? Are you, um, doing anything...for lunch?" his mid-sentence stops, now utterly convinced him that he must sound like a complete idiot.

This was not going well at all. He was not his normal, confident self. His words stumbled out of his mouth. Much to his chagrin, his confidence had abandoned him at the worst possible time. He received no outward signals from Rita, other than her mesmerizing stare. Their conversation was becoming increasingly unsettling to him. "Damn her and her gorgeous face," he thought. Keith suddenly had an extremely awkward thought that Rita could read his mind, which would be a *bit* of a problem. His fear led him to the idea that she could play professional poker. Or should.

Although his invitation didn't come out *quite* as eloquent as he had planned, he did get the feeling she got the gist of it, even if he had sounded like a buffoon.

Rita was amused. She could tell he was struggling to find the right words to ask her out for lunch. She found it endearing that he fumbled his invitation, especially since he didn't look like the kind of man who would ever unravel around women. Contrarily, he looked as if he should have women flocking to him. Her 'hunk-o-meter' had been redlining from the moment she saw him earlier in the day. *And* she knew he was attracted to her by the way his eyes quickly darted up and down her body several times, when he thought she wasn't looking. She would take him up on his offer—but not because she was hungry.

"Listen Rita, since I'm making a perfect fool out of myself at the present and…." Keith shook his head and continued. "I don't quite know why this isn't coming out right, so let me try this again…Rita, would you like to go to lunch at Cheers with me?" he asked. He relaxed a little as he felt some of his confidence return. However, he still couldn't understand what it was about this woman that had him feeling so awkward. There was *something* about her. Maybe he just needed to get laid—it *had* been a while—and she *was* distractingly attractive.

To his surprise, and relief, Rita gave him the answer he had wanted. "Yes, Mr. Vintner…Keith. I'd love to, but I should call Cheers and get our names on the waiting list, otherwise we'll be in for a long wait to get a table. I've really only got an hour for lunch. Don't worry, I know some people," she said and gave him a heart-stopping wink.

Rita tidied up her desk as she made the call to the famous pub, and then called Colleen to let her know she was leaving for lunch. "Colleen, I'm catching a cab to Cheers. The original. Taking another tourist to experience one of Boston's most famous spots, and you know that place is always packed for lunch, so we'll probably be a bit longer than an hour. I'll be back as soon as I can though."

Rita grabbed her purse and popped out of her chair. She said, friskily, "Once again, follow me." She thought it might be entertaining to watch him fall over himself. On the other hand, she hoped he would be able to relax so she could get to know him. He looked like he had all the right equipment, but maybe he was a shy, handsome genius who needed to work on his self-confidence. She found this hard to believe, but from their brief conversation, it appeared he was like any other guy: all talk until it was time to 'pay the bill'.

Rita felt Keith's lovely smile—and his ogling—as they walked under Cheers famous awning. Always the gentleman, Keith opened the door for Rita, and after closing it behind himself, saw Joe, the Maître d.

As Joe looked up from his reservation list, checking to see who'd just entered his domain, he noticed Rita. A wide smile appeared on his face. Joe's smile was ample evidence that he recognized her, and knew her well. The mammoth man gave Rita a big hug, released her, grabbed her shoulders, and bent down to kiss her on both cheeks. He leaned back to look at her, holding her firmly. In a baritone voice, he growled, "Lady, you are lookin' good. When are you going to go out with me? You know I've had my eye on you for a long time." He laughed while completely ignoring Keith.

The behemoth released Rita and continued in a voice that sounded like a low roar. "Before you tell me 'no' again and remind me that I'm happily married. Let an old man dream a little. Tell me 'maybe'. Lie to me," he said, and gave her a wink.

Rita smiled from ear-to-ear as Joe's laugh resonated the rafters, his barrel chest heaving. "Ho, ho, ho,"

Keith thought this guy probably had a Santa Claus job during the holidays. "Hmmm," thought Keith. "*You'd* better be good for goodness sake."

Joe finally released Rita and stepped back. He proudly proclaimed, "I've reserved the best table in the house. Just for you. It's a good thing you called. You know how crowded it gets here during the lunch rush. Oh...and before I forget, I gotta' tell ya', my granddaughter, Penelope, just loves the book of prehistoric fish that you recommended we get for her birthday. I told the missus that you really knew what you were talkin' about.

"Penelope said she had a wonderful time on her field-trip to your 'fish bowl'. She loves all those fishies. You folks made quite an impression on the kids. I had no idea that little girls liked sharks and killer whales so much. I thought they just went in for those cute ones, you know, sea horses and jellyfish and such. Just goes to show ya' what I know about kids these days. Anyway, enough about my family. How's yours? All healthy and happy I hope. I won't ask about Simon, I got nothin' to say that's nice about 'im, so I won' say a thing," Joe said. His forehead crinkled as he made no attempt to show his disgust at the thought of Simon.

He noticed Rita seemed to be uncomfortable with the direction of the conversation, so Joe got back to business. "There I go ramblin' on when you two kids are probably hungry. Let me get you seated so you can get eatin', I'll stop by and chat later."

He weaved among the packed pub gracefully, not unlike an extra-large ballerina, sans tutu, and seated the couple at a great people-watching booth. Cheers was filled to capacity with tourists—and locals who, regardless of the slowly waning fad still frequented the popular watering hole.

After two orders of fish-and-chips was served, and they had finished their meals, Keith finally loosened up a bit. Rita realized that Keith, though initially nervous, was intelligent, eloquent, and interesting. And his self-deprecation was very charming. She had begun to feel more comfortable around him by the minute.

After their delicious meal and delightful banter, and after Rita said goodbye to Joe, Keith paid for lunch and purchased a hoodie at the counter. He figured it would be perfect to wear after surfing or a dive.

During their cab ride back to the aquarium, Keith realized that if he wanted to ask Rita out for a *real* date, his immediate options were closing fast. Rita had to know by now that he had amorous intentions. There was no mention of a boyfriend—just that she had a psychotic ex-husband, Simon, the guy Joe had revealed earlier. As their cab approached the aquarium, Keith's confidence had returned to full strength and he decided to give it a shot. He would keep the request for a real date low-key. Since he knew very little about the local cuisine, and since he was soon going to be staying in Boston for the next several months, he ought to let Rita know he was interested in getting to know the city, and her, in more than just a casual way. Now if he could just *say* something like that.

Keith once again felt confounded by the fact that he was having difficulty asking Rita for a date. Something told him to tread carefully in this situation and he usually followed his instincts.

As Keith opened one of the large main doors to the aquarium, he turned to face Rita. "Thank you for having lunch with me today, and at the risk of assuming that you had as much fun as I did, I'd like to ask you out for dinner tonight. I've got to go home to California in the morning but I'm coming back here next week, and will be staying in Boston for the duration of the project. I'm normally pretty good at this courting game, but for some reason… I'm, um, not with you. What do you say? How about going on a *real* date with me? You can even choose the restaurant," he teased. "It's obvious you know quite a lot of people and places in this town. How about it?"

Keith really enjoyed Rita's company, but the idea of something beyond friendship was more a hopeful longshot than a sure thing. Rita was a jewel and Keith's instincts told him that she must be involved with someone, even after divorce. But maybe not.

Rita, with a not-so-feigned look of puzzlement, was pensive, as if she was unsure of how to respond. Keith seemed like a nice man, and if it didn't work out, she was certain they could keep their business relationship. From what little she did know about Keith, she believed that would be easy. "Take a leap, Rita," she told herself. "Do it! Say 'yes'. What do you have to lose?"

She looked in his eyes for signs of ulterior motives—and saw them. She felt ulterior motives of her own, but still wanted to go slow. She had not been on a real date in a long time. She had gone out with friends—some of them single—but always as part of a group. <u>This</u> would be her first real date since college. With Simon.

She quickly debated what to do while she tried to disguise her anguish. She didn't want to seem too willing—she liked Keith— what she had seen and heard so far, but she didn't want to dive into something that would be considered a rebound affair. "Your heart has been broken enough, thank you very much," she reminded herself.

The fact that Keith *was* very good looking was difficult to ignore. He was in great shape—his suit filled out in all the right places. He was eloquent, well mannered, and seemed like a real gentleman, down to earth, not someone who would become a vagabond surfer or diver dude as he got older. "Just do it!" she beseeched herself.

"Yes...yes, I'll go to dinner with you. But *just* dinner. I have to get home early tonight. I've got a batch of reports to finish first thing in the morning for Pete...Dr. Sneed. Meet me in your hotel lobby at six o'clock sharp, I know just the place for dinner," she said quickly.

Keith didn't know if what she had just said meant he ought to take it slow with her, or that she just wanted to be friends. He thought he might have come across as being interested in her romantically, which was true, but he deliberately kept the afternoon's conversation all business. The problem was that he liked Rita and hoped to learn more about her. Physically and intellectually.

"Six o'clock sharp." He said.

8

The Loser

Having heard every excuse in the book, Theodore 'Tank' Schmotz, Simon's supervisor, knowingly dismissed the verbal flatulence Simon had just expelled. Tank felt duty bound to agressively handle the situation. He had little doubt that Simon was an alcoholic. After all, Tank hadn't just fallen off a turnip truck. He had seen it too many times from too many people. Tank shook his head with disbelief thinking about how irresponsible Simon was, before he happily executed the coup de grâce. "Cathcart! Shut the fuck up! I know a line of horseshit when I hear it. Change your attitude. Do yourself...and me, a favor. Get your ass here on time, every damn day...sober! And give me a full day's work *every* day. You're officially on probation now, which means *no more fuck ups*! Got it, Cathcart?"

Simon truly didn't believe that he deserved the humiliation and abuse Tank had leveled at him. He acquiesced—his jaw tightened. He nodded. "Good, now get the hell out of my office. I've got work to do," Tank grumbled.

Tank reached for his coffee, took a sip, opened a manila folder, and stared at it. After a few seconds, he looked up, surprised to see Simon still there, visibly upset by the wrath Tank had just unleashed on him.

To Tank, some people were just clueless. "What the fuck are you still standing there for? Go home and think about what I just said good and hard. Keep that feeling of humiliation in your

58

Neanderthal brain. It'll do you some good. And think about how lucky you are to still have a goddamn *job*!"

"What a lousy-ass life I've got," Simon whined. He had just been kicked out of his foreman's office. Put on probation. Chewed out for continually being late, doing a less-than-stellar job, and having a bad attitude when asked to put forth additional effort. To compound the problem, Tank had sadistically waited until the end of the day to lower the boom.

Well-known for rattling off multi-word, multi-syllabic expletives, Simon made a feeble attempt at exoneration. "What an *asshole*."

9

"Henry!" Simon shouted across the crowded bar. The Tin Horn was filled to the rafters with patrons all looking for solace or companionship. Or both.

He realized the time had finally come for him to find another place to hang out. The Horn had changed—it was no longer a local dive. It had become a popular watering hole for trendy, hipster dudes to meet up after work.

"Look at all these worthless clowns," Simon thought. After elbowing his way past several of the patrons in an attempt to reach the bar, he suddenly felt uneasy. Dirty. "Great. Now I'm gonna' have to take a shower. Fuckin' vermin," he thought as he wiped non-existent microbes from his forearms.

Upon taking proprietorship of The Tin Horn, the new owners had immediately proclaimed that tabs—nightly or otherwise—would no longer be extended. This applied to regulars as well as new customers. This new policy was also posted in in several prominent locations. "Bastards!" Simon seethed.

They had redecorated the 'Horn' in a pseudo-western motif, which Simon considered to be "downright hokey." And to top it off, they now had an openly gay bartender, Henry. "What's the world coming to?" he moaned.

Most people would consider Simon to be hateful. But additional words were needed to truly describe his personality: bitter, disingenuous, racist, spiteful, cruel. The meeting with Tank did nothing to soften any of these qualities.

When Henry finally acknowledged him, Simon angrily shouted, "Double shot and a draft! Sometime today!" He hoped his contempt for Henry and his ilk was detected.

He was desperate for a drink. He *needed* a boilermaker to help him get out of the funk he was in after his meeting with Tank, discovering he would have to pay cash for all his drinks, and being surrounded by people he considered beneath him. Henry's obvious indifference to Simon pushed him that much closer to the edge. Could Henry not hear him? See him? Simon was now desperate for the magic potions that would calm him down. "Fuck Calgon," he thought. "Jim Beam will take *my* cares away.

No one, it seemed, paid attention to Simon these days: Tank, Henry, the guys at the dock. No one. Simon figured it all started with "that bitch of an ex-old lady" of his, Rita. He was convinced that she was the one who started his downward spiral of contempt for his fellow man. And women. Especially women.

During their divorce hearings, Simon guessed that Rita must have brainwashed them all—slept with them? She made them all her little lapdogs—turned them against him. He had seen her talking to them—conspiring to take him down. "Conniving slut." She did her best to change him, finally realized that was not possible, and abandoned him. "*Bitch*! No one leaves Simon Cathcart! Not without payback, that is," he fumed.

As soon as his drinks arrived, Simon inhaled them as if they were the essence of life itself. He began to recap his undeserved existence again: his life sucked, his job was boring, his boss was a certified asswipe. In doing so, he had inadvertently stressed himself out even more than he already was, so he decided to have another boilermaker. "Henry, hit me again. And hurry!" he shouted.

Henry's back was turned to Simon, either intentionally or indifferently. "Kiss my ass, dipshit. You're going to have to wait," Henry chuckled to himself. Henry had clearly heard Simon's request, but he knew Simon was homophobic and took great delight in deliberately antagonizing him. "What'll it be, big boy?" Henry winked at Simon, and intentionally, antagonistically added a diminutive lisp. He didn't care one iota if that intolerant Cathcart ever set foot in *his* bar again. Henry was now half owner of The Tin Horn—the working half. The decider.

"Just give me a fuckin' Jim Beam and an PBR. Sometime today!" Simon replied insolently. Simon was clearly disgusted by the way Henry was treating him. Who the hell did Henry think he was? Simon had been coming here long before Henry showed up. Who was Henry to be treating Simon this way? Like a lowlife. "Fuckin' fag," he thought.

Simon downed his last two drinks, slipped off his stool, placed a twenty-dollar bill on the bar for his drinks—which didn't cover the bill let alone a tip—turned and headed toward the door, but not before bumping into a seemingly endless slew of hipster dudes and yuppies. "Fuck you all. Now I gotta' go take a goddam shower!" he blurted out in a drunken, not-so-quiet rant. That was it. He was *never* coming back here again. No way.

Still agitated by his recent confrontation with Tank, he muttered to himself as he weaved his way to his car. "Lame-ass excuses for putting me on probation. Is he better than me? No. Who made him God anyway? Who the fuck does Tank think he is anyway? He's a fuckin' jerk, *that's* who *he* is."

While the contempt for his boss was still fresh in his mind—festering—Simon began think of ways to get back at "that son of a bitch, and the rest of the backstabbers in his life." Simon wanted payback for all the injustices he believed were enacted on him by them. All of them.

Simon desperately wished he could just quit his job. "Fuck 'em," he thought. "If I didn't have those pain-in-the-ass alimony payments to that bitch Rita, my life would be better. *Rita! All* this shit started with Rita. This whole goddamn mess was *entirely* that stupid bitch's fault. Why did I ever get involved with her in the first place? What was I thinking? Fuckin' Ski. I always knew it was a mistake to get hitched. I coulda got pussy any time I wanted, but *no*, I *had* to go and get a wife! Fuckin' ball-and-chain!" Simon now fully understood that enduring aphorism. "Wives, even ex-wives, are nothin' but punishment, from which one can never truly be free."

———◦———

Three sheets to the wind, Simon stumbled through his apartment door, grabbed a cold beer, then plopped himself on the sofa to sort out the mail that had been piling up in his mailbox. He tossed the junk mail directly into the trashcan, then recognized with disgust, an envelope from Rita's lawyer in the State of Massachusetts. The envelope contained a *friendly* reminder that he was late on his alimony payments, and that they didn't *want* to resort to garnishing his wages, *again*, but they were more than willing to do so, if he didn't make good on his past due payments.

"What bullshit! Who do they think they are?" He had car payments to make. And rent to pay. And the utilities bill. And booze to buy. Simon chuckled to himself, "They're trying to get milk from a bone. That bitch and that fucker she hired are really askin' for it. They'll get payment all right! Over my cold, dead, achy-breaky body."

Fixated on Rita, he desperately wanted to give her a piece of his mind. "Why the hell did she leave me anyways? That connivin' bitch had someone waitin' in the wings the whole time. That had to be it. She was seeing someone else before she left me. I knew it! Having her cake and eating it too, sucking money offa' him and this guy, Mr. whoever he the hell he is. I'm going to find out, damn it, and right now. I'll put that bitch in her place. Fuckin' A right I will."

Drunk, he impulsively called Rita's house. Rita wasn't there, or didn't want to answer. Did she know it was him calling? "Bitch." He didn't leave a message on her answering machine. Then he called her cell phone, guessed he would only get to her voice mail—he was right.

"*Shit!* Who the hell does she think she is, unleashin' her junkyard-dog lawyer on *me*, sending *me* threatenin' letters!

Demanding *money*! Bitch, I'm not the one who'll be paying. You'll be payin'. Oh yeah. You'll pay all right. Yes you will."

———————

Simon was obsessed with his Rita. He felt sorry for himself and felt unloved and alone. The real reasons Rita had left him never even occurred to him. He only knew that he had been victimized and that he missed her. He missed being the only thing in her life, the center of her attention. He thought school would be the end of her outside yearnings. He couldn't understand why she needed another man. And a job making good money. He was confused. Didn't know why Rita wasn't satisfied with their marriage.

In his current extremely inebriated state, the simple truth eluded him. He tried to focus on reasons why he should forgive her and just let her live her new life in peace. But this gave him more reasons to hate her. As far as Simon was concerned, she took *everything* away from *him*, and he was not going to just sit back and let *anyone* do this to him. No one! Not even *sweet, adorable little* Rita.

He slammed the phone down. "She's gonna' to get *more* than a piece of my mind." He went to the kitchen and grabbed a bottle of rotgut whiskey off the counter. He took a long pull. Another. And another. Feeding his hatred with the foul-tasting brown fuel.

"Call her at *work*!" the thought popped into his head as if from the gods themselves. "That'll teach the bitch who's who."

10

Keith couldn't wait for dinner. His stomach wasn't the issue, he was anxious to see Rita. Uber-anxious. It was only five-thirty, so he put on his wicking garb and sneakers, left the hotel, and jogged at a brisk pace for about three miles. After that, he visited the hotel gym and lifted some weights in an attempt to ease his increasing anxiety. Sweaty from his energetic workout Keith went back to his room, showered, and shaved. Again.

"Damn five o'clock shadow," he groaned.

Keith opened his laptop, connected to the Internet, logged in to the Scripps private network, and responded to some emails.

He then opened a real-time flow-analysis program he and some of his colleagues had developed. Since he still had some time to kill he thought he would try out some new ideas that had been gnawing at him. It was only 5:10—still an hour to go before he would see Rita again. He deftly keyed some variables into the program, moused his cursor with precision, and sat back to watch a simulation of water flowing through a virtual aquarium's circulation system—rainbow-hued colors swirled across the screen graphically depicting the circulatory patterns created by the suction and dispersal of the water through the virtual system. To laymen, it probably appeared to be psychedelic new-age art. But to the trained eye, the vibrant colors, whirls, vortices, and eddies, meant something quite specific to Keith's new aquatic design.

11

After their lunch, Keith dropped Rita off at the New England Aquarium. She rushed back to her desk, put on her headset, and with nervous excitement dialed Colleen's extension. Before Colleen could finish uttering her standard greeting, Rita butted in. "Colleen, are you sitting down? I've got some news that will knock your socks off. You won't believe me, but that nice looking man from Scripps asked me out for dinner tonight, and I said 'yes'. I can't believe I actually said 'yes'. Am I crazy?"

"Whoohoo!" Colleen replied jubilantly. "It's about time someone asked you out. I saw you walk him back to the boardroom and was wondering who that hunk was. I'm so happy for you Rita! Finally gettin' some! That's my girl. What's the plan?"

"Whoa! Slow down Colleen. First things first. We're just going to dinner! Not to his *hotel* room. I told him I had to be back at the office first thing in the morning, which is true, and that I had to make it a short night. This 'excuse' seemed to make it easier to accept his invitation, and you know, I don't want to seem *too* easy." Rita giggled. Colleen did too.

"Girl, by the way he was checking out your behind, dinner was *maybe* the second thing on his mind when he asked you out. I'm jealous. I'd like to get with him for a few hours. He has a nice form, if you know what I mean."

"Colleen. Pulease!" Rita fired back. Thoughts of Keith's nice form suddenly assaulted her consciousness.

Thanks to Colleen's intimation about Keith's sculpted body, Rita worked that afternoon as if possessed. She attempted to concentrate on her work, but thoughts of Keith's body kept creeping in. Rita checked her watch. Then checked it again. She still had at least thirty minutes of work to wade through before she could leave the office and then head down to the Marriott to meet Keith for dinner.

Try as she might, she couldn't keep her mind on her paperwork. Her brain, having a mind of its own, decided it was much more fun to daydream about a pleasant evening with Keith. An evening Rita felt she deserved, and was a long time coming.

Then her phone rang. She glared at the it with disdain. On a normal day, she would have answered it in a heartbeat, even after business hours. But today, right now, she had too much paperwork to finish before she could call it a day, and see Keith again. And now *this*. "Aarghh! Who on earth could be calling at almost five-thirty in the afternoon? Why can't they give me a break?" she grumbled. She tried to justify ignoring the call. That was a tall order for 'Rita the Dependable'. 'Rita the Professional'.

She figured it was probably a grouchy member who had not as of yet received their annual parking pass in the mail, or was not aware that extended summer hours started *next* week. The incessant ringing caused Rita to resent, uncharacteristically, whoever was calling. Moreover, she felt resentment toward *all* of the members. "Didn't they *read* their member magazines or newsletters?"

She then chastised herself for thinking ill of others. "Come on self, go the extra mile. *That's* what you do! What the hell, there's only a million other things to do! What's one more phone call gonna' hurt?"

"Thank you for calling the New England Aquarium, Rita Haley here. How may I help you?"

Simon loathed hearing Rita use her maiden name. He had heard through his network of spies that she had reverted to it immediately after their divorce, completely severing her association with him. At least on paper.

Hearing her refer to herself as Rita Haley triggered his inebriated rampage. "What the hell're doin' havin' your lawyer sendin' me nasty grams? Huh? Wha' ya' think tha's gonna do? You can't get blood outta' a turnip little girl, grow up. You'll get what I damn well wanna' give ya', no matter what your fancy-schmancy lawyer tells me to do. Go 'head an' try to rob my wages, you bitch. Wait 'n' see what that gets ya'. I know your roootine, know where the checks go…where ya' live. Don' ya' think I been pas' there keeping an eye on ya'?"

Simon Cathcart, her ex-husbad, the last person she ever wanted to hear from, was the one keeping her from leaving to meet Keith. Simon was drunk again—his slurred and incoherent rambling evidenced that. But what really worried Rita was the fact that her suspicions about his stalking her were correct. She *knew* she had seen him parked outside her home. And now she knew it *was* him she had seen occasionally drive slowly by and stare through her window. *He just admitted it.*

Rita took a deep breath and exhaled slowly. She felt resilient and tough—her once fragile psyche now battle hardened after their divorce proceedings. "No, Simon," she responded calmly. "I didn't send my 'fancy-schmancy' lawyer after you for more money. If you had looked carefully, you would have seen that the notice came from the State of Massachusetts. My lawyer called me to see if you were current on your monthly payments. I told him that you were not one, or two, or three months late, but in fact you are now four months in arrears. So what the hell are *you* complaining about? You want to get the state off your back, and keep your *hard-earned* wages from being garnished, just give me what you owe me, which is practically nothing anyway."

She elevated her voice for emphasis and chose her next words very carefully. "And Simon Cathcart, you drunk prick, don't ever call me at work again, and don't you *ever* threaten me!" She wouldn't give him a chance to respond—she defiantly pressed her finger on the line button, disconnecting the call, and broke a fingernail in the process. "Damm'it!"

The call had rattled her. Simon had just threatened her and she knew what he was capable of doing. "What a way to screw up a perfectly good day."

She tried to calm herself down but failed. She needed to talk to someone—Colleen would still be here. Rita dialed Colleen's extension. "Simon just called," Rita cried out.

"What did that snake say?" Colleen hissed. Colleen's hatred for Simon was marrow-deep and she didn't hesitate to express it.

"He *threatened* me Colleen. I told you I'd seen him around. Stalking me. And he confirmed it just now. Oh Colleen, I don't know what to do! Do you think I should I break off my date with Keith tonight? What if Simon comes to work right now? What if he follows me tonight and confronts Keith?"

Colleen felt duty bound to calm Rita down—get her composed. "What are you talkin' about? Why would you break your date? That's looser talk. Of course you should go out tonight. You can't let that dirt bag control your life anymore. Don't let that piece of shit get to you, Rita. You know he's just a big bag of hot air. He's just trying to scare you, that's all."

"Colleen...I...I *yelled* at him. Right here in the office. Oh, God, I hope no one heard me," she said, trembling.

Colleen smiled at the thought of Rita pushing back at Simon. "Good for you. Now you listen to me, and listen good. You go out and enjoy tonight. But, Rita, we need a plan. Promise me that first thing in the morning you go to the police station and get a restraining order. Then, at least the next time that creep shows up you can get him arrested."

"Colleen? Why won't he just go away?"

Rita suddenly worried about how she would hide her Simon-induced anxiety from Keith. And how he would react to the news that Simon was stalking her. The last thing she wanted to do was drag him into this ugly mess. "One step forward, two steps back."

At 5:50, fearing she would be unable to appear composed and be herself after the latest unwelcome abuse from her ex, she closed her eyes and took several deep breaths, and thought about Keith. A few minutes of silent contemplation turned her emotional tide.

Rita left the aquarium and confidently, albeit still a bit shook up, strode to the Marriott Long Harbor Hotel. During the entire short walk to Keith's hotel Rita forced—commanded—herself to move literally and figuratively forward. Of course, when she glanced back twice for any sign of Simon she told herself that was only natural. After all, he was a legitimate threat.

As she paced the last 100 yards to the hotel, she said a silent prayer. She felt better and decided that Colleen was right—that Simon just wanted to scare her.

Keith was in the lobby reading the Boston Globe's sports section when she arrived. He had had deliberately seated himself at the perfect angle, in the perfect spot, to see anyone who walked into the hotel. He glanced up just as the doorman opened the door for Rita.

Something seemed *wrong*. She looked calm, yet she furtively glanced over her shoulder, and then her eyes quickly darted around the lobby. What troubled Keith the most was that her beautiful smile—the one that captivated Keith just a few short hours ago—was gone. Even from across the room he could tell she was somehow different.

"Was she there to cancel their date?" he thought, his heart fluttered wildly.

12

A New Plan

In the entryway at Lou's On Clark, Michael shook off the raindrops, accumulated from a brief Midwest-style deluge, from his overcoat and umbrella, and greeted the hostess. He said he was meeting someone for dinner, didn't have reservations, and would wait in the bar for a table.

He walked over to the well-seasoned, solid oak bar, found a couple of empty stools next to each other, hung his overcoat on the back of one the stools, sat, greeted the bartender, and ordered his usual—Maker's Mark on the rocks.

When Lou found out that Michael was there, he rushed out the 'in' door of the kitchen, briskly strolled past the other patrons without so much as a glance at them, or even a quick 'hello', and then quietly crept up behind Michael, and tapped him on his shoulder.

Michael turned, thinking it was probably Sarah, letting him know she was there. Lou looked nothing like Sarah. "Lou, you old bear! I knew I'd see you tonight. How the hell are you?"

To which Lou replied, gruffly, a big smile—as always—on his face. "Ah, you kids these days, no respect for the elderly." This was followed by Lou's trademark booming belly laugh.

Michael told Lou he had already arranged for a table for two, and had specifically requested Eddie to be his waiter. "Lou you've got a real winner in Eddie. The kid did a great job last time."

Michael noticed Lou's face light up when he mentioned he had requested a table for two, so he attempted to circumvent

Lou's interrogation as to whom Michael would be dining with this evening. "Sarah's joining me. Chuck's on duty at the fire station for the next 24 hours and she has a hankering for a big plate of your legendary 'Linguini alle Vongole'. She spent the entire day talking about it. That and Isabella's tiramisu. When she found out I didn't have a date for the evening, she invited herself to have dinner with me, here. I suppose I could have done worse for a dinner companion," Michael laughed mischievously.

"I couldn't disagree wit' ya' on *that*," Lou said. A big smile broke out on his large round face. "Sarah ain't exactly hurtin' in the looks department, and she's a spunky one, that's for sure."

Lou's smile suddenly faded. "But ya' know, Michael, ya' deserve someone of your very own. Kinda' like Sarah, but, um, different... you know what I mean?"

Michael, shook his head and cracked a smirk. "Lou, now you're starting to sound like Sarah."

"Michael, you should...." Lou stopped short.

"Tssk, tssk. It seems like we're going to have to have a little talk," a familiar voice directly behind Michael chimed in.

Michael smelled a set up. Sarah had more than likely been standing right behind him the whole time and Lou didn't let on. "That crafty old coot!" Michael's back had been turned away from the front door, and he knew Lou must have seen Sarah as she entered, but Lou let him continue rambling anyway.

"Sarah!" Lou boomed. He flashed Michael a quick smirk. "As always, good to see you. Gimme' a hug."

"You dirty old man. Sure, I'll give you a big hug, *if* you promise to make some of your famous clams for me. You think you can do that for a poor, starving, underpaid architect?" Sarah very gently stroked Michael's thick main of hair, knowing that would get a rise out of him. "I'm tellin' you Lou, this guy works me too hard."

"She *is* a firecracker." Michael thought.

"Sounds like I'm getting the better end of the deal here," Lou said with glee. He then gave Sarah a big bear hug, not unlike those he gave everyone in his 'family'. Sarah knew as well as anybody that everyone was family at Lou's On Clark. Lou looked directly at Sarah and brought her up to speed on his and Michael's current conversation.

"Not that the sighta' you doesn' brighten my day...but I was tellin' Michael that I was hoping that *he*," pointing at Michael, "was waiting for a someone else. Not that you're not worth waiting for, Sarah, it's just that, ya' know, I wish he would start datin' for *real*. But I know his mind is...how you say...preoccupied with work."

"Lou," Sarah countered, as if on cue, "Michael here doesn't *have* to work so hard. I've been on him forever to start dating, even tried getting him to register at the online matchmaking service that brought Chuck and I together, but he's brushed it off time and time again. You and I need to do something Lou, I'm tellin' you. Forever buried in his work is not *healthy* for Michael. We've got to break him out of this perpetual holding pattern he's in. Wanna' help me, Lou? For old time's sake? And Michael's?"

Lou, in an uncharacteristic, for him, subdued tone—not his usual jovial self—looked at both them intently and spoke softly. "You know I'm here for the both a ya'." He set his ham-sized hands on their shoulders, gave a little squeeze. "Both a ya'."

Convinced he had made his point, Lou removed his large hands from their shoulders. "Ok, that's enough of this chit chat for me. You know they can't run the kitchen without ol' Lou." His big grin returned, he looked at Sarah. "I'm goin' get yer clams ready for a jacuzzi." He turned and strode away—kitchen bound. This time he used the proper door.

"Hey boss," Sarah, changed the subject, "care to order me a dirty martini?" She slid on the stool next to him and grabbed a bread stick from the basket on the bar. "I hope our table will be ready soon. I'm famished." Twirling the breadstick in her fingers, Sarah quickly changed the subject back to the original topic— Michael's love life. "Another Friday night, and no date. What's the matter Michael? What's going on? I thought we talked about this already. We're losing the old Michael. Lou and I are simply going to have to rectify this situation," she frowned. "Where oh where has he gone? No glow, no verve. Just work. What's up with that?"

He knew Sarah's heart was in the right place, even if she was a bit over the top on the matter of his personal life. "I know you care about and worry about me. But I'm fine. And besides, I just don't want to any effort into finding someone. I've got my work. It's my life. I enjoy it and that's enough for me. Really. That's...all I need right now."

"That's a crock of shit and you know it. I'm going to connect you with Jillian's matchmaking service. You just wait and see."

13

Over the Edge

Simon revved the engine, manhandled the gearbox, and peeled rubber, leaving behind dual black streaks and billowing flumes of smoke. He arrived at Rita's home minutes later and stopped directly in front of her ground-level garden condominium.

Peering through the opened curtains Simon saw no lights or movement inside her condominium. Ever since Simon started stalking Rita, he had never seen anyone one going in or coming out of her apartment, except the cable guy, and he was in there for about fifteen minutes, long enough to set up her cable box. But, Simon *knew* Rita was playing him—he honestly believed she had a lover. She had not come home yet, so he concluded, as much as his inebriated brain could conclude, that she must still be at work. It *was* only 5:30, so he still might be able catch her as she left the aquarium—rattle her cage a bit, just for fun.

"No one hung up on *Simon Cathcart*!"

———⟫⟪———

Simon was parked on the street across from the New England Aquarium when he saw her walking, not toward her apartment, but heading east on Old Atlantic Avenue, toward State Street.

He got out of the car, indignantly ignored the parking meter, and tailed her. Sloppily. She seemed intent on reaching her destination—she obviously didn't see him trailing a half block behind her despite the fact that she looked over her shoulder a two or three times.

Rita walked down State Street and into the lobby of the Marriott Long Harbor Hotel.

"Was she meeting someone?" He had to know. Simon snuck across the street, found an advantageous observation point, turned, and looked toward the hotel. "Should I get closer?"

He was contemplating his next move when he saw Rita suddenly leave the lobby with a rugged, good looking, tall guy—smiling, laughing, chatting. Simon saw the look in the guy's eyes. He was certain this guy wanted to fuck Rita. It was obvious—maybe he already had. So, *this* was her new boyfriend.

He wanted go over there and confront them right then and there. Simon figured he could take the guy out—he didn't look that tough. Simon cringed as he watched Rita laugh. He felt nauseated as he watched her fawn over her new boyfriend—lover. Simon recognized the signs—Rita was giving the green light to this guy to let him know he could have his way with her. "What a whore! Gettin' the proof I need to stop my money from goin' to her is going to be the easiest thing I done all week," Simon chuckled. "She's probably bangin' him good, and takin' his money too. We'll see who's smarter. Won't we?"

Simon's egotism was deeply rooted—his malevolent brain already calculating his next step.

14

Rita had chosen a restaurant close to Keith's hotel in the harbor for their date—within walking distance of her home, just in case Simon reared his ugly head. "Why do I keep thinking about Simon? Fuck him!"

She *was going* to be in control of her own destiny. She *was not* going to let her ex-husband ruin her life. She did her best to push all thoughts of Simon to the back of her mind, but, old habits proved hard to break completely—her eyes darted warily around the hotel lobby looking for Simon. Keith was a strapping man, but Simon with his frequent uncontrollable anger could undeniably do some damage if he did make an apperance.

Rita saw Keith, and the visions of her lunatic ex-husband dissolved instantly. Keith, handsome and well built, must have been a model sometime in his life, she thought. He was the kind of man any woman would go for—gorgeous, in a masculine, GQ, Robert-Redford-way. Her natural, glowing—beautiful—smile quickly replaced the Simon-induced scowl. As far as Rita was concerned, beyond being a prime-grade American male, Keith Vintner was something special.

———⟫●⟪———

To her delight, the evening went smoothly. They discovered that they had many things in common—both had active lifestyles, loved their families, and loved their jobs.

Rita nervously divulged to Keith that she was not used to being on the dating scene and told him she really needed to get out and meet people again after her recent, unpleasant divorce.

She was pleased that Keith didn't seem to mind talking about her divorce. She had always assumed men naturally dreaded hearing about exes—how bad they were, and how they were so much excess baggage. Keith actually seemed to embrace the subject. He told her he had good relations with all his exes—still talked to and was friends with them. Told her he had never met the right woman for a long-term relationship. Rita couldn't believe her ears.

Concerning exes, Keith didn't understand what was wrong with someone like Simon—seemingly determined to make someone else's life so difficult. He felt sad for Rita. He could tell she had wished for a loving, meaningful relationship, but like so many other relationships-gone-bad, evidently, so had hers.

Their pleasant and comfortable conversation lasted through dinner—each gradually disclosed a bit more about themselves. As evening turned to night, both were delighted to find, the more they learned about each other, the more they liked what they heard.

After dessert, Keith began calculating a method to get closer to Rita, without coming on too strong. She didn't *seem* hell bent against all men after her bitter separation battle, but he didn't want to be presumptuous. "Rita, I know you've just gone through a nasty divorce, as you put it, and probably are pretty cautious about relationships in general, but I'd like to see you again. Would that be all right?"

Truth be told, what he really wanted to ask was, "Rita, will you come upstairs to my room and have wild banshee sex with me all night long?" But obviously that particular tactic would put the kibosh on any chance of him advancing to home plate with her, not to mention his desire of sliding into third. "Damn!" he thought. "What a lousy time to be a gentleman."

15

S imon shadowed Rita and Keith to the restaurant. When they didn't come out for a few minutes, he figured he would just wait and see what would happen—he had nothing else to do.

He spotted a liquor store's neon sign a few blocks down the street and made a beeline for it. He grabbed three forty-ounce bottles of malt liquor, paid the guy behind the counter, and left the liquor store with saying a word. He found a darkened alcove across the street from the restaurant where Rita and Keith were dining, kicked out a street urchin, battened down the hatches, and downed one of his cold brews. And waited. He took a heavy pull from the first bottle of malt liquor and belched loudly. "At least I got me some beers" he chuckled.

"Finally." Simon lamented as he saw the couple exit the restaurant. They were laughing and holding hands. "I knew it! She *does* have a sugar daddy! Got her now!"

As he stood up the muscles in his back screamed. He had been squatting in the same position for over two hours, a necessary imposition to remain anonymous from unwanted attention. His muscles ached from lack of circulation.

They appeared to be going back to the hotel—he figured this would be an easy tail. The short walk to Keith's hotel would do him good—his body still unkinking itself from hunkering down for what seemed like forever in the darkened alcove. Simon stayed on the opposite side of the street, a half block behind the couple. "Should I follow them in? Sure, why not? Maybe I can find out what room they're going to be fucking in. Whoa! What the...?"

Rita and Keith stopped in front of the hotel and turned toward each other. Rita leaned forward and gave Keith a quick peck on the cheek. Then she turned and walked away. Keith went quickly inside the Marriott.

"That's interesting...this may work out to my benefit," Simon thought. Simon crossed the street—saw Rita turn to do a little window shopping—and slipped into a small dark doorway. He decided it was too soon to pounce. "That money grubbing bitch has a sugar daddy, alright. Probably thinking about spending his money right now on a sexy little number to slip into."

Simon quickly worked himself into frenzy as Rita started to walk down the street toward him. He held his breath as he pulled back into the shadows. Rita passed right by his hidey-hole, and as she did so, he quickly made his move. He wanted to surprise her and give her a good scare—just for kicks.

Sneaking up stealthily behind her, Simon snatched one of her arms and spun her around to face him. "Say bitch, 'ave a nice night with your sugar daddy? Is your evenin' o'er, or jus' started? No won'er my money doesn' mean anythin' to you. He looks like a rich fuck."

Rita looked around for help, but saw no one. Traffic was stopped at a red light a block away. "*Shit!* Simon was going to kill her! Why did she say those things to him? Oh my god he stinks of beer!" The stench was so bad that she momentarily forgot about her perilous situation.

The surprise attack brought dread and panic—her mind froze. She couldn't scream. Her lips opened to cry out for help but no sound came out.

"You money grabbin' whore, scammin' offa' two guys. I shoulda' known. Who is he? Who *is* he?" he screamed in Rita's face.

As traffic started to flow once again, he became bolder—louder. He shouted at her brazenly—used every obscenity in his repertoire. What he was saying made no sense. It was just vulgar gibberish. Even though she was scared out of her mind, she could not rid herself of the thought that he absolutely reeked.

Simon shoved Rita into a doorway, against the sidewall, and she thought he was getting ready to beat her. Tears formed in Rita's eyes as she shielded her face with her arm—the only defense she had.

———◆———

Ted Edmonton, and his beautiful wife Sylvia, had just finished having dinner as they walked along State Street. They continued their mealtime conversation about the activities of Beantown's criminal community. Sylvia was a District Attorney. Ted was a homicide detective with seventeen years of service protecting the citizens of Boston under his belt. He had seen every horrible thing an officer could in a city of this size.

At the intersection, for the rarest of moments—all stoplights were red—all engines idled. While they were preparing to cross the street, Ted and Sylvia heard shouting, and turned toward each other in unison, just as they had done on the dance floor hundreds of times. They both saw Simon harassing Rita, and watched him shove her into an alcove. "Honey," Ted said, "call for backup! I'll be over *there*!" Ted darted across the street, using the passing traffic as a visual shield so Simon wouldn't see him as he approached. Ted hoped the thug was distracted by the blaring horns as he dodged in and out of traffic—receiving several one-finger salutes and four-letter expletives for his effort. Ted was livid—this kind of violence grated on his nerves. He got really irritated at men who abused women and children under *any* circumstances. According to the 'Gospel of Ted', this particular derelict was the lowest form of human being that existed. He decided that *someone* was going to get a lesson in manners. And he was that lesson.

Simon, *didn't* see Ted. And just as Simon's right arm uncoiled to coldcock Rita, Ted lurched and gripped Simon's arm, stopping him from doing any damage to Rita's face. Using a much-practiced maneuver, Ted twisted Simon's arm behind his back and slammed him into a wall. Simon's nose hit the wall with a crack—a stream of blood began to gush from Simon's now broken nose. Before Simon knew what hit him, Ted grabbed his other hand, and brought it back with the other, handcuffing him in one fluid movement.

"On your knees! Now! And don't move a muscle, or you'll see what I'm like when I'm in a bad mood," Ted shouted at Simon. Simon kneeled in submission while Ted read him his Miranda Rights. Ted looked over at Rita, who was paralyzed by fear at what just, in a blur, happened. In a subdued tone Ted asked, "What's your name young lady?"

"Rita...Rita Haley."

"Are you hurt?"

"No, I'm all right."

"Ok, Rita, do you see that pretty woman across the street over there?"

"Yes."

"Good. Her name is Sylvia. She's a District Attorney. And she's my wife. Go across the street...carefully...and stay with her until the patrol cars arrive. They're going to want to get a statement from you. Now, go! I need to tend to this scumbag."

As a District Attorney, Sylvia didn't take violent behavior lightly—evidenced by her ruthless courtroom skills in defense of the victims. From where Sylvia stood, the young woman didn't look like a street person or look like she was hooking—she was very attractively dressed but not provocatively so. Sylvia watched as Ted subdued the thug, appeared to talk to the young woman, and pointed toward her. She watched anxiously as the young woman raced back and forth through traffic, and then watched as she zigzagged across the street. The sound of horns honking and the din of traffic increased the tension of the chaotic situation.

"Careful! Over here!" Sylvia shouted, waving her arms at the young woman. "At least she's following Ted's instructions and coming to me, not running away," Sylvia thought. A temporary sense of relief enveloped her. "So far, so good. Almost here." When Sylvia was certain she had caught Rita's attention, she held out her arms as a sign that *she* was the young woman's lifeline. After what seemed like forever, the young woman reached the curb where Sylvia stood waiting.

"Are you hurt?"

Rita shook her head.

"What's your name young lady?"

"Rita. Rita Haley."

"Rita, do you know that man who was attacking you?"

"Yes."

"And?"

"He's my ex-husband."

"Ex-husband," repeated Sylvia, nodding, absorbing the information about the disturbance she had just witnessed. Bile from her dinner journeyed up Sylvia's throat. Sylvia wouldn't admit it, not liking violence of *any* kind, but she was glad Ted had slammed that man's face into the wall. As she watched the event unfold, she was certain that Ted was extremely overzealous in apprehending the thug, but found solace in the fact her husband had inflicted some damage.

"Do you want to file charges against him?" Sylvia asked the trembling Rita. "I think you should." Sylvia continued. "You need to at least get the process started so when...notice I said *when*...he gets violent with you again we can nail his ass to the wall."

Tears began to stream down Rita's face. Sylvia's voice got firm—prosecutorial mode kicking in. "Do you have a restraining order against him?" Rita's head shook sideways. "I really think you should. This isn't going to stop, you know. Trust me, I've seen this before. Here, let me help you." Sylvia offered her hand in greeting, and introduced herself. "Sylvia. Sylvia Edmonton. I wish we would have met under different circumstances, but I'm glad we met anyway."

Officers Ian O'Malley and Jane Chikowski, after a chat with Ted, examined Simon's bloody proboscis, determined it *was* broken but did not require immediate medical attention—after all, it *had* stopped bleeding—and carted Simon off in Squad Car 54. He would spend the rest of the night in jail and he would be arraigned the following morning.

After Rita had answered all of their questions, Sylvia and Ted escorted her to her condominium and assured her she was safe. Like the many choreographed dance moves the couple had practiced over the years, they simultaneously proffered their business cards.

"Really, I'm ok, really."

Ted and Sylvia were not so sure.

Rita tried to decide whether to tell Keith what had just happened. She wanted badly to have Keith hold her in his strong arms and console her. She decided not to mention it to Keith, thinking she didn't want to get him any more involved than he already was. She hadn't told Simon who Keith was, so she didn't feel Keith was in immediate danger. Rita concluded that there was no need to ruin Keith's evening, and besides, she feared all of the drama would frighten Keith away. That he would not want to see her again after learning what Simon was able, and willing, to do.

She just wanted to get home and sort this out in her head. And she wanted to talk to her big sister Frannie.

16

"Holy Crap!" Frannie's command of the English language was sometimes limited, but she always seemed to get her point across. "A cop and a DA were right there? How friggin' lucky is that? Did Simon hurt you? If he did, I swear I'll come out there and rip his shriveled dick off myself."

"Frannie, I'm all right. He didn't really hurt me. He didn't have time. The only thing he did was shove me against the wall. I may have a bruise or two, but that's it. Please don't tell mom and dad, you know how upset they'd be. I don't want them stressing over me any more than they already do. Promise me, Frannie. Promise me you won't tell them."

"Only if you promise to take the DA's advice on gettin' a restraining order against that bastard. That's my offer, take it or leave it. Deal?"

"Yes."

"Cross your heart?"

"Yeah, yeah."

"Done. I won't say anything to mom and dad...yet."

"All right, enough about that. Now let me tell you about the dreamboat I had dinner with. He's sculpted, real GQ, at least six-feet two-inches. You wouldn't believe what a gentleman he is. And he is *so* smart, a doctorate in this, a Phd. in that. It's all very impressive...but he doesn't put it in your face. He's a regular guy. Just a really smart regular guy. We went to lunch this afternoon, and then when he dropped me off at the aquarium afterwards, out of the blue, he asked me to have dinner with him. Can you believe it? He designed the new tank and exhibit we'll be building at the aquarium. I told him I had to be at work first thing in the morning, so it had to be a short night. Just dinner. Which was the truth. That, and you know, I didn't want to sound *too* willing. We went to a wonderful restaurant, right down the street from his hotel. I had just left him at the front door, so thank heaven he didn't see the altercation with Simon."

"You should thank heaven the cops were there, that could have been ugly. You are *so* lucky, Rita. What a day, huh? So, you think this new guy might be somethin', huh?"

"Yeah, Frannie. He might be somethin'. We'll see."

17

The Courtship

Keith was now in Boston working fulltime with the New England Aquarium team and his staff to build the new exhibit. Ground already broken the curvatures of the exhibit started to take shape. A hands-on guy, Keith loved to get into the meat and potatoes of a project and to rally the troops as it started to take form. He was most certainly in his element.

Like a couple of school kids, Rita and Keith would break away from their respective responsibilities to enjoy each other's company as soon as, and whenever, possible. It became a daily ritual. Keith would time his departure from the worksite around lunchtime, head to the front desk, and strike up a casual conversation with Rita. Then he would politely ask if she was free for lunch, fully aware she would be waiting for him to show up precisely at noon to ask precisely that question. Everyone around them saw the sparks. Rumors ran rampant.

Keith wanted to take her California, show her his place in Malibu, and introduce her to his family. He couldn't wait to ask. This would surely be a defining moment in their relationship. Keith told Rita his plans: the trip to Malibu to meet the Vintner family—who were not unlike her own family in Chicago. He managed to convince her everything would be fine—that they would love her. After meeting his family, they would go on a statewide journey to see the sights and meet his friends. Especially Sammy.

It took all of two seconds for her to say 'yes'. Rita just could not believe how much different—better—Keith was than Simon.

Keith's self-confidence was grounded in real achievements, not like Simon's false sense of self-importance from various, ludicrous trumped up dreams. Keith was an ordinary guy with extraordinary sensibilities. And even though he was a genius he was extremely modest and grounded.

Part of Keith's charm was the way he always reminded himself and others that human beings had very little understanding of our planet. That there were still places on Earth where no human had ever been. Canyons deeper than Mount Everest teeming with unseen, unknown life forms in our oceans. Countless forests and rivers had still yet to be discovered, navigated, and charted. Keith loved to explain, to anyone who would listen, about the marvelous, amazing things he had learned on his various treasure-hunting experiences and travels.

Keith was not the kind of guy—unlike Simon—who would get angry with those around him who didn't see things *his* way. Again, the contrast to Simon was striking. And Rita fully, genuinely appreciated Keith for all the ways he set himself apart from "that piece of shit" she had married. Thought she loved.

Rita was nervous about the trip, of course, but being with Keith, she felt right. And safe. And loved.

To Rita, this is what a relationship was *supposed* to be like.

18

Hooked

"Sammy! Aloha! How's the reef?" Keith asked Sammy, who was using a satellite-linked phone.

Sammy was off the Great Barrier Reef filming a diving expedition for The Discovery Channel about the countless sharks that frequented Australia's 1,000-mile natural wonder. Sammy was more than Keith's best friend—they believed they were twin brothers from different mothers. Their intertwined relationship started while they were roommates during their sophomore year in college, and were practically inseparable until their careers took them in different directions. Since then, their paths still crossed regularly—if not by chance, by choice. They were truly birds of a feather.

Sammy, not interested in remaining a bachelor like Keith, married Keilana—a native Hawaiian—as soon as she graduated from USC, a year after Sammy and Keith had. The newlyweds didn't waste any time making babies. They had two kids: a girl, Kololia—'Kalo' for short—the English translation for 'Gloria', honoring Keilana's maternal grandmother, and a boy, Kika—Hawaiian for 'Keith'—as a tribute to Sammy's surrogate brother.

Sammy, who didn't leave the halls of USC after graduating, was now a professor at USC's School of Cinematic Arts. His passion, naturally, was wildlife documentaries. Sammy got the urge to make a documentary. He would pinpoint an interesting subject or locale and travel wherever he needed to make his films. It didn't matter if the subject matter had fur, scales, or some combination of the two, Sammy could expertly weave a compelling story and capture it on film. Whenever Sammy needed time off from his professorial duties at USC, he requested additional paid days-off to complete his latest documentary. Of course, USC would oblige Sammy with the resources he requested, albeit with the usual grumblings. After all, Sammy *had* won six Oscars which were prominently on display in the halls of the USC School of Cinematic Arts. Moreover, he might very well bring them another, to put right alongside those of Spielberg and other famous USC alumni. Such notoriety bought Sammy high-favor from the USC board members and boosters.

"Aloha, Brother! The reef is hanging in there, but barely. You wouldn't *believe* all the trash we see around here. Keith, it makes me want to puke. I'm thinking about doing a documentary solely on the trash in the reef. I think I'll call Greenpeace to see if they want to go in on it. Otherwise, everything is going great. Most of the sharks are very accommodating to us. We got some incredible shots that I can't wait to show you. Oh, and you'd positively salivate over the new digital equipment we got from Kodak. It's some very cool gear, brother."

"Sounds like you're having fun," Keith chirped. "If I wasn't so damn busy here, I'd be there, you know that. Hey, are you going to be back in L.A. soon? There's someone I want you to meet. I'm bringing her out with me when I go back to Malibu for a long weekend, and then we plan on visiting some other parts of the state, see some of the sights. You'll like her Sammy. I think she might be the one. I'll be taking a short break from the aquarium project in Boston in a few weeks. As for the project, everything is moving along nicely, thanks to an outstanding crew."

19

Keith and Rita flew to L.A.—first class. Keith, after they departed the airport, was beaming with pride as if he was on the California Tourism Board. But after excitedly pointing out "over there is downtown L.A., and there's the famous Hollywood sign, and there's Sunset Boulevard," he realized he was rambling and promptly curtailed his instinctive enthusiasm. He really did want Rita to see the real Keith—for her to see that he was just plain folk.

———⊰•⊱———

'Mom' Vintner, excited about meeting the new flame in her son's life, had insisted the first thing the couple do was to come to his childhood home for lunch.

"Keith. My son, it'll be almost noon when you get out here and you'll need to eat anyway. You might as well bring Rita by to meet the whole family right off the bat, and get that out of the way before you go wandering around who-knows-where. Knowing you as well as I do, I'm guessing you'll start in San Diego, work your way up through Big Bear, drive through the mountains up to Tahoe, head over to San Francisco, zip down to the coast to Monterey, then south to San Luis Obispo, then drive back home in that little sports car of yours. All that after a stop at 'the shop', of course. Am I right?"

Keith's mother knew her son very well indeed.

⸺➤●◄⸺

Rita found it a bit ironic that Keith described himself as plain folk as she sat in the passenger seat of his customized Porsche 911 Carrera as they roared up the Pacific Coast Highway in a blur of cobalt blue.

Although his Porsche looked a bit ostentatious with its aerodynamic modifications and perhaps sounded non-eco-friendly, the little sports coupe was powered by a bi-turbo, four-cylinder engine that went from zero-to-sixty in just over four seconds all the while sipping biodiesel. It attained an impressive seventy MPG on the freeway and sixty MPG in the city. The engine and seven-speed gearbox were crafted from a design Keith and a group of fellow students at USC put together for an international scholastic engineering competition. Keith smiled smugly as his little fireball responded soundly to the paces he inflicted on it while driving up the snaky California coastline.

A concerned environmentalist, and proud of it, Keith's other vehicles were similarly eco-modified in some way. His Toyota Tacoma 4x4 was also converted to run on bio-diesel, had custom gearing, and a solar panel on the roof of the camper to power his research equipment and mini-kitchen while he was in the field doing research. Keith purchased the truck to carry his research equipment and the various accoutrements needed for his sporting ventures. The truck, when not in use, was parked next to his boat—a 32'er—powered by modified, highly efficient Volvo Penta bio-diesel engine.

⸺➤●◄⸺

The whirlwind plan was to meet the Vintner family, then Sammy and the gang while in Southern California, spend a night at his house in Malibu, then zip down to Scripps in San Diego.

The San Diego area has a world famous zoo and aquarium, Sea World, and the Scripps Institute in their back yard. These were all must-see places for Rita. After that, they would drive up to

Northern California, then work their way back down south to his home in Malibu. After all of that, they would fly back to Boston on the first non-stop flight out of LAX.

"Welcome to my world."

The list of California facilities, organizations, and attractions dedicated to the sea and its inhabitants is as long as it is cherished—a breathtaking, 1,000-mile coastline. Keith planned to show Rita as many of these attractions as time allowed. The list of Keith's associations with California marine institutions was practically endless. Keith, who of course had a VIP guest pass to all ecological attractions in his beautiful home state, wanted to show Rita *everything.*

He was especially excited to show Rita 'the shop'—the salvage business he and Sammy jointly owned. And to show her off to the tight-knit group of ecologists, preservationists, scientists, archeologists, divers, robotics engineers, and ships hands. All members of 'the shop' and united by a common cause to search the world for the next great ecological, historical, or archeological discovery. All members of 'the shop' had their own individual passions and were on their own quests for adventure and knowledge.

Each member had made proposals to Sammy and Keith more than once, trying to get them to fund an expedition, and, of course, to share any discovered treasures. Sammy and Keith had rejected as many of these sometimes far-fetched requests as they had funded. Keith and Sammy were seriously considering funding the search-for-Atlantis venture Giuseppe Artiolani had recently proposed. "He *might* be on to something," Keith thought.

20

The entire Vintner family was crowded around the kitchen and great room catching up on the latest developments of each other's families, swapping fishing stories/lies, and talking about their respective careers. Every few minutes someone's hand was swatted by Keith's mother Wanda—who also answered to 'mom', 'mom Vintner', 'momma Wanda', 'grandma', 'sweetheart', and 'Mrs. V'—for snatching pieces of the not-yet-ready dinner.

"Grandma! Look! Look!" One of Wanda's grandsons greeted her, arms outstretched with a bowl full of Roma tomatoes, fresh out of her garden. "Look, Grandma, I got *roman* tomatoes for you...I picked them all by myself," he said proudly, beaming from ear to ear.

Wanda took the bowl from her youngest grandson, a warm smile spread across *her* face as she accepted his offering. "Thank you very, very much." She noticed that not only did he retrieve some of her prized tomatoes, but also in the process of doing so, like most little boys he had gotten a little sidetracked playing in the dirt. "Now go wash your hands, dinner's almost ready," Wanda said.

Wanda's grandson didn't budge. He stared at her with his big brown eyes, and asked, "Is it time to ring the bell Grandma? I'm tall enough to reach it now if I use, the, uh, counter. Wanna' see?"

Wanda replied, "No, I don't want to see you get on the counter so you can reach the bell. I'm sorry sweetie, you know the rules. To answer your first question, yes, it *is* time to ring the bell. Go and find Melissa and tell her that it's her turn."

Wanda wondered how many times had she told the children—generations of them—that unless they were able to reach the bell, without the use of the counter or any other aid, they had to wait until they were a little bit taller. Those were the rules.

Bending over, not as far as she used to be able to, she gently took his disappointed, angelic, mud-smeared face in her hands, and kissed him on his forehead. "I know you want to help Grandma, and I *also* know you are very, *very* hungry. Your next job for Grandma, my handsome little mud man, is to round up the whole herd, and tell them to wash up for dinner. That includes *you. Now*, off you go."

———<>———

In one whirlwind day, Rita had met Keith's entire family and most of his friends in Southern California. She already loved his family, especially Wanda. She could see where Keith acquired his enthusiasm. The fruit certainly didn't fall far from this family tree.

From Ralph and Wanda's house, they went straight to Sammy's home so Rita could meet him, his wife, and their two kids. While Sammy and Keith had a beer and talked about the good old days, Rita and Sammy's wife had coffee and looked at Tagaki family photo albums.

After that, Keith dragged Rita on a tumultuous tour. He proudly introduced her to all of his old stomping grounds and most of his friends.

———<>———

The distance between Keith's backyard and the Pacific Ocean changed regularly. Sometimes caused by the tides sometimes caused by other forces of Mother Nature. No matter where the border was on any given day, Keith took great pleasure in knowing that the silky white sand leading to the azure sea was never more than a few steps away.

The sun was about an hour away from setting. Rita gazed at the intense iridescent orange blaze on the horizon. She felt like she was in heaven. "No, this isn't heaven," she laughed, "but it's certainly a close second."

As promised, Rita called her sister Frannie to check in and let her know that she was ok, and that everything Keith had said about his family and friends was all true. Certain that Frannie would answer—Howard and their kids never did—Rita immediately went into the details about her trip. "Frannie, you wouldn't believe half the stuff I've experienced, already! I must be dreaming! You wouldn't believe the toys this guy has. My goodness he has it all, though he really is some kind of eco-nerd. His *Porsche* is even eco-friendly. You wouldn't believe it if you saw it with your own eyes. And his house! What a view! It's totally secluded and overlooks the ocean. You could get naked and no one would see you! From the street, it looks like a typical beach cottage, but like everything Keith owns, it's also eco-friendly. The roof tiles are really solar panels linked to a battery system that powers the whole place. All his neighbors are filthy rich, of course. Everyone has a Rolls-Royce, a Mercedes, or a Ferrari. Talk about lives of the rich and famous. And he knows them all...says some of them are arrogant jerks, some are regular people, someone you could have a beer with. Kind of like you and Howard."

"Honey, ain't *nobody* like Howard and me in Malibu," Frannie countered. "Come on, isn't California filled with fruits and nuts, the human kind as well as the kind you eat?"

"Frannie behave. It's nothing like that at all. Everyone is *so* nice. I met Sammy Tagaki and most of his family. Sammy is Keith's best friend. Sammy's mother and father are the best. They're first generation Japanese Americans. They ended up in an internment camp in the San Francisco area during the war. It's a sad story that I'll tell you later. One that, as an American, I'm not too proud of. They're *really* nice people. We're going out to meet more of Keith's friends after dinner. I just wanted to call and tell you how fantastic this place is and that I'm ok."

Rita suddenly heard Keith shout from the deck. "Oh, that's Keith now. He says dinner will be ready in five minutes. Oh yeah, I forgot to tell you. He cooks! Can you believe it? We're having surf and turf for dinner! What a guy! He could teach Howard a thing or two around the kitchen, by the way. Ha! Anyway, if I don't call in the next few days it's because I'm having too much fun driving around California in a Porsche. I'll be home in a week and call you then. Love you! Bye!"

Now it was Colleen's turn for an update, but Rita had to be quick. Rita heard the receiver on the other end of the line pick up. "Greetings from California!" she exclaimed. "I told you I'd call. I've only got a few minutes because we're about ready to have dinner. Oh, Colleen! It's so beautiful here! I can see why so many people migrated here. Keith's family is wonderful. His friends a hoot. And Keith is *quite* the perfect gentleman. He even set up his guest bedroom for me. He didn't want to presume that just because I flew out here to California with him that we'd sleep together."

Colleen was truly happy that her friend had finally found someone who was not a flake, or a user, and someone who showed respect to the female half of the species. "Sweet thing, you know he wants to get in your pants," Colleen teased, "but I'm glad he's not pushing it. In fact, I think you should get with the zeitgeist and make the first move! It's obvious he's waiting for you to make it. You said he was being a perfect gentleman, and I don't want to sound like a tramp or anything, don't even of think going there Rita, but seriously, it seems to me that the right time is now. It's been a long famine for you, and, um, you know, you're not getting any younger. I hope the last time you checked everything was still working down there...it is still working? she teased.

"Colleen!"

→➤●◄←

Keith had a room at the Marriott, and during their courtship, had never insisted or pleaded for Rita to come up to his room after one of their nights out on the town. Keith felt she was truly delightful to be around, even if the upshot would probably be only a gentle kiss on the lips. However, it had not escaped his attention that those kisses were starting to have some heat behind them. He felt ensnared—helpless by her powers. When the time came for them to make love, he knew it would be phenomenal.

He was hopeful that that time would be soon.

21

Finally

Dinner was ready. Keith had prepared everything. The dining table on the veranda was replete with candles, fine silverware, and luxurious 600-thread-count Egyptian cotton napkins and tablecloth. A bottle of expensive sparkling wine was sweating in a sterling silver ice bucket.

Sunset was at hand, creating an amazing orange-blue aura on the horizon. As far as he was concerned, the only thing missing was Rita, and she was walking toward him at that very moment. The sunset created a remarkable glow around her as she approached the table. Keith pulled her to him and kissed her tenderly. She enthusiastically responded in kind.

Most of the doubts she had recently about Keith had faded away. She was convinced that he *loved* her. He had not rushed their courtship and clearly respected her reluctance to delve into another relationship so quickly after her divorce.

Keith knew to take it slow. Not to rush. Nevertheless, his feelings for her intensified daily—hoped hers were in sync with his—that *he* meant as much to her as *she* did to him.

He pulled her close and relished their embrace. They kissed. When their finally lips parted, in the moment, Keith couldn't—wouldn't—refrain from sharing his feelings with her. "I love you Rita Clarisse Haley."

Rita was in love too. She realized that Colleen's advice was perfect—she would make the first move right after dessert.

———>➤●⊰———

They cleaned the kitchen and dishes together, after which Keith suggested they take a late night swim and relax by the pool.

Reclining side by side in a doublewide chaise lounge, the couple gazed out at the ocean and star-filled night sky. "If you'd like, I have a real comfy bathrobe you can get into after we take a dip, so you don't get cold," Keith said. An impish smile slowly spread across his handsome face. "Just sayin'," he whispered, provocatively.

———>➤●⊰———

Keith slipped into his bathing suit, and then, while Rita changed into hers, he knocked on her bedroom door. "Here's your robe," he said. He opened the door just wide enough to slip his forearm through, and offered her the robe.

Rita opened the door fully, modestly clinging to a towel to cover herself. Keith gazed at her shapely silhouette. "*Oh man*, that is enticing. Calm down, man. Calm down. No bulges now!" he thought, feeling the blood rush to his head and other parts. The notion that Rita could read his mind popped into his head again.

"Thank you," she said. Having similar thoughts as he, she wondered if he could read *her* mind. Rita took the proffered robe. "I'll be right out." Rita started to shut the door but stopped as she caught him checking out her exposed rear end in the bedroom mirror—a blissful smile plastered on his face. She closed the door and smiled herself.

"Ok. I'll be in the pool," he said. Keith was excited and it showed. He had only ever seen her in slacks or occasionally in a dress when they went out at night. He fantasized about what she would look like in a bikini or a form fitting one-piece. "Either way, I win," he thought.

———>➤●⊰———

As Keith emerged from the pool after a one-and-a-half gainer—pike position, very well executed—off the one-meter diving board, he saw Rita, ensconced in the fluffy white cotton bathrobe. She glided to the chaise lounge, and in one smooth motion, disrobed, revealing much more than Keith was expecting. What he saw, in cheerful disbelief, was Rita's naked body.

"Very well done," she commented nonchalantly. She took notice of the incredulous expression on Keith's face, pleased to know she was the reason for his obvious elation. "I admit to knowing nothing about diving scores, but I'd give you a '10'," she teased.

Keith said the first thing that popped into his head. "Nice suit. I take that back. *Very* nice suit, although, frankly my dear, I *was* expecting something with say...some fabric. I must say, you are incredibly provocative, Rita."

"Got to keep you guessing."

"And you are *very* good at doing just that."

"I thought you might like this look. And while I did consider wearing my one-piece, I just thought that, since I've done so many new things on our trip, I thought I'd try something I always wanted to do. Something I've *never* done before. And that *thing* was to go skinny dipping."

"Well then, I guess I should slide out of this," Keith said, as he slipped out of his trunks and flung them out of the pool without taking his eyes off of her body.

She dove in the pool and met him in the middle. He grabbed her and held her tight against his body. They kissed. For the first time, they touched without boundaries.

———————

After a playful, suggestive swim—and countless shooting stars spotted—Rita and Keith both felt that the time for chitchat and flirtation had come to a timely and promising end.

Fully reclined on the chaise, Rita wantonly gazed into Keith's eyes and took his hand. She held it up to her lips and kissed it softly. "Thank you, Keith. The flight. The trip. For introducing me to your family and friends. For everything. But most of all, thank you for this." She leaned over, took his head in her hands and placed her open mouth tightly against his, passionately. She broke their kiss then unabashedly removed her robe, then his, and pressed herself against him. They eagerly kissed again.

Their hands explored with willingness—his fingers finding moisture, hers finding an erection that didn't feel like it would be going away any time soon.

Rita positioned herself on top of her man, and slowly, guided him into her. She began to grind. Her intense passion overwhelmed her.

Afterward, she leaned down, and whispered in his ear. "I love you too."

22

In between sips of her lunchtime clam chowder, Rita gave Frannie the Cliff Notes version. "Frannie, he is the kindest man I've ever met. He's gracious and *so* smart. He's got more letters *after* his name, than he does *in* his name. And," she giggled, "he's absolutely one-hundred percent man."

Frannie wanted to hear more about Keith, but she was worried because her little sister was still in grave danger. Frannie's spidey-sense tingled. She *was* happy for Rita—that she had finally found the kind of man she deserved. But, Rita's ex-husband was still around and they both knew he was dangerous.

"Rita, it sounds like your trip was an awful lot of fun, and I'm *glad* you had a good time. Really glad. We definitely need to talk some more about Keith. Like a lot. I want to hear all the juicy details, trust me, but right now, I'm more concerned with your safety." She voiced her specific concerns. "Have you seen Simon or his car since you've been back?" Frannie asked. "He's outta' jail you know. He's been stalking you even with the restraining order against him. He really scares the shit outta me. Boyfriend or no boyfriend, come home Rita. Where it's safe. Don't make me come out there and drag your skinny ass back here myself 'cuz you know I'll do it."

Can you imagine what would have happened if Keith was there when Simon attacked you? It could have been… and still could get real ugly, sis. It wouldn't surprise me one bit to know that he's even gone so far as to get a gun. Get out of Boston, Rita. Get out now! I'm pleading with you. I promised I wouldn't tell a soul about any of the shit that's been goin' on with Simon's stalking, and I haven't, but this has already gone way too far, and you know it. Don't you?"

23

Changes

Sammy heard the rumors about Keith going around the USC campus, and he intended to have them confirmed or denied. "Keith! Sammy. Aloha!" Then straight to the reason for his call. "What's up with you? I heard through the grapevine that you've been considered for the curator position at the Shedd Aquarium. Is that true?" Sammy asked.

Keith laughed—knew the question would come up sooner or later. "Oh Sammy, you're too much. I don't want to know who...or where you heard that from...but yes, it's true. The Shedd made me an offer I shouldn't refuse, but I'm having a little trouble deciding what I should do. What do you think, Sammy? I'm glad you called, by the way, I need your...."

"What are you, *nuts*?" Sammy asked. "I *wish* I could have my own public aquarium to tinker with. And in Chicago! Of *course* I think you should go for it. You're the perfect man for the job. You've got the vision to take them to the next level, buddy, trust me. What's the problem, Keith? Why are you even thinking about *not* accepting?"

It suddenly occurred to Sammy that maybe Keith was thinking of turning down the job because of Rita. But why? He *had* to ask. "Is it Rita? Are you telling me you're thinking of not accepting the job because of Rita? What does she have to do with the Shedd appointment? What's going on brother? I gotta' know. Is she turning out to be someone you want to get serious with, and even so, why would you turn down the job because of her? I mean, she seems like a wonderful gal and all that, but I've got to ask if she's worth *that much* to you, man. What you're telling me is...." Sammy stopped short. Truly puzzled, he wondered if his good friend—the definitive bachelor Keith Vintner—was about to take the plunge.

Keith realized that if he didn't put a halt to the one-sided conversation, Sammy was going to continue down the wrong path. "No, no...that's not. I'm...I mean, I'm not going to turn the job down, and I wouldn't turn the job down because of Rita."

"So, what *is* the problem? I thought Rita is from Chicago."

"Yes, she is. But she's finally turned the corner on her failed marriage. And she's started to make her own life and her career is finally on track in Boston. I...I wouldn't, can't take that away from her."

"Well the way I see it, you'd be doing her a huge favor. Isn't her ex still living in Boston too?"

"Yeah."

"So do you love her?"

"I've really fallen for her. You met her, Sammy. You have to admit she's a gem. I got it bad, Sammy, real bad. I don't want to let her go. The problem is that I don't know how to tell her about the job offer and having to move to Chicago."

<hr/>

Keith was restless. A lot of things were going on in his life in addition to putting the finishing touches on the Boston project, and he had to find a way to break the news to Rita about the job offer in Chicago. The importance of the disclosure required kid gloves.

During their time together in Boston, Rita had taken him on a culinary tour of Boston's finest restaurants—some chic, some not so, and some mom and pop places only a local would know existed.

But *this*. This had to be *his* idea. *His* plan.

Rita had contacts in high places, but Keith had connections of his own, and he decided it was time call in a favor. He set the wheels in motion for a truly special night.

24

Back at Lou's On Clark

Sarah politely burped into her napkin. Her stomach was full and quieted. She had devoured the entire portion of clams Lou had prepared exclusively for her. She didn't want to let Lou down, and besides, she did tell him she was hungry.

She further demonstrated her affection for Lou's On Clark's fare by asking Eddie, whose nametag identified him as Eduardo, for some of Mrs. Santorini's homemade tiramisu and a cappuccino. She was decidedly satiated, but convinced herself that there was still room for Isabella's wonderful tiramisu.

"Right away, ma'am," Eduardo said courteously.

"He's a good kid. Very attentive and a hard worker. He deserves a good tip," Sarah thought. "I just wish he wouldn't call me ma'am."

"Now where were we? Oh, yeah, I was telling you about the gal who hooked me up with Chuck. Jillian Lyman. She is the best matchmaker in the city. Listen to me. I mean, what is so weird or demeaning about using a matchmaker, huh? Come on, tell me. What are you afraid of? Finding the love of your life? After I told her about you, she said that if she couldn't find you a match, she'd refund your money. I wanted to bitch slap her when she said that! She didn't give *me* that kind of deal," Sarah griped. Her forehead wrinkled.

Michael stifled a laugh. He imagined how difficult it must have been for this Jillian woman to have found Sarah a suitable partner. As far as Michael could tell, it was not that Sarah and Chuck were polar opposites, but individually, the one just didn't seem to compliment the other. In reality, when the two of them were in the same room, it was like something out of a fairy-tale. True romance. "Maybe I should hear Sarah out on this matchmaking thing," he thought.

Sarah noticed the quick change in Michael's expression and attempted to close the deal. "For me, Michael? Do it for me. Come on. Have a talk with Jillian, for me. So I can keep my promise to Liz. I loved Liz. And I love you too. I promise you, Jillian will find you someone. If she can't hook you up, then I'll stop being a pain in your ass. Really. Cross my heart."

Sarah felt bad for using the memory of Liz in this manner, but she had made a promise to her, and was determined to keep that promise. She watched Michael's emotional ramparts slowly crumble. "You're going to do it then? You'll talk to Jillian?"

"Yes, I'll talk to Jillian."

"Hot damn, here we go! Where's my tiramisu?"

25

His reservation at the restaurant confirmed and the tickets to the opera in his wallet, Keith strode down State Street, freshly pressed tuxedo in hand.

With his free hand, he reached around to scratch an itch on the nape of his neck when it suddenly occurred to him that he needed a haircut. His hair—scraggly, unkempt—was in dire need of some maintenance, so he detoured to the barber shop near the Marriott—Franc's Fine Hair Salon.

The owner, Franc O'Herlihy, offered Keith a seat next to the window in Chair Number 1, and started to give Keith's thick mane a much needed grooming.

⎯⎯➤●⬤●◄⎯⎯

Franc, 66-years-old, was never one to shy away from voicing his opinion with anyone who sat in one of his chairs or the regulars who hung out in his barbershop. His candid comments frequently led to heated discussions.

Whether the topic du jour concerned the Red Sox, Bruins, Patriots, Raquel Welch vs. Gisele Bundchen, or the Kennedy's, 'frank talk' was a tradition in Franc's shop.

For nearly forty years, he spent twelve hours a day, six days a week in his cramped but immaculate shop. Over the last fifteen years, when he wasn't at work, other than taking in games at Fenway Park to see his revered Red Sox play night games, and the occasional visit to see his younger sister Carol who lived in Nashville with her ailing husband, Franc spent his time upstairs—his home. After his wife Theresa passed away, Franc sold their two-story brownstone in Brookline and moved into the apartment above his shop. He sold their car, which was useless for a townie anyway. Thanks to Boston's intricate inner-city transportation system he could be at 'The Fens' in less than thirty minutes from the moment he left his apartment.

⟿⊱⊰⟿

Shortly after getting started, Franc—nee Francis—spotted an oddly shaped growth on Keith's neck. He had seen many a splotchy rash covered neck in his day, usually due to overexposure to the sun.

Franc figured he would say something to Keith before Ellis Langley showed up. Langley was a frequent patron and a gossip—the regulars who congregated at Franc's shop had affectionately dubbed him 'The Voice of America'. Franc glanced at his watch and realized Ellis would be by any minute for his monthly trim and his two-cents work of political pontification.

"Young man, I don't know you from Adam, but have you ever had this growth on your neck checked out? As a barber, I've seen more than my share of skin cancer and, um, you know, I'm not tryin' to sound like an alarmist or nothin', but you should have someone take a look at it." Franc grabbed his hand-held mirror and handed it to Keith. "Here hold the mirror, I'll show it to ya'."

Franc spun Keith around on Chair Number 1—well-worn with countless posterior impressions—so Keith could see the growth for himself. Franc instinctively knew where to stop the chair's rotation. "See what I mean? Do you see it?"

While Franc went about his business of grooming his new customer, Keith adjusted the mirror to see what Franc was talking about. "*Damn*," Keith said, with a hint of surprise in his voice. He did see it. An irregular shaped thumbnail-sized growth, or sunspot—or something. Keith's first thought was that it must be

110

an old wound that didn't heal right—he had plenty of those. He quickly assumed that it was probably nothing. He was healthy and faithfully used SPF 70 whenever he was outdoors. Keith's second thought was that Franc was right—he should have it checked out. "Better to be safe than sorry," he thought. He decided to have it looked at by his doctor when he got back to California. "Thanks for spotting that Franc, no pun intended," he said with a laugh which was really more of a concerned snort. "I'll have my doctor take a look at it when I get back home."

"Well then, you're good to go my young friend." Franc considered anyone under the age of sixty to be young. "That'll be fifteen bucks." Franc then nodded toward Keith's tuxedo. "My guess is that you're wearing *that* tonight. She must be something special."

Keith handed Franc a twenty-dollar bill. "She is. Keep the change." Keith grabbed his tuxedo and headed for the door, paused, and turned to look back at Franc. "Oh, and Franc, thanks a lot for the advice."

26

"Where the hell were they going?" Simon wondered. He had been following Keith and Rita for about twenty minutes. He stayed a few car-lengths behind them and a lane over. He maneuvered his car with care so as not to draw attention to himself from Rita, or worse, the police. The last thing he needed, he thought, was to be pulled over with all the empties strewn about in the back seat and floor—and the 12-pack box that still had two beers in it.

He quickly glanced at the back seat. "Damn, I shoulda' cleaned those out. I didn't think I drank that many beers after work last night. No wonder I feel like shit." he thought. The pain between his ears overshadowed the remnants of the high from the previous night's binge. He did his best not to lose sight of them, stay inconspicuous, and keep himself calm, which was difficult in and of itself due to his throbbing headache. Simon knew the empties—evidence—would probably amplify the facts that he was currently stalking his ex-wife, violating the terms of his restraining order, and driving while technically intoxicated. The police were unlikely to be appreciative of the fact that he had not littered the streets with the empties and 12-pack box.

"Where the hell were they goin'?" he wondered. Then he saw their car stop at the valet parking service of the Boston Opera House on Washington Street. The newly remodeled theater, first built in 1928, was a magnificent venue—everything from vaudeville to Wagner had been performed on its revered stage.

"The opera? What a joke. This guy is a fuckin' snob. The opera!" he scoffed.

As Rita exited the car, Simon noticed her dress. It was stunning. He couldn't recall a single time she had dressed like that when they were together. Simon, the egomaniac, could not fathom that the reason she never dressed up like that for him was that he never took her anywhere other than a Red Sox game or The Tin Horn.

27

"Romeo and Juliet? The opera? Are you insinuating that I need some refinement?" she asked contemptuously.

Keith calmly replied, "Rita, let me start at the beginning. You know we're almost done with the new tank, so my job here in Boston will be wrapping up in a couple of months."

Then it hit her. Romeo and Juliet! Fleeting love! Rita didn't like the sound of this. It seemed as if Keith was graciously telling her goodbye. "This is some kind of sick way to let a girl down," she thought. "Like something Simon would do. I've fallen for him, and now this!"

Keith immediately noticed her body flinch at the mention of his impending departure and realized he should carefully explain to Rita what was going on. "The curator of the Shedd Aquarium in Chicago announced that she is retiring at the end of the year. And the museum's board of directors asked me if I would be interested in taking over her job."

Rita's eyes widened.

"Rita," Keith continued, "it's an offer anyone in their right mind would snatch up. The job is high profile, with a lot of responsibilities. Designing new display tanks and wave machines is one thing, running an aquarium is another. I suppose if they didn't think I could do the job, they wouldn't have offered it to me. It would give me a lot of street cred, as the kids these days say. The other thing that is compelling me to say 'yes, I'll take the job' is that I know you've got family in Chicago. And I thought if

I moved there that you might want to go back there and, maybe… move in with me. I mean, it's such an amazing career opportunity. One I shouldn't pass up. They know I'll be finished here in Boston in a couple of months. And I can wrap up the rest of my projects for Scripps by the end of the year and move to Chicago to start the job on the first of January. I haven't given them my decision yet, because I wanted to share the news with you and get your feedback. I respect your opinion. And…. What I'm trying to say Rita, is that I really want to be with you. I've been holding in my feelings for a long time. I want you bad, not just physically…but emotionally. For the rest of my life. I've fallen deeply in love with you. And I picked Romeo and Juliet because the story encompasses the way I feel when you're not with me. Heartbroken. No pressure, you don't have to give me an answer now." Keith's words were not coming out in the sequence he had rehearsed. He hoped she understood.

Rita was stunned. And embarrassed. At first, she thought Keith was telling her goodbye but what he was actually telling her was that he needed her in his life. That he wanted her to move to Chicago with him. That he cared for her. And that he loved her. "I love you too. I feel the same way when you're away, like a piece of me is…missing. Take the job Keith. You're right. Any one in their right mind would take it. What an incredible opportunity! And I just know you'll do great! As for me moving to Chicago and living with you…well…I'm going to have to think about that. It's a pretty big step."

It was a bold move, committing to a relationship, but she knew he meant every word. She kissed him tenderly on the cheek. "You've already made this evening *so* special. Don't worry. I won't take long to make up my mind. Let's go see the show."

28

Despite the fact that it was nearly midnight, the moment Rita walked in her front door, she knew she had to tell Frannie the news.

"He's moving to *Chicago* to be the curator for the Shedd Aquarium! They said he'd be perfect for the job. And he asked me for my advice on what he should do," she blathered, barely able to get the words out of her mouth. "He said he loves me! And I believe him! He wants me to move in with him in Chicago!" She took a deep breath and exhaled slowly. "He told me all of this tonight. But," she sighed, "I'm not sure I'm ready for that last part. I think the best thing for me to do is to move back home to Chicago then see what happens after that. I know that's a lot of stuff to unload on you Frannie, I'm not sure what to do. What do you think?"

'Granite' Frannie—used to hearing her little sister babble on excitedly—was stoic. She coolly replied, "What I think is you need to pack your bags right now. You can stay here with Howard and me until we find you a nice place. Suzie's living on campus 'til June so you can stay in her room. We'll work out the details later. Hold on, let me tell Howard."

Moving the handset away from her mouth, Frannie shouted to her husband Howard, who was relaxing in his Barcalounger, ice-cold Old Style in hand, while he watched the Cubs play their archrivals, the Cardinals on WGN. "Rita's moving back to Chicago! She's gonna' stay with us 'til she gets her own place! Isn't that great?"

Deeply engrossed in the game, Howard, a man of very few words responded to his wife, "Great." He finished his beer and decided it was time for another.

———————

When Rita told her parents that she would soon be coming back to Chicago to live, they could not contain their joy. Sheila Haley broke down in tears. "My baby is coming home!"

———————

Rita was in her bed, reminiscing over the kiss Keith gave her as he dropped her off at her home that night. Before she got out of the car, he turned to face her, kissed her fondly, and said, "Rita Haley, I will love you forever." He held her as she nestled her face against his chest. She wanted that moment to last forever.

She was so enraptured by the moment that she briefly considered telling him that she would indeed move in with him in Chicago. But, just as quickly, she realized that she needed to make sure she was ready for that kind of commitment. So she decided to sleep on it.

———————

Their next night out, after she finished her corned beef and cabbage dinner, Keith suggested they order desert. He said he wanted something that embodied her essence. Something sweet and tempting—a concoction with the words cocoa, swirl, whipped cream, and chocolate.

"I have some news," she said casually, even though her stomach was teeming with butterflies. She had been waiting for the perfect moment to tell Keith that she had come to a decision. She knew he had been extraordinarily patient with her the past few days. That he had respectfully given her the time she felt she needed to make this important, life changing decision.

They had been talking about the new exhibit's grand opening for the entire meal, which was fine by her. The new aquatic tank was nearing completion. The media proclaimed that the it would be the crown jewel of Boston's cultural community. The staff and board members, and Keith's team, were in frenzied anticipation of the exhibit's forthcoming unveiling. There was much more work to talk about, but her news—her decision—was more important.

She had already told Colleen, who got very emotional—tears of happiness and sobs of sorrow. After all, she was losing her very dear friend, but deep down, Colleen was elated that her Rita found someone, and she was thrilled that her very dear friend would finally be able to get away from Simon. Nonetheless, Colleen would *miss* Rita.

"So? What's the news?" Keith asked.

"I've decided to take your advice and move back to Chicago in two weeks and could use your help," Rita fitfully explained. She realized the words had not come out the way she meant them. Instead of backtracking, she moved forward, fully aware of the effect her news had likely affected Keith. "I can fit everything I own in a small truck. We can make the drive in a couple of days, if both of us are driving, and make a weekend trip out of it. Being the big he-man you are. Whadya' say, want to help a girl out?"

Keith's face went slack and pale. The news was exactly what he had hoped for, yet he was conflicted. He was excited that she would be moving to Chicago and far away from Simon. Nevertheless, he was disappointed that she had decided to get a place of her own and, consequently, they wouldn't be cohabitating.

Once more Rita seemed to know precisely what Keith was thinking. This was hardly the case because his facial response to her news was a dead giveaway. She adored him, but if they were ever to play poker, she was certain she would take all his chips in no time. "Keith, darling, I know you want me to move in with you, and that will almost certainly happen…in time. First things first. I need to get away from Simon now. He's…dangerous. Not only to me, but to us. The sooner I get out of here the better. And besides, look at it this way. I'll be waiting for you when you get there," she said as she leaned over to kiss him.

29

Rita had finished packing her possessions into the moving boxes. She was exhausted. Colleen, Rita and Keith—the packing crew—were covered with sweat despite the chilly early-fall easterly wind. The boxes were stacked as high and tight as they could be in the U-Haul truck. The boxes were jammed against the few pieces of furniture she managed to wrest from Simon after their divorce. The only things dear to her heart that were not packed in the truck were waiting for her in Illinois, or standing next to her.

Before Keith left to pack his belongings, he took a few moments to soak in everything that happened and was happening. He was so proud of Rita. She had come so far. After everything that she had gone through with Simon, and landing her first job so far away from her home. He believed that he had helped her in some small way as she came into her own.

Rita wanted some time to say goodbye to Colleen and her neighbor Diana, so Keith said a quick adieux to Colleen and gave Rita a quick lip-kiss. "Love you. See you in an hour or so," he whispered.

Rita's heart ached as she said goodbye to her dear friends. She was emotionally troubled that neither of these supportive and unforgettable women would no longer be part of her everyday life. Yet she also knew that her life with Keith was about to begin. It was at once one of the saddest and happiest times in her life.

Exactly one hour later Rita arrived at the Marriott to pick up Keith and his belongings. It would be an exhausting trip for him. First, driving to Chicago and helping Rita unpack once they got there, and then immediately flying to California to tie up loose ends, and move his possessions to Chicago. He was still experiencing ambivalent emotions—happy yet sad. Rita would be waiting for him in Chicago, which was a good thing, but the fact that she insisted on getting her own place disturbed his psyche. Especially the way she put it, saying she 'had no intentions of being a kept woman'. He voiced his concerns over her choice of words so she explained how she would 'feel awkwardly indebted' to him if he were paying her living expenses. That she could 'take care of' herself. 'And, besides, she told him, she 'hadn't yet decided' to live with him.

She told him that Frannie had found a little apartment for her in Lincoln Park—a nice, safe, upscale neighborhood—close to the red-line station. She reiterated that she wanted to deal with things one step at a time, and she would think seriously about living with him when he finally got to Chicago. Keith admired her spunk, but he admitted that he could not help feeling a little hurt. His heart spoke to him loud and clear. He wanted to be with her every day and night.

⎯⎯⎯➣●◄⎯⎯⎯

The trip to Chicago was uneventful—the good kind of uneventful: no blown out tires, no leaky radiator hoses, no cows or deer hit crossing the highway. *That* kind of uneventful. Smooth sailing. The trip took the entire two days they had allotted, each of them taking turns at driving and sleeping. They stopped off the interstate at diners for meals—and pee breaks. They journey was more or less a straight shot: I-90 to I-84, then to I-80, then on to I-90 again. They traversed the 1,000-mile distance at 55 miles-an-hour, the maximum speed the truck's engine-governor would allow.

Along the way, they talked about her family, how Keith was nervous about meeting them, the places she would show him in

121

her home city, and about Rita's career plans. She had already agreed to be the manager of the Membership Services department at Chicago's Museum of Science and Industry. Rita told Keith how she was thrilled by her ability to find a good job on her own so quickly. She just as quickly admitted though, all it took was a call from Pete Sneed, her now former-boss at the New England Aquarium, and she was in like Flynn.

—————>●<—————

With a new place to call her own and a new job, it felt great to be back home. When Keith arrived in a few months, her new life would really take off.

30

Bad News

Keith was back home in LA where he began the tedious tasks of wrapping up his projects for Scripps and some personal matters, and informing his family and friends of his new job and the move to Chicago. Even though they would all miss him they were all very happy for him.

Keith decided to rent out his house in Malibu—he couldn't justify selling his piece of heaven. He planned to ship his Porsche, truck, furniture, household items, and research equipment. And his boat, so Rita and he could cruise around on Lake Michigan on weekends.

The Scripps board made a counter-offer to Keith—his considerable talents *were* valuable—but they could not convince him to stay. From the very beginning of their relationship with Keith, they knew it was inevitable that he would ultimately head off to greener pastures one day. They would miss his intellect immeasurably.

It was while Keith combed his hair in the morning that he nicked the small lump Franc had found a couple of weeks earlier. He decided to make an appointment with his physician. After all, it *was* time for his annual checkup, so he might as well have it looked at before he headed to Chicago. Until then, there was much that needed to be done and very little time to do so.

——————>•<——————

Keith's doctor carefully examined the abnormality on Keith's neck. He made a few 'hmms' and 'huhs' as he poked and prodded. Afterward, he was blunt. "I'm very concerned about this, Keith. I know you've been exposed to copious amounts of sun and you've put yourself at greater risk for skin cancer, regardless of your faith in high-SPF sun block. You of all people should know of the damaging effects of the sun, even on cloudy days. I realize that in your profession there was really very few precautions you could have taken, and unfortunately this lump on your neck, I suppose, is the price you've paid for your career choice." Then in rapid-fire succession, "How has your energy level been? How've you been feeling? Any unusual aches or pains?"

"So much for making me feel better, Doc" Keith chuckled nervously. "Yes, I'm feeling fine, plenty of energy. Do you really think it's serious?"

"Yes...I do. This growth on your neck is more than likely melanoma. I want to remove it now, run a biopsy to make certain, then run a series of other tests to see if it has metastasized into any of your other tissue. We'll get results back in a few days. Then we'll see what we have to do...if anything. Despite my suspicions, I want you to keep a positive attitude. We've got an excellent team here."

——————>•<——————

Keith instinctively pushed any and all negative thoughts out of his head while he waited for the results of the biopsy tests. He had not told anyone of Franc's initial finding or the fact that he had gone to see the doctor for anything other than his annual checkup. He certainly didn't tell anyone what the doctor intimated or what he was afraid the results would show. He felt that crying wolf would not help him or anyone.

———⟫●⟪———

But his worst fear became his reality. The biopsy tests came back positive—Keith had stage four melanoma—and it had already spread to some of his vital organs. In fact, if it had not been detected when it had, he would very soon be feeling its devastating onslaught.

Regarding his overall health, Keith's doctor was amazed by how hearty Keith appeared. "Keith, even though your body is fighting an enormous battle internally, it isn't obvious by your energy level. Or your attitude. I'm astounded, really. It is a tribute to your lifestyle and character...and, I'd have to say also, your genetic makeup. However, you're going to need all that and more in this upcoming battle for your life."

———⟫●⟪———

Keith, after a great deal of procrastination, finally called Rita and told her he had cancer. The line suddenly went silent. Keith thought the call had been dropped. "Rita?...Rita?...Are you there?" Keith asked. He desperately tried to repel the image of her standing there, in shock. This was the most difficult news he ever had to share.

"Yes...I'm still here...." Rita's synapses were firing at warp-speed. "Why is this happening just when things were finally looking up?" she asked herself. "What's going to happen now? Is Keith going to die?"

Overwhelmed by utter-disbelief—and anger—she slowly collapsed on her hide-away sofa.

31

Snap

Keith was under the care of the USC Norris Comprehensive Cancer Center's finest doctors. No expense would be spared, no procedure or option disregarded. After all, one of its own was in need and they were going to do everything in their power to get their guy healthy again. They would begin Keith's initial operations in two days.

———◆———

Keith's doctors were as aggressive as they could afford to be, given his current state. They successfully removed all existing cancerous growths. Afterward, the plan was to halt the spread of his devastating opponent quickly. They immediately began an extremely vigorous series of treatments—chemotherapy and radiation—to relentlessly attack the cancer from every possible angle. Through it all Keith was a trooper—a great patient. He patiently tolerated the bombardment his body received fully aware that he was literally being destroyed right along with the cancer. Unfortunately, Keith adversely reacted to the cycles of innovative chemotherapy and radiation designed to eradicate the deadly malaise.

It was while in the transfusion room receiving treatment—felt the corrosive fluids progress through his body—when the combination of ravenous chemicals reached his brain. He he felt a distinctive snap, which caused his psyche to crack like Humpty Dumpty's shell. Through closed eyes he saw a bright flash, his synapses briefly, painfully short-circuited, manifesting in an ocular burst of color. The doctors had cautiously, deliberately set the dosage as high as they could, without killing him out right. However, this time, for this patient, the dosage was too much. It was a tricky thing, dosing. Not enough and it wouldn't do the patient any good—too much and complications would surely arise.

Keith suddenly went berserk. In his hallucinations, there were people in white coats jabbing needles in his arms, and big machines, whirling, breathing, pulsing and pumping—forever pumping foreign substances into his veins. He had to escape! Illusion and reality merged. He violently thrashed, twisted, and convulsed. Equipment was strewn about helter-skelter as Hurricane Keith continued his uncontrollable seizures. Spittle sprayed as he frantically screamed at the nurses and doctors. He yanked the needles out of his arms, which caused blood and chemicals to spatter everywhere and on everyone in the room. He flailed about wildly in an effort to escape the room. He viciously attacked and verbally assaulted the staff. "What are you doing to me? Where am I? What am I doing here?"

Five minutes of mayhem ensued. With the assistance of four huge orderlies he was finally pinned down and restrained. The infusion room was trashed. They kept him strapped-in and sedated for twenty-four hours. When he was lucid enough to speak coherently, they determined he was no longer a threat to them, or himself, they freed him from his restraints. They kept him in the ICU for a few more days, during which they performed numerous physiological and psychological tests, and eventually concluded that he was well enough to discharge him, with the caveat that he agree to return for regular checkups. On a cool September morning, with cautious optimism, they released him back into society.

Although he still talked like Keith Vintner, the overdose—neither the hospital nor the doctors called it that—had *changed* him. All eight cylinders weren't firing as they should be. Quite like the story of the famous egg, all the king's doctors couldn't put him back together again.

A small team of fine doctorial minds, and Keith, were assembled in a conference room around a large table deep in the bowels of the sprawling medical complex. Although the room was in the administration section of the facility it had the sickly sweet smell of a surgical room.

Chris Plesari, world renowned oncologist, one of the team, spoke up, interrupting the conversation between Keith and one of the other doctors—an ex-school mate of Keith's. "Keith, I'm going to be brutally frank...you deserve that." Keith knew what was coming would not be pleasant. "What I must tell you now is that we really can't do anything else for you at this point. Your body reacted violently to the chemotherapy. This last batch damn near fried your system. And the radiation therapy hasn't accomplished what we hoped it would. The best we've been able to do is remove all the tumors we knew existed and try to stop the advance. But," Dr. Plesari cleared his throat, "um, it's spreading, Keith. Too fast. Faster than we're able to combat it. Keith, it hurts me to say this, but...you don't have many months left. Even if we were to continue with other alternative chemotherapy treatments, which we would if you want us to, but at best, you'd have maybe six months. You must understand we're doing everything we can. This is one of the finest oncology teams in the world...but Keith, although we *always* give it our best shot, we can't always win these battles. We didn't find it soon enough to make this a fair fight."

Keith appreciated Dr. Plesari's candor. That he would not survive his battle. And he appreciated their willingness to do everything in their power to combat the enemy. However, Keith concluded then and there that it was time to throw in the towel.

He respectfully nodded his head, acknowledging everyone in the room. "Ladies and Gentlemen, it's time to cease these attempts to save my life. You know anything else you can do for me will just exacerbate my problem and deteriorate my mind, what's left of it. I've got some things to do before I literally give up, and I need all of my wits in order to accomplish these things. I want to thank each and every one of you for giving it your best shot. I know how you must feel, and I know you've given it your all. But the time has come for me to step up to the plate and face the pitcher. I plan to go down swinging, as you all know a home run this late in the game is not very likely. All I ask of you now is to keep me out of pain so I can concentrate on taking care of the last details of my life."

***

Keith was stretched out on the chaise by his pool. He gazed at the warming sunrise and tearfully reminisced about the night when Rita had laid next to him on this very chair. He vividly recalled the spectacular sex they had that night. It all seemed so long ago.

***

Keith was unable to sleep. Wide awake all night, his brain—even though it had been decimated, performed better than the average person's—raced at NASCAR speeds. His mind refused to let himself relax enough to rest and there was nothing he could do about it. There was that and the pain. The nagging pain.

His laptop on and online, he took a sip from his steaming cup of green tea, and swallowed a couple of oxycodone pills to take the edge off. The three-inch gashes in his cheeks, from the last of the operations he had allowed to be performed, ached profusely. Time short, outlook bleak, his mind turned inward. An introspective, a replay of his life's movie streamed across his mental screen in vivid color and remarkable clarity. Keith's life could have been so different. Life with Rita sailing across the oceans of the world, drinking wine, sunbathing nude on Mykonos, cruising up the Amalfi Coast, diving off the Great Barrier Reef. There were so many places he had wanted show her. Some many things he wanted to teach her. All the possibilities unfairly cut short. "Fucking cancer! Why? Why now? Why me?" he quietly sobbed.

He stopped himself. "Damn it man, get rid of those thoughts!" he said aloud to no one. "Knock that shit off!" He refused to have pity party for himself. He had lived a wonderful life. Had his time in the limelight. He did *not* have time to waste on self-pity, but felt he did have time for closure.

Keith had always been philanthropic as evidenced by his contributions and involvement with dozens of charitable organizations. Now, there just was no *me* in the equation—just what he could do for others while he was still in the game. After all, it was not as if he felt he *needed* to leave a legacy, just to make a big enough dent so his spirit could remain long after his physical departure. 'Go big or go home' was one of his favorite self-motivational mantras.

Keith's condition had deteriorated very rapidly. Although his family and friends would find out soon enough—only his doctors had seen how ghastly he had become. Not that they, or anyone, could save him. As far as the rest of the world was concerned, he was on sabbatical leave. Not that he *was* eccentric, but he *was* wealthy enough for the story to fly.

He called the Shedd in Chicago and told them he wouldn't be able to take the job after all. He was deliberately vague about the reason for his decision. They didn't need to know—it was none of their business. He expressed his gratitude for the opportunity, but he made it clear he had already made up his mind. They reluctantly accepted his decision but the Shedd's board members wondered what had gone wrong—asked if there was something on their end of the bargain that had soured the deal. Keith assured them this was not the case, that the decision was made strictly for personal reasons and he hoped that they would accept that. The board members wondered how they could have made the wrong choice in the first place.

The media hounded him incessantly day and night. The local media outlets had caught wind of his Shedd appointment and his subsequent rejection. If word of his illness hit the media's sails they would have a field day. He could see the photo captions: 'Rich playboy Keith Vintner as he exits the USC Norris'. Then in gory detail: 'Look how horrid he looks. Word on the street says he doesn't have much longer to live. Who'll get his millions?' He wanted to be alone to figure out how close his life with dignity and privacy. "*Bastards.*" His opinion of tabloid journalists was not very high.

More importantly, he didn't want his family or friends, especially Rita, to go through any paparazzo inquisitions. Not now.

Keith had spread his wealth around as easily as he seemingly had accumulated it. Every Vintner family member had benefited from Keith's success. It was in his nature to take care of everyone and everything he cared about. He determined that he would have made a great father. With a still barely-certifiably sound mind, Keith documented his desires—parsed his estate between family and friends. He sent the final draft of his will to his lawyer, along with a princely check and the instructions that he stipulated must be adhered to, un-contentiously, upon his death. Keith knew his lawyer would want to talk to him after he received Keith's letter. They would talk, but there would be no need for chitchat, or additional correspondence. Everything was straightforward.

Frederick Jr., Keith's cousin, would get his boat. Cousin Ruth would get his truck—she was always saying how she could use a good 4x4 to travel to her remote mountaineering locations. Sammy would get Keith's diving equipment, although he would have even better equipment lying around than Keith owned. Keith promised his doctors that he would sell his Porsche. He wanted to assure them that he would not end his life via four wheels, regardless of his fragile mental state. Besides, he was on oxycodone and didn't want to be tempted to take just one more cruise up the PCH.

Years ago, Keith had set up substantial trust funds for his siblings and parents. He had also long ago paid off his parent's mortgage as an anniversary present.

The Malibu house would go to Rita, and if she didn't want it, to the Vintner family. He resolved to leave her his financial portfolio—which was now worth over $400,000,000—and his share of S and K Enterprises' assets—its holdings in treasures alone was now worth over a billion dollars. Keith owned fifty percent. Rita would probably reject this but she knew she meant the world to him and he hoped she would take that into consideration before making any rash decisions. With her charming personality, her charitable nature, and her passion for life, she could put that money to good use, and she would make a great business partner for Sammy, *if* she wanted to enter the private sector. If not, as stipulated in Keith's will, she would have to sell her half of S and K Enterprises to Sammy for one dollar.

Keith never told Rita exactly how much he was worth. She never asked. He liked that about her. She, too, would be set for life and never have to worry about finances ever again. She would truly be independent.

"But would she be taken care *of* for life?" he wondered.

32

For the first weeks of his treatments and surgeries, he kept in touch with his family, with Sammy, and Rita, to give surety that his treatments were going well. But after his mental meltdown, he stopped calling everyone—unable and unwilling to tell any of them what had happened. What was happening. What he had become. Broken. Sickly. Emaciated. Ugly. He was defeated and had retreated.

As for Rita, her new—old—surroundings were again part of her normal life. However, this did include a lot of intrusions and distractions. Visiting with family and old friends, catching up on all the latest happenings in their lives, what had been happening in hers.

All the while, despair had consumed her downtime—the notion that Keith really was not as well as he let on, draped over her like a thin veil of anguish. It had been an entire week since she had last heard from him. He didn't return her calls or emails. Panic shadowed her constantly. Convinced something was wrong, she called Sammy at his USC office and left him a voicemail. Fortunately, for Rita, he was still in town and he returned her call. "No, Rita, I haven't heard from Keith. Don't worry, babe. If I can't get a hold of him ASAP, I'll drive up to his house and see how he is doing, face-to-face. The minute I know *anything* I'll give you a call."

Sammy felt uneasy after talking to Rita. Before Rita called him, Sammy was not overly concerned that *he* had not heard from him recently. During that time, he assumed Keith would have been communicating regularly with Rita. Her alarming tone was contagious and caused Sammy to fret. The last time they spoke, Keith convinced Sammy that his cancer was in remission and that he was going to 'beat this thing'. He immediately called Keith, but was greeted by the sound of Keith's recorded voice. Extremely frustrated, Sammy left a message on Keith's answering machine. Despite his concern for Keith's health and MIA status, Sammy tried to sound upbeat. "Keith. It's Sammy. Just checking in. I wanted to let you know Rita called me today. Asked me how you're doing. She hasn't heard from you in a while…like the rest of us. How about it good buddy? Give Rita, or your folks, or me, *someone*, a call and let us know how you're doing, ok? It's about four o'clock. If someone doesn't hear from you soon, like by eight-thirty tonight, I'm coming over. We're worried stiff. Take care. Love you man."

———⟫●⟪———

He would try to live the time he had left with as much grace and aplomb as possible although that was not going to be easy as the realization of his imminent death had practically derailed his conscious thoughts. To make matters worse, if things could actually *be* worse, he recently suffered another setback—incontinence. His muscles simply wouldn't do the things he commanded of them. They clearly had developed a mind of their own. The idea that, at thirty-five years old, he needed adult diapers humiliated him. He felt trapped in the body of a ninety-year-old man. Keith hired a live-in caregiver recommended by a local hospice, but not before demanding a signed oath of confidentiality. He completely rejected the idea of a family member taking care of him—that was something he would not allow to happen. As far as they knew, his chemotherapy treatments were working, he was recovering, and was back on track to good health.

Keith heard Sammy's message over the speakerphone as it came in. After he was released from the hospital following his mental breakdown Keith started monitoring his incoming calls. The paparazzo calls were incessant—all day and all night. "Fucking leeches," he thought. "What's a guy got to do to get some goddamn respect around here?" After he listened to Sammy's message a tsunami of guilt crashed over Keith. "Why am I alienating everyone?" He felt terrible for not taking Sammy's call.

Sammy was his *best* friend. For Sammy to take the time to check in with him—voice concern from Rita, Keith's family, and himself—highlighted that fact in a way that was at once elegant and heartbreaking. He would call Rita at once. After that he would call his parents and then Sammy.

"Hi sweetheart," Keith spoke into the phone, trying unsuccessfully to sound like his old self.

Rita was an emotional wreck. She thought it was Sammy calling her back to tell her bad news about Keith. Her voice audibly wavered as she answered. "Hi...how're you doing? I'm so happy to hear your voice! Like everyone else, I've been worried sick about you. No one has heard from you in a week. Keith, please tell me what's going on? Is...is something wrong?"

"I'm ok, I'm just really tired. I'm sleeping a lot lately. Sorry for not calling you." Keith told her the standard lies, that he was going to be all right and that there was no need for her to worry. Or to lose any sleep. He reminded Rita that he had the finest doctors in the world who were fighting hard for him. "You don't need to worry about me, kiddo. I'll navigate this gauntlet. I just hit a rough patch of water, is all."

They both cried uncontrollably after their conversation ended.

———>●<———

It hit him like an arrow from on high: he needed to find Rita another soul mate! That was what she deserved. Someone to take his place who truly cared for her. He would find that someone. It was as simple as that. He was on a mission from God. He was resolute in his objective, even if it took his last breath to complete. His ultimate purpose in this life, and after, was to take care of Rita.

"*Damn.*" He wished their life together could have been longer. Rita would have been a great wife. They were truly a match made upstairs. But that was the root of his dilemma. He had to undo all the love she had for him and he had to redirect that love toward someone else. Before he died. Keith knew Rita was still fragile. Wary. He had seen firsthand what 'once bitten, twice shy' looked like.

It was time to get things done. Wrap this trip up with a nice shiny bow.

33

Partners in Crime

Keith searched through endless profiles on various matchmaking websites in search of the right man. A daunting task, but he felt his determination would overcome any and all obstacles. Except for time. His obsession manifested in his quixotic quest—only he was not chasing windmills or treasure. Surely, he was not the only man on the planet worthy of her love.

It wasn't going to be an easy task to find the man who would meet his criteria. Her new partner had to be in good physical shape and athletically inclined. Height-, financial-, and mental-issues would be instant disqualifiers. The ideal candidate had to be personable, compassionate, and devoted—and financially secure. Keith would diligently weed out the money grabbers. The best, and *only* the best, would do. The plethora of dating websites was overwhelming. Most of them were thinly veiled meat markets or pretenses for people of various sub-cultures to meet. The majority of men he found were nothing but johns—guys just looking to get laid or searching for some kinky relationship with a female. Not a single one suitable for Rita. Those who were not pigs were otherwise unworthy of consideration. It dawned on Keith that these things were a natural culmination of modern technology and the current temperature of humanity.

Keith realized he needed to step back and rethink the problem. He honed the terms he used to scour the web and finally stumbled upon a dating service for intellects and professionals. One in particular caught his eye—Professional Matchmakers Inc., an upscale matchmaking firm in downtown Chicago. He checked the Better Business Bureau for complaints about PMI's services, and found none. They seemed to be legitimate. He sighed, took a moment to collect his thoughts and then called their main number, impatiently navigating his way through the voice prompts.

Finally, he got transferred to the New Member Services department. "Jillian Lyman, how may I help you today?"

"Hi Jillian, my name is Keith Vintner, and I have a very, uh, unusual request. I hope you don't think I'm some kind of weirdo, although I have to admit it's going to sound a little farfetched. But what I'm about to tell you is the absolute truth."

"Oh dear! This guy sounds a little off his rocker, not-playing-with-a-full-deck-of-cards kind of guy. What have we here?" Jillian thought. "What exactly is your request, Mr. Vintner?" she asked.

"I'm looking for a man for my girlfriend."

"Oh no, not one of these," she thought. "Why was he coming to her when it's so easy to find this kind of arrangement on the Internet." This was a just a bit out of her comfort zone. To Jillian, it didn't matter if these kind of guys could afford PMI's services or not, company policy left it to her discretion to accept or reject new clients. She decided that she would guide this guy elsewhere. "Mr. Vintner, I can assure you that Professional Matchmakers is not *that* kind of service. You can easily find *that* kind of arrangement on the Internet," she said with more than a hint of rudeness in her voice. "This guy is a freak. Damn! The world was full of nut-jobs." she thought. Jillian was just about to disconnect the call when she heard Keith quietly sobbing on the other end of the line. She was instantly taken aback. "What's going on here, Mr. uh, Vintner is it?" she asked.

"Help me please. I'm not a weirdo. Or a pervert. I'm *dying* and need to find someone to take my place. I'm sure this sounds crazy but I don't know how else to go about this type of thing. Or where else to go. I've never had to do *anything* like this before. I thought your website spelled it out quite clearly, that your company is the 'finest matchmaking service in the city.' Is that true or isn't it?" Keith added indignantly.

"Why do I always get the strange ones? Why?" she thought. The life of a professional matchmaker was not an easy one. "Yes, that is what our website says Mr. Vintner, *if* that's your real name." she replied.

"Yes, yes, I assure you, it *is* my real name. Do you have web access right now?"

"Where was this guy going with this?" Jillian wondered. "Yes. Why do you ask?" she enquired.

"Try googling 'Keith Anthony Vintner' and 'treasure hunter' and see what pops up."

She keyed in the search terms he gave her into duckduckgo. com and hundreds of posts were returned—most of them were news articles about his personal and professional achievements and endeavors. A couple of them displayed photos of him with gorgeous women. One photo showed him standing alongside another guy, both of them in wet suits. They were standing on a ship, next to a huge chest, which, according to the article, the two had recently salvaged from the bottom of the Atlantic Ocean. The man identified as Keith Vintner was holding what appeared to be a very large ring in one hand and flashed the victory sign with the other. The article stated that the chest had been retrieved from a sunken Spanish galleon and it was filled with gold coins and jewels. The article stated that there were fourteen other chests just like it. "No wonder he looks so happy," Jillian thought.

"So I'm to believe this is you?" Jillian asked with a hint of suspicion in her voice.

"Yes, that *is* me. See! I'm not a freak!"

"Well, I will say that the man in these photos doesn't appear to be a freak, to coin your phrase. But how can I be sure this is you? I mean, if you want me to find someone for you and your girlfriend, I'd need to be sure this isn't some kind of hoax or prank."

"Are you able to video chat online?" Keith asked.

"Yes."

"Good, we'll do a video call. Hang on while I log in."

Jillian logged in as well. Keith's face was now displayed on her screen in real-time. "Oh my God! He looks like the pictures on the web! But...his face is...*distorted*," she thought. A shiver ran up her spine. No matter, it was clear to Jillian that the guy in the photos was the guy she was talking to and could see on her screen at this very moment.

He heard a slight gasp on the other end. "Do you believe me now?" Keith crowed.

"All right. I'm convinced that you are Keith Vintner. Now let me explain the way we do things at Professional Matchmakers. You'll need to consent to our thorough screening process, just like all of our new members. All contract fees are due up front, and if you don't get results in six months, which in this case would be that we couldn't find someone suitable for your girlfriend, you'd be eligible to receive an additional six months for free, after which you could renew your contract or allow it to expire. Is that agreeable?"

"Thank you Jillian, yes, but I'm afraid we...I don't have that long."

"Oh, dear. I'm so sorry. I...I don't know what to say."

"It's ok. Don't worry. I've gotten used to this fact. You seem like a nice person, Jillian. Thank you for helping me."

"It would be my pleasure to help you. Oh, and one more thing Mr. Vintner. Please understand that, while we don't guarantee results, we do have a very successful track record."

With the initial tension and emotions out of the way, Keith, gave Jillian additional details of his background, right up to the day when he learned that he had cancer and that he would soon be as dead as a proverbial doornail.

He realized that he had to trust this woman, so he told Jillian everything. He expressed how truly, madly, and deeply he loved the woman he mentioned. And, of course, how he felt responsible for her happiness. Most importantly, how he feared for the woman's safety—in no small part due to her ex-husband's outbursts of violence and trouble with the law. Then he told Jillian everything about Rita, everything he knew—her family, friends, her likes and dislikes.

Jillian took a deep breath. "Excuse me Keith, but Rita doesn't know anything about this, does she."

This was a tipping point. Keith knew Jillian might not be willing to help him because Rita was in the dark about Keith's plan. He *had* to convince Jillian to go forward. "No, she doesn't know anything. She can't. Ever. It would crush her to think I was giving up on life. And on her. On top of that, she would be extremely pissed off thinking I was manipulating her, which by all accounts could be construed as the truth. However, I prefer to think of it as increasing her odds for happiness after I'm gone. Jillian, I'm going to be dead in a very short period of time. Jillian, I'm not going to demand that you find someone for Rita to marry before I'm dead. I just want you to find a life partner for her, introduce them somehow, and let fate take its course. That's all I can reasonably ask."

Jillian took another deep breath. "All right, I'll try to find someone for you, or rather for Rita. But 'who' and 'how' are the next questions to solve." Jillian was certainly in uncharted waters with this one. This was a far different scenario than hooking up a couple of love-starved people searching for like-minded partners. She had never been asked to find a soul mate for someone who was going to need one, and didn't *know* it! "What kind of hornets' nest have I stirred up?" she wondered.

Her video call with Keith over and done with, she resumed her research on Keith and Rita. She needed to be absolutely certain about them. Then, if everything panned out, she would begin to search for a match for Rita. The more details she uncovered on the two of them, the more genuine they seemed to her.

Keith—engineer extraordinaire, holding multiple patents in fluid technology that revolutionized the industry—eco-visionary philanthropist who was filthy rich but didn't flaunt it—already gave away half his vast fortune to various charities because he said 'he didn't need that much money'. Once the press got a hold of that tidbit, more money came pouring in to his affiliations because of his rock-star-like notoriety, boosting his income stratospherically. Jillian reviewed countless articles about Keith and came across one about the construction of the new aquatic exhibit at the New England Aquarium in Boston. The article also mentioned

Rita: 'Rita Haley was the latest project associated with Dr. Keith Vintner'. "Very interesting," Jillian mused.

She keyed in 'Rita Haley' and hit enter. There she was! Rita Haley attended Northwestern University, and then transferred to Northeastern University as a junior to graduate the following year with a BA in Business Administration. Her pictures matched the ones in the online magazine with those Keith had emailed her. She was quite attractive, not unlike the other women Keith had been photographed with. Rita's first job after graduation had been with the New England Aquarium where she worked her way up the ranks quickly. When Jillian went to the Science and Industry Museum's web site, a snap shot of her as the museum's Manager of Membership Services was there. Same job description. "Hmmm."

Aside from what Keith had told her about Rita, which was quite detailed coming from a guy, not much else could be found about Rita Haley with the exception of her being a Chicago native. Nothing exciting. A brief mention of her family and a few friends.

Something tickled the back of her mind, but she went with her instincts. Her gut had never let her down before. "Man, this all just seems so bizarre," she thought. Then it hit her: her friend Sarah's boss, Michael, would be a perfect match for Rita. And Sarah could even help her figure out how to make it work. It seemed absurd to Jillian, but truth was stranger than fiction. "That *was* the saying, wasn't it?" Jillian thought.

⇒➤●◄⇐

"Good morning, Halloran Associates, Sarah Clancy here. How can I help you?"

"Sarah? Jill. Got a minute?"

"Sure. What's up? I haven't heard from you in a while. I was starting to wonder how you were. And about ready to give you a jingle to see if anything had come up for Michael yet?"

"Ms. Clancy," Jillian giggled, "*That* is the very reason I am calling. I've got this situation. So I'm sitting at my desk today, and

I get this call on the new member line looking for a guy for his *girlfriend*! At first I thought this guy was a pervert. You know, 'I want to find a fuck buddy for my girlfriend'. I just about puked. I told him to go search the Internet...that there were plenty of websites that catered to *that* kind of thing. But he suddenly broke down in tears and finished his story. It turned out to be very interesting. He's from California, but looking for a life partner for his girlfriend here in Chicago. Why? Because he's dying! And soon! And wants his girlfriend to have someone special, not a pervert or a screw up. He's leaving her a lot of money and doesn't want a money grabbing dirtbag to take it from her, so he wants me to find him a good man for her, well-off in his own right. It seemed a little strange at first. Not unethical, just...strange. So I did some research and confirmed all the information on him was true. He checked out as clean as an operating room floor. His name is Keith Vintner and he's for real. Quite rich. You should see some of the stuff I read about him. He's worth almost a billion dollars, and that's *after* he gave half his fortune away. He and his business partner found a sunken treasure worth over eight hundred million bucks, and that was only *one* of the treasures that he and this... Sammy Taga...Tagaki, his partner, found. That was their first major discovery. They went on to discover three treasures that are much more significant.

"Keith's been a confirmed bachelor, dating some famous, and some not so famous women, all gorgeous, until he met this Rita gal. Now, what the press hasn't caught onto yet, is that he's dying of some kind of cancer and won't live to see next year! Sarah, this is the strangest request I've ever had in all my years here."

"So what does this strange request have to do with Michael? Get to the point," Sarah, agitated, prodded.

"Ok, ok, I'm getting there." Jillian, the backstory exposed, was ready to jump into the grist. "So here is the juicy part of the whole situation. I'm thinking that this Rita gal...call me crazy...but in my professional opinion, might be the one for *Michael*! I know Michael's deal, but you know him much better than I do. So? Will you help me decide how to proceed with the set up? I can't think of a single reason why not to, and can't quite figure this one out on my own. Not a word of this gets out, ok? Mums the word. Got it?"

Sarah jumped at the chance to get involved. "Hell yes I'm in! This will be fun. Let's get busy! Oh my heavens," Sarah snickered, "I can't believe I'm hooking my boss up with a blind date per a request from her boyfriend! Setting him up with a woman who is devotedly attached to a man who's dying of cancer. Who lives in Malibu. Is rich. Bighearted. And good looking! Reality is stranger than fiction!" Sarah chirped.

"I know! That's what I said!"

<hr />

Two hours later, a plan preternaturally fell into place. The first step would be for Keith to write Michael an eloquent letter.

34

Sarah was anxious to tell Michael about her conversation with Jillian—about Rita and Keith—but she didn't want to reveal her involvement, fearing it would lessen Jillian's credibility. And damage her relationship with Michael.

But it occurred to her that she *could* tell Michael that Jillian asked her to find out if he was available for a short phone call. Finding an excuse to call Michael was easy enough—they had several projects in progress, and she could casually bring up Jillian's request.

"Hi Michael. It's Sarah."

"Oh, hi Sarah. What's up?"

"Just checking to see what else I need to do to get the Kopinsky model ready for the presentation."

He was tired. She could tell by the sound of his voice. He had probably been at it for two days straight. He was an extreme workaholic—like no one she had ever known. The techno-geeks who regularly pull all-nighters could learn something from this man. However, even machines need to be switched off occasionally for maintenance.

Michael expounded, "The model looks really good. George and I tested all the moving parts and it works just as everything else he creates: flawlessly. I think we're good to go. I'm tweaking my presentation to give it some extra zing. I intend to go for the jugular with this one."

"Cool, as long as there is nothing else that I need to deal with, I've got something else I wanted to talk to you about. Something… personal."

"What do you mean *personal*, Sarah?"

"Well, I was talking to Jillian today," she giggled slightly.

"No more dating requests, Sarah, please. I'm bushed."

"No, no, no. This is not about blind dates. Jillian kindly requested that you call her when you get a minute."

"Do you know what's it about?"

"I have no idea," lying through her teeth. "Really, I was just chatting with Jill, and she said since I was going to be calling you in a minute anyway, to let you know you should call her. That's it. Really. The Kopinsky job update, and a request from Jill for you to call her, those are the only reasons I'm calling. But…I've got to say Michael, you've been working *too* hard again."

"Why do I think something else is going on here, Sarah?"

"Just call Jillian, would you? Shit, lighten up. I'm just the messenger here."

"I'm sorry, Sarah. Really, I haven't been myself lately. You're right. I've been pushing myself too hard. Like you said the other day, all work and no play has made me a dull man. I'll call Jillian. See what she wants. Thanks, Sarah."

"For what?"

"For caring."

"Good night boss…I love you too."

35

Jillian

His first two dates were nothing special. Although the women Jillian had chosen for him *were* elegant—each had great personality and style—sparks didn't fly, butterflies didn't flutter. Celene, his third date, was a violist for the Chicago Symphony Orchestra. She was extremely attractive and a nice person, but a second date with the violist wasn't in the cards. It suddenly occurred to Michael that maybe the problem was *him*.

⟫●⟪

"Jillian Lyman speaking."

"Hi Jillian, Michael Halloran. Sarah said you wanted to talk to me."

"I do. Let me tell you about a situation that's popped up."

Jillian told Michael about her conversation with Keith, the letter he had written, that Keith wanted Michael to read it. And, if after reading the letter, Michael wanted to move forward, Keith would like to do a web call and come up with a plan for Michael to meet a woman named Rita Haley.

36

The Letter

Michael opened Keith's letter. "Oh well, here we go," he thought. "Let's see what we have here."

———⋙●⋘———

Dear Michael,

I have an idea that I'd like to put forth for your consideration. My idea is very difficult to explain in writing without turning it into a novella, but I'll do my best to be succinct. My idea includes one very lovely lady who is also very beautiful, inside and out, who's in love with, and loved deeply, by someone. That *someone* is *me*.

Please understand that this is not a scam or anything immoral or illegal, and I urge you, or rather beg you, to keep reading. I care so deeply for this woman that I am desperate to find someone else for her to love. And someone else to love and protect her in my stead. She is *very, very* special.

Why am I doing this? I am dying of cancer. She knows I have cancer, but thinks I'm going to pull out of it. I'm not.

I searched the Internet and personal ads for weeks trying to find someone, but to no avail. Luckily, I stumbled across Jillian and asked her to help me. Obviously, Jillian was skeptical and a bit apprehensive about helping me, but she and I had an online video chat after which she did her due diligence, checked my background, my social status, finances, and so on. I'm so very grateful to Jillian for overcoming her initial revulsion to my idea. I can never repay my gratitude to her.

She convinced me that you're exactly the type of person I'm hoping to find for my ill-fated soul mate. After reading about you on the web and hearing what Jillian has told me about you from her personal and professional knowledge of you, I concur that you are a good man, self-sufficient, philanthropic, and to me most importantly, not misogynistic. And, if I may be straightforward with you, guy-to-guy, from what I can see from your recent photo, are quite handsome.

Jillian might be right about you. However, I want to be as certain as I can be. I hope you can understand how important it is that I remove any possible doubts. And I'm sure you will want similar assurances.

If you'd like, Jillian can arrange for us to meet online, at your discretion of course.

Michael, I have no doubt this is probably the oddest letter you've ever received, but this is a very real plea for help, from one human being to another. I don't know why I'd think someone would accept or even consider this, but if you are looking for a chance to open your heart to, and possibly share your life with, a wonderful, caring, beautiful woman, I beg you to consider my idea.

If I don't hear from Jillian by next week, I'll assume that you are not interested.

Sincerely,
Keith Vintner

———>➤●◄=——

Michael carefully read the letter and when he finished he called Jillian back. "Hi Jillian. I'm intrigued. More than a bit skeptical, but interested enough to check this out. Set up a web call."

37

And So It Began

Jillian just finished setting up the video link as Michael strode into the conference room. On his end, Keith logged into the call and switched on his web cam. He realized that it was time to let fate take over. "If it's meant to be it will be."

The audio synced first and then the video slowly came into focus. Jillian spoke first. "Hi Keith, this is Jillian. Can you hear me?" Silence. "Can you hear me now?"

"Hi Jillian. I'm here and can see and hear you fine. Can you hear me?"

"Hi Keith, there you are. I can see hear and see you too. Michael is here with me. Per your request, Michael has read your letter about your...situation, and Rita, so it's time to get the two of you acquainted, and get the details of the plan hammered out. Keith Vintner, meet Michael Halloran."

Michael had read the additional information Jillian had collected on Keith and Rita, but was still not sure he was ready to move forward. Now that he could actually see Keith onscreen, he realized he was looking at a person who had undergone radical surgery. The digital transmission was clear, with no pixilation whatsoever. The man who Michael stared at on-screen had a grotesque clown-like countenance.

"Hello, Keith. I've read your proposition. I have to admit, I'm not totally sold on the idea, but I'm willing to listen to what you and Jillian have in mind. Your story is really fascinating, Keith, as is the background information that Jillian provided. Being recently widowed myself, my wife succumbed to a short battle with cancer, your request struck an unnerving chord in me. And then, as I read your heartfelt story, it began to make sense. You see, just before she died, my wife Elizabeth, implored me to start dating and open myself up to someone new once I'd gone through the grieving process. She even convinced one of our friends to promise to help me find another woman to share my life with. Elizabeth told me that I would know when the time was right. After reading your letter I believe she may have been right after all."

Michael's eyes welled up as he recalled his wife's last days and wishes. "At the time, I, I...sorry" Silence. Michael cleared his throat and continued "I got quite angry, not understanding how she could possibly want someone else to feel the love I had for her. I truly believed my love was for her alone. She tried to put me at ease. Told me that obviously she could no longer be there for me. That I was going to be left here alone and that I needed someone to share my life with. That I deserved it. Looking back, I appreciate how unselfish that was of her to say. She was...correct. I *did* feel it when the right time finally arrived. So, here I am, taking the chance that I'm not a hopeless fool!"

Michael turned toward Jillian. "Ok you two, give it your best shot. Convince me to go through with this."

Michael then shifted his attention back to the screen, at virtual Keith's sad and grotesquely deformed face. "Tell me everything you know about Rita Haley."

38

The Plan

Keith described Rita's physical characteristics in detail, which, to Michael, sounded almost too good to be true. Keith explained how he and Rita had met. Their whirlwind romance. Their illfated feelings of love for each other. He quietly and calmly told Michael all the reasons he loved Rita. Spoke of her beauty, her sparkling personality, and her wonderful quirks.

After Keith finished, Michael told Keith of *his* past. His upbringing. His philosophies on women, religion, and politics. After a lengthy conversation, the two men delicately scrutinized each other—asked various probing questions.

Keith had already made up his mind—Michael passed with flying colors. He had found his man. As far as Michael was concerned, nothing that Keith had said so far had been off-putting. He had to admire a man that would go to such painstaking lengths to protect—and provide for—the woman he loved.

During a rather long anecdote about one of Keith and Rita's adventures, Michael realized that he wanted to proceed. For now, he decided, nothing else needed to be said. With uncharacteristic impatience, he interrupted Keith's story. "Keith, if you feel after this last hour or so of talking, that I'm the guy for Rita, that you're confident I would love and take care of her, then I'm in. Provided of course that Rita and I bond. But, I have to wonder. How do we *do* this?"

"All right, Michael. Fair enough. Let me tell you how." Keith shared his plan with Michael and Jillian. The trio spent 30 minutes on the various logistics to make sure everyone was on the same page. Michael's 'innocent' introduction to Rita was set to take place the next day.

"Michael, I cannot tell you how sincerely grateful I am that you are even considering this."

A sharp pain in his face brought Keith quickly back to his grim reality. "As you both now know, time is not my friend."

39

The Chair

Rita, friends, and family, constantly called and emailed Keith trying to goad him into revealing some sniglet of information about his health—these attempts were in vain. Their spoken and written words and concerns might as well have been thrown against a brick wall. On rare occasions when Keith did reply, it would be feeble hyperbole: 'I'm fine' or 'the treatments are going well' or 'it's looking good'.

He had built up his defenses well. Begrudgingly, he offered some brief statement of hope to which they could cling. Most of them believed Keith was lying and was deliberately withholding the truth about his condition. They rightly assumed the worst.

The truth was, Keith decided, not something they needed or indeed wanted to hear. Good news was no longer in Keith's vocabulary. There was not even a shred of hope for Keith's continued existence.

―――→►◄←―――

"Why talk when you have nothing to say? Should I tell them about the mundane rigors of my existence, the aches of my cancer, or the results, or rather lack of results, of my treatments?" Keith asked Zeke, matter-of-factly.

Zeke Tarkanian: pale, sleight yet chiseled physique, unintentionally unkempt Einstein-hairdo, large dark-brown bespectacled eyes—thin-framed black glasses perpetually perched halfway down his nose.

He attentively listened to Keith.

To most people, Zeke exemplified the archetypical psychoanalyst: compassionate, fatherly, statesmanlike. Zeke felt at ease studying the nadir of mankind's mental illnesses. For the last twenty years or so of his thirty-year-career, he specialized in treating those unfortunate souls suffering with the same type of terminal illness that had intruded upon Keith's life.

In the large, overstuffed, wingback, maroon leather chair in which Keith now reclined, Zeke had counseled literally every socio-economic ethnicity, profession, and gender on the planet. The very chair that a much younger Dr. Tarkanian had reupholstered after finding it at a garage sale for a pittance so many years ago.

Zeke was fresh out college. His internship completed successfully he started his own practice in the private sector. Not yet polished or experienced, Zeke was not yet earning the kind of money he hoped to be when he chose his profession.

"It's perfect," the cash-starved Zeke thought when he spotted it. The chair was tattered, covered with old clothes, debris, and small boxes of various sizes containing more junk for sale. During the process of redecorating his office, Zeke decided that he wanted something that could provide a certain artistic esthetic. Something that he could afford. He haggled with the chair's owner until the price was right. Finally, Zeke had his first piece of office furniture. He had the chair reupholstered at a greater expense than the chair itself cost, but over time, the effort and expense had worked out in his favor. And his patients'.

The chair had been with him ever since. It was *the* place for Zeke's patients to relax in—just the right size for an adult to almost fully recline and rest their head on the huge, comfortable wings. Years and thousands of patients later, Zeke frequently puzzled over the fact that no one ever chose to sit on his modern, more expensive sofa.

Keith was semi-reclined in the chair with one leg stretched out over a wing. This was Keith's favorite position. He had plenty of room to toss his hands in the air for emphasis to complement his words.

Zeke sat back and looked at Keith over his spectacles as Keith explained why he had distanced himself from his loved ones and colleagues. Keith described how talking to them about his condition and prognosis had become redundant and boring and how it had become laborious to think of new or less obvious lies about his condition. Keith's brow furrowed as he told Zeke that this task was getting more difficult by the day. Although he knew that his loved ones would have to deal with his death, post-mortem, he was determined to make it as uncomplicated for them as possible, pre-mortem. These days, he felt there just wasn't much to share that would not be depressing in nature and he didn't want his loved ones to be worried about him any more than they already were. This was the way he wanted it. The way he wanted to die. End of story. Quietly. Nonchalantly. Sullen. Guilt-ridden. Most of all alone—without anyone hovering over him. He didn't want to leave this earth with that image imprinted in his mind, playing over and over like a scratched vinyl-record as he faded into oblivion.

Zeke empathetically listened as Keith described the first time he had an out of body experience. He told Zeke that his doctors had recently described to him, in gruesome detail, the survival rates, symptoms, and affectations of other patients in the final stage of terminal cancer. Keith knew with miserable certainty that by *other patients*, the doctors now meant *him*. His chances of survival were nil. Although they never beat around the bush, he confided to Zeke they didn't have to—that their anecdotes and facial expressions said it all. In the days leading up to the biopsy results he had prepared himself to accept any outcome and meet it head on if the results came back positive—the irony of the semantics gave Keith an oh-so-brief respite from his moribund destiny.

Even though it was obvious to Zeke that Keith was mentally prepared to accept his death, he wondered if this was even something humans were actually capable of doing.

Keith stared out Zeke's window and tried to visualize that inevitable, fateful moment. Then as if he had read Zeke's mind, blurted out, "Who could ever be ready for *that* kind of news?"

"No one, my friend," Zeke sighed. "No one can truly be ready for *that*. Keith, as a professional, I hate to sound trite. You were blindsided by your illness just like everyone else who's ever been in your situation."

Zeke looked directly at Keith. With every fiber of his being had to force himself to hold back the tears that constantly threatened to appear at times like these. He spoke softly, "Keith, I truly wish I could impart some wisdom for you, for anyone in your situation, in order for you, and them, to be prepared for the end, but no one knows the secret of how to be prepared. We only know how to... react. To respond. For some, faith in a higher power, some deity, or self-awareness *can* help. But even if one believes in a hereafter, no one can ever truly prepare for the shock...is that the right word?... that finality brings."

Eyes still transfixed on his patient, Zeke continued. "I honestly don't know how I'd react. I've never been on that chair, only this one. There was nothing in your life that would hinted at such an event. You were physically fit. Active. Young. And strong. You took good care of yourself." Zeke needed to force the session onward, emphatically, but with subtle instruction. "My job is to help you deal with this the best you can. I'm very good at what I do, but all I *can* do is help you work through this with high spirits. The rest is up to you. Is there anything else on your mind? Anything you want to talk about?" Zeke figured he had heard every story, delusion, denial, frantic scheme, or mental rationalization that could be articulated, conjured, or elaborated from the occupants of that chair.

He was wrong.

40

Sweet Home Chicago

Completely independent for the first time—she was at ease—in a familiar yet somehow different place. Rita immersed herself in her work. And with the support of her now nearby family she was able to calmly accept what was happening to Keith. And to her. In spite of Keith's secretive behavior in recent weeks—or because of this—she believed everything would work out for the better.

She dedicated most of her time to her responsibilities at the largest science museum in the Western Hemisphere—Chicago's Museum of Science and Industry. A keystone of knowledge, invention, and discovery, it frequently added exhibits to reflect the evolution of society and our knowledge of the planet.

———⟫●⟨———

It was home to the original Zephyr, the famed Silver Streak, and Germany's U505 submarine. A Wright Flyer and a Boeing 727 flamboyantly hung in the main gallery. It housed an eco-friendly Smart Home and the famous Whispering Gallery—one of the oldest exhibits. And a domed IMAX theater which presented movies about the wonders of our planet and universe.

Visitors to the museum could learn about the history notable local scientists—their accomplishments and contributions to better our world through knowledge. The region arguably produced the most Nobel Laureates in the world.

For visitors who wanted to see everything the museum had to offer—every display, movie, and presentation—it took three entire days.

———›❂‹———

Rita was the Director of the Membership and Donor Services department. Soon after she took the position, membership revenue and visitor attendance began to soar. Even in a depressed economy, the organization was flush with donors, mostly as a direct result of her marketing and promotional campaigns.

From the time she arrived in the morning and throughout the day, she greeted everyone—visitors, members, groundskeepers, janitors, parking lot attendants, and docents—with a smile and a cheerful 'good morning' or 'good afternoon'. *Everyone* knew and liked Rita Haley.

Rita's presence illuminated every room she entered. Her personality made everyone around her feel special. Her short, cinnamon-tinted tussled hair, rustled in the breeze that *she* created by her exuberant stride around her workplace.

———›❂‹———

Rita was in the basement of her parent's house searching for mementos to decorate her new apartment. She came across a large box which was full of Haley family photo albums. She puffed and wiped the layer of fine dust off the box and marveled at its contents. Her mom and dad's wedding photos. Pictures of the familiar house in Wrigleyville, but with the old, smaller porch. The Haley children and friends playing in the front yard. First teeth. New bicycles. Cubs games. New cars. Prom dates. Weddings. In-laws. Outlaws. Grandchildren. Life. She fondly remembered the good times and bad portrayed in the aging photos, and realized the fact that the majority of good times in her life were in this very house, with her family.

"How sad," she sighed. Tears began to flow down her rosy cheeks—and she let them. She knew this was part of her life's journey—to set free what once was, to embrace what is, and to dream of what could be. She set aside the photos she wanted to take home, wiped her nose, took a deep breath, and then exhaled deeply. "Ahhh, better."

Rita believed that her life *was* moving in the right direction. Her sense of self-worth grew stronger as the time that separated her from Simon passed. Like so many women, satisfaction and happiness of others defined her existence. That her career was going well and her professional accomplishments were recognized certainly played a large role in her current state of mind. And she loved her new apartment, even if it was just a humble studio. It *felt* like home.

She felt one thing was missing in order to make her life complete. Rita was steadfast in her belief that Keith's doctors were going to cure him. Bring back to her the love of her life. Create harmony in her universe. She promised him that she would wait for him forever, and longed for the day they would be together again.

41

Collaboration

With his plan to find someone to take care of, and to love Rita underway, he shifted his focus to solving the last part of the equation—Simon. Keith had to figure out a way to get Simon out of the way and permanently out of Rita's life. He knew that Simon—while a few cards short of a deck—was smart enough to find Rita in Chicago. Hunt her down—maybe even kill her. As far as Keith was concerned, in a perfect world, Simon belonged in a dark, dank hellhole.

An inconvenient truth nagged at him. How could someone be imprisoned if that someone had not been caught doing anything illegal? He wracked his brain for ideas, but, as he had just swallowed two oxycodone tablets, the logical part of his brain began to cloud. Keith decided to tell Michael about his new idea—thought he could come up with a solution. He would call Michael at his home in the evening. "Probably not a good idea to have this kind of talk from his office phone," he thought.

<hr/>

He had spent most of his day deep in thought on a concept-community project that he planned to present to a client the following week. In the evening, he was still thoroughly engrossed in his project, when the phone rang. He didn't want to be disturbed so he let the answering machine intercept it. "Maybe it's Sarah. Or one of the team," he suddenly thought. Most of them worked as hard and as long as he did. He pressed the talk button on the answering machine and picked up the handset. "Good Evening. This is Michael."

"Hi Michael. Keith here. I hate to pester you again, but there is something else that hasn't been, um, resolved yet."

Michael, annoyed by the fact that it was Keith, uncharacteristically let impatience get the best of him. "What the hell is this guy calling about now?" he wondered. "Ah, hell. Whatever it is, I'd better find out what's on his mind. It's obviously urgent, at least to him."

"No problem, Keith. What's wrong?" he spoke into the receiver.

"Well, I've told you about Simon, Rita's ex. His abusive tendencies. How he's stalked Rita. Threatened her. It's really starting to gnaw at me. He's violent. I'm also worried that I might have put you in harm's way as well. It's weighing heavy on my mind, so I figured I should tell you what I want to do to nip this thing in the bud. I thought if you knew what you're up against you might have a...solution. I've been beating my head against a wall trying to find a way to, um, take him out of the picture. Maybe catch him committing some petty crime or something. I'm pretty certain that that fucker is always up to no-good. I want to *help* him get thrown in jail where he belongs. Or otherwise get him out of the way. But short of killing him, I've got nothing. Do you have any...*advice?*"

"So this is what was bugging Keith." Michael thought about this dilemma—the ramifications quickly entered his mind, but he dismissed them just as quickly. He did have a lot of connections though he rarely asked any of them them for favors. Certainly not something of this nature. Quite suddenly, a solution to the problem made its way from Michael's subconscious, through his cerebrum, and directly out of his mouth. "Keith, I've got it! Maybe. You said Simon works on the docks in Boston slinging freight, right?"

"Yep. That's what the scumbag does alright. Not exactly an artisan."

"If Simon were offered a job...say on board a ship bound for some exotic destination...for big money, do you think that he'd take it?"

Keith huffed sarcastically. "Pfft. According to Rita, Simon's middle name is 'Greed'."

"Good. I've got connections in the freight forwarding industry. At Vittorio. I'll make a call and get back to you."

"You know people at *Vittorio?*"

———◆———

Michael indeed had contacts at Vittorio. His very good friend and one of his best clients was Salvatore 'Sal' Vittorio—Italian shipping and cruise-line magnate. Sal owned a fleet of luxury cruise liners and large fleet of tankers and freighters that hauled goods across practically every body of water on the planet. Halloran and Associates had designed interiors and staterooms for Vittorio since Michael's grandfather ran the firm.

"Buon giorno, Vittorio," Angelina Cosentini answered the call.

"Buon Giorno! It's Michael Halloran calling. Is Sal available?"

"Michael! It's Angelina! How nice to hear your voice! When are we going to see you again?"

Angelina Cosentini, Sal's niece, had a crush on Michael à la '9 1/2 Weeks'—but he never knew. Her interest in Michael began when she interned for Halloran and Associates after she had graduated from The University of Chicago.

"Hi Angelina, I thought it was you. It's good to hear your voice as well. To answer your question, I believe your uncle wants me to come out there soon to work on his new fleet. How are you and the rest of the family?"

Angelina was more than happy to chat with Michael before transferring the call.

———◆———

"Michael! How the hell are you? I haven't heard from you in a while. How are my designs coming along?" Sal asked in perfect English but with a telltale Italian accent.

"The plans! Oh! Uh…the plans. They'll be complete next week, a couple of months early. I can visit you and show them to you whenever you want."

"Molto Bene! That's great news! Can you fly out soon? I'd love to see the model."

"Of course. I'll make the arrangements as soon as I hang up." Getting to the point. "Sal, that's not the reason I'm calling. I need a favor. A big favor. Here's the thing...."

Sal listened to Michaels plan and agreed to help his old friend. Sal would make Simon an offer he couldn't refuse—a job on the next freighter out of Boston bound for Hong Kong.

"Sal, you're a great friend. Thank you. I owe you one."

———

Sal called Vittorio's Boston office and told them to make an offer to a *certain guy* in the Boston dockworkers union. Someone at the Boston office contacted Simon's foreman, Tank, and relayed the message. Tank thought that the pay was a little high considering the assignment. "What the fuck, if Sal Vittorio wanted this guy on one of his ships, it's no skin offa' my teeth."

———

Simon was overjoyed when he received the job offer, especially when he found out about the money. He was also very happy to 'get out of this rat hole of a city for a while'. To Simon, the timing of the opportunity couldn't have been better. He was about to be evicted from his apartment and the idea of free room and board for a while suited him just fine. Moreover, his car was mere days away from being impounded—he had missed the payments for three months in a row. As far as he was concerned, they could have the car—he would buy another one with cash when he returned to Boston. The chance to make better money was great, but the icing on the cake was a free trip to Hong Kong. He knew that there were women in Hong Kong that would do anything for a little money.

"Gonna' have to go pussy shopping while I'm there," he chuckled.

42

Keith's health was rapidly declining and he didn't have the nerve to tell Rita. He wanted to be the *old* Keith again. The *strong* Keith. For her. But the *new* Keith was no match for his formidable opponent. Powerless to change what was happening to him, he cried as his once toned body deteriorated before his eyes like a Hollywood slow-motion special-effects scene. He had accepted the fact that he could no longer satisfy Rita's physical or emotional needs, if such acceptance was possible for him—or any man. The ravenous cancer and the radiation and chemotherapy treatments shriveled any chance of a mutually rewarding sex life with Rita. The pills created by the mega-pharmaceutical companies to enhance men's sex lives did nothing for him—their claims were farcical.

His desire for bonding—sexual or otherwise—plummeted. No matter how talented his fingers and tongue, or how sweet his words, he would never again be the lover Rita needed. He was regrettably, tragically, no longer capable of loving her the way she deserved.

———⇒●⇐———

Keith shared this torment—his sexual desperation—with Zeke. How his attempts to bring back some form of desire had turned against him—caused him deep humiliation. And frustration. And anger. He told Zeke about his daydreams—of making love with

166

Rita. How he had attempted to masturbate to this daydream fantasy. And how even that had proved fruitless. His body was unwilling to cooperate. He described to Zeke about another attempt to masturbate, this time while fantasizing in the shower. Desperate to have an orgasm he violently stroked his penis until he finally succeeded. His head in his hands, Keith shamefully told Zeke that while he stared down at his dripping penis, the extremely brief moment of pleasure he had experienced vanished like a wisp of smoke. Tears filled his eyes as he told Zeke that he had ejaculated without even having an erection. His semen swirled down the drain faster than it had trickled from his withering genitals.

Keith reached for the box of tissues conveniently placed on the glass and wood coffee table next to the chair, wiped his eyes, and continued. "Doc, I'm a mess. I know I'm not going to make it and I don't have the balls to tell her. I'm such a pussy," he sobbed.

"You're not a wimp," Zeke interjected, using a politically correct term. "You're afraid of hurting Rita. You love her deeply. In addition, considerate, caring people don't want to hurt those they love. Intentionally or otherwise."

Keith gained his composure, wiped his eyes once more, and decided to confess his plan to Zeke. Keith expected Zeke would be taken back a notch—would likely say Keith was crazy, but Keith already knew he fit that classification to a tee. Although the legal classification would have a fancier, longer name. "I love Rita so much. I want her to have a happy life. I know you're gonna' think I've completely lost it, but I have to tell you something. I've started to look for a man to take my place. I know it's an insane idea, but that doesn't matter to me. I can no longer be there for her and I'm grasping at straws to take care of her any way I can."

A rushed, yet detailed description of Keith's plan ensued. He told Zeke how he had fastidiously searched for the perfect mate for Rita. That he had scoured the personal ads on websites and how he ultimately found Jillian at Professional Matchmakers, Inc. "Jillian actually found a potential match. His name is Michael. He's good looking, kind, and wildly successful. You know, not just any replacement will do. Men are such pigs," Keith spat. "Most guys looking for love on the Internet really just want to get laid. Not that there's anything wrong with no strings attached sex..." he added, "but I want her to have the loving, strong, considerate mate that I can no longer be." Keith admitted it was ludicrous to think he and Michael could pull it off without Rita realizing that something was amiss. But maybe they could. He had no doubt that it would be difficult. But his determination was unwavering—his resolve solid.

In Zeke's estimation, Keith's endeavor sounded too complex. Then, as if he too could read Keith's mind he voiced his concern. "Keith, that is a very...interesting...and considerate, albeit unethical plan, but, have you considered Rita's feelings? How do you think she would feel if she knew what you're up to?"

Keith laughed. "If she knew I was searching someone to take my place, she would be livid. She would undoubtedly believe I had already given up hope of recovery and my return to her arms. And she'd be right. Doc, you *know* I've got no chance of beating this thing. I've fully accepted the fact that I am going to die...very soon, and the only hope I have now is to find someone else for her to love. And for someone to love her."

Zeke, slowly, dramatically took off his glasses, bowed his head, and rubbed his eyes. Then he raised himself off his chair to indicate not-so-subtly that their session had ended. He looked directly at Keith, his mind searching for the right thing to say. He finally broke the silence. "Keith, I just don't know what to make of all this."

43

The Courtship

Michael paced uneasily in his plush office at Halloran and Associates—one of the city's oldest and largest architectural firms, which hailed back to the glory days of Mies van der Rohe, Adler and Sullivan, and Frank Lloyd Wright. These were the very same four walls in which his father and grandfather had toiled as they built their empire of unique progressive architectural designs. By all accounts, Michael had advanced the firm's standing more successfully than had his progenitors. He had created some of the most beautiful, functional, and eco-friendly structures on the planet. In its current embodiment, Halloran and Associates employed over two-hundred architects, designers, and engineers. Michael was proud of his firm—rightly so. It had the best and brightest architects in the industry and a backlog of projects on four continents. Business was good. His professional future held no worrisome uncertainties. Until recently, his personal future seemed to be heading down a distinctly different path.

Tired of pacing—having practically worn a groove in the hardwood floors—he finally deposited himself in his chair. "If I don't have any worries then why am I so worried? What is my problem? I run an incredible company. Negotiate contracts with some of the largest companies in the world, yet here I sit in my office, all alone, hands wringing with sweat, stressing over a phone call for a blind date. The chance of a successful outcome was far from a sure thing. I must be going nuts. How did I allow myself to get into this?" Of course, he knew how. Sarah coerced him into joining a matchmaking service.

He made the requisite video. Endured the long and detailed interview process. Replied to several potential candidates. Had a couple of dates. And now he was preparing to make a telephone call to an unknown woman and ask her for a date. "Ok, here we go," he said aloud to no one. He called the Museum of Science and Industry's main number. "Remember," he reminded himself, "you're just calling to find out about purchasing a membership. It's as simple as that."

After several rings, someone at the museum finally answered his call. "Thank you for calling the Museum of Science and Industry. How may I direct your call?"

"Um…hi. I'd like to purchase a membership."

By chance—or fate—all of the other lines were busy. Calls to the Membership Services department were automatically forwarded to Rita's phone whenever the team was overwhelmed. The glut of calls during the current membership promotion triggered just such an event. "Good Afternoon. Membership Services, Rita Haley here. How may I be of assistance?"

Michael was startled by the fact that Rita had answered his call. "Err…umm, I'm, uh, I'm interested in a membership for the museum. How much are they…is it?" he stammered. "I'm such a dork," Michael thought. "Get your act together man, or you'll blow it!"

"To whom do I have the pleasure of speaking with?"

"Michael. Michael Halloran."

"Well, Mr. Halloran…."

"Please call me Michael. Mr. Halloran is my father," he said, weakly attempting to inject humor. "There," he thought. "That was better. Loosen up."

"Well, Michael, is this a membership for your family or is this a gift membership?"

"Er…aahh…this is for myself…but I might want to get one for my parents. They live in the city and enjoy going to museums."

"Ok then," she replied. She then began to deliver her oft-delivered membership options spiel and asked Michael if he knew which plan he would prefer.

Rita enjoyed her job and the people she worked with immensely—she gushed over her colleagues who contributed to the museum's expansion and growth. She knew the right questions to ask—had the right answers. Her verve for the museum, and its contract with the public to preserve historical artifacts, was contagious. She courteously and professionally informed new prospects of all of the museum's membership and donation options. She was clearly very passionate about her responsibilities and about the museum's charter to preserve history and educate the community.

———————

Outside of the work place, Michael was uncomfortable having a conversation with members of the opposite sex. He was suddenly overwhelmed with flashbacks of recent failed attempts at dating. The women were nice enough, attractive enough—one was even famous—but the dates had not turned out the way he hoped they would. There were no fireworks. He figured Elizabeth had set the bar too high. He questioned the validity of love at first sight. The logical side of his brain determined that true love could only develop through friendship first, then, with luck, romance.

As he listened to Rita talk about the membership options, he began to feel confused and flustered—blood rushed to his face. *That* thought suddenly worked its way into his conscious again: maybe *he* was the reason his recent dates had failed. "Why am I thinking all this bullshit right now?" Carrying out his part of the plan was proving to be harder than he thought it would be—should be.

Eventually, to his great relief, the conversation with Rita started to become less strained. Less nerve-racking. Rita made it easy for him. He could tell that there was nothing pretentious about her. He found her articulate and helpful—and very charming.

Michael purchased a membership for himself, one for his parents, and he made a generous donation to the museum. He felt a civic responsibility to support the museum's noble undertaking.

Rita decided it had been a good day. She had just booked two new memberships and over $50,000 from a new donor, all in a single phone call. It might not be a record, but it *was* $50,000. She looked around and saw no that one else was in reception area. She couldn't hold in her excitement. "*Yippee!*" Her excitement for a job well done was short lived. "Hmmm," she thought. "What a nice guy."

"What did I just do?" Michael pondered. Then he answered himself because no one else was around to comment. He chuckled, uneasily, "You just cut a check for $50,000 all because of a mesmerizing voice." He had just had a brief glimpse of what Keith already knew. Her personality was effervescent and charming. Michael was certain that these qualities actually radiated out over the phone lines. He decided that he liked her.

He had seen the pictures of Rita that Keith had sent him. Keith told him they didn't do her justice—that she was much more attractive in person than in two dimensions. "Could that be true?" he mused.

44

Michael wanted some time alone to ponder his role in this devious yet honorable scheme. He absent-mindedly disregarded the posted speed limits as drove home. It was providential that the highway patrol was seemingly inattentive that evening, otherwise, a ticket, along with a hefty fine would be justifiably awarded to Michael.

Immediately after he arrived home he called Keith to recap his conversation with Rita. He explained how he faltered at the onset and then steadily became comfortable in his repartee with Rita. Michael was obviously excited. He rambled on about how he was going to visit the museum the next day during an extended lunch break.

As the conversation moved along, Michael exhibited signs of pessimism, which elicited a stern response from Keith "Get a hold of yourself man! Just be yourself. Don't back down now Nervous Nellie. It'll be fine, trust me. Just go on up to the front desk and ask for her. It's *that* simple. Then strike up a conversation. If something clicks, then go for it, ask her for a date. If she agrees, great. If not, no harm, no foul. Come on Michael, I need you to do this. See it through. I told you that you'd quickly find out how truly incredible she is. You'll see what I've been talking about, about Rita. You won't be disappointed, I promise."

"What if she isn't attracted to me and turns me down? Or...?"

"Then," Keith interrupted, memories of his own self-doubts rushed back, "we've determined it wasn't meant to be. I'll continue my pursuit, and you're out nothing but $50,000 to a worthy cause."

"Alright! I'll do it!" Michael said enthusiastically—confidently. At that exact moment, Michael realized he had had another momentary lapse of reason—he had promised to call Sarah and tell her about his conversation with Rita. These lapses were getting more frequent, especially when the topic was Sarah. This realization baffled Michael.

Sarah recognized the number on the caller ID and didn't bother to say hello when she answered. "Well? How'd it go?"

"I'm going to meet a potential date tomorrow."

"Yes!" she screamed like a diehard Blackhawks fan after a goal.

45

He woke up periodically throughout the night—worried that he wouldn't be able to pull off the charade. An hour before his alarm was due to go off he got out of bed. Michael felt awkward attempting to woo someone else's woman with assistance from that *someone else*. The situation was unscrupulous tabloid fodder.

He showered and shaved. And then ate a breakfast of fruit, cereal, and had one cup of black coffee while he scanned the headlines from the morning papers. In the local section of the Tribune he read about the plans for a new annex at the Museum of Science and Industry. Something clicked—he recalled Rita's remarks about the undertaking.

A hole opened up in Michael's life—a hole that was not directly connected to, but related to Liz's constant and devoted companionship. It was due to his sudden lack of community involvement. Together they had been tremendously active in their community, generously volunteering their time and monies to various causes. After she passed away, those activities ceased. He spent the last three years obsessed with his work and attempts to increase his client base. He had inadvertently neglected the philanthropic aspect of his life. "It's time for me to get back in the community involvement saddle," he thought, earnestly. He was certain that everyone—Keith, Sarah, his parents, his colleagues— would be pleased.

Michael's anxiety increased as each minute passed. Not because he was finally going to see Rita with his own eyes but because he was furtively fretful about a woman who could drive another man to such acts of desperation and trickery.

Meetings kept him focused on business from the moment he arrived at his office, but his mind intermittently wandered off in anticipation of meeting Rita, which caused an unusual lack of concentration. His mobile phone alarm went off at 11:30—time to get going. The museum was a convenient short walk from his office. On the way, he practiced the words he would attempt to utilize effectively. As he strode up the broad concrete stairs to the museum's entrance, he hoped that he was not making the biggest mistake of his life. He checked his hands. Clammy—not a good sign.

The Membership Services desk was on the east side of the museum's main atrium. He glanced around as if he were looking for someone he knew. And he was—sort of. He had to force himself to appear calm as he walked toward the desk. He felt like a young boy about to ask for a dance at his first sock hop. He noticed that the woman sitting behind the desk fit Rita's description. Short, cinnamon hair. Obviously tall even though she was sitting down. He wiped his clammy hands on his pants and he felt like he was going over the first drop of a very high roller coaster. He approached the desk with trepidation. Rita deftly handled some paperwork and was obviously unaware that someone was there until he spoke. "Excuse me," Michael said, interrupting her focus.

Her head whipped at the sudden intrusion—brought her back to the here and now. "Yes, how may I help you?" she instinctively responded.

"I'm looking for Rita Haley. She was a great help yesterday when I called to purchase a membership. She was so enthusiastic about your programs and the goings on here that I ended up joining and made a small donation as well. Ms. Haley told me I could stop by and pick up my free gift or she could mail it to me, and since my office is right down the corner, I thought I would just pick it

up in person. Save you guys the hassle of mailing it to me. So...
here I am."

"I'm sorry...and you are?" she queried. Then a thought quickly
popped into her head, "Could this be the same man who donated
$50,000 yesterday? Here so soon? It had to be, she hadn't heard
of any other donation yesterday."

"Michael Halloran."

"Oh," she exclaimed. The visual linked with her audio memory
recall. "Here he was...in person," she thought.

"Hello, Michael. *I'm* Rita."

"Damn, it *is* her! Calm down, Halloran. You're just picking up
your free gift," he assured himself.

Rita took some items from her desk, got up, and strode pertly
to the other side of the desk, set the items down, and offered her
hand. "Thank you so much for your generous donation to the
museum. Like I said yesterday, we'll be having your name engraved
on our wall, which should take a month or so. Which free gift
would you like? The World Almanac and Encyclopedia DVD set
or the Wonders of the World coffee table book?"

He shook her hand and marveled at the softness of her skin.
"Which do you recommend? I plan to give it to my niece."

"How old is she?"

Michael laughed aloud. "Twelve going on twenty-four. She is
very mature for her. What a fireball she is. A wonderful child. She's
so intelligent for her age, she drives her parents crazy, which, by the
way, is extremely entertaining to watch. For me at least," he said
giving her an awkward wink. "As soon as she turns eighteen and
graduates from high school, she wants to travel around the world.
Concerning her parent's frustration, I'm afraid I'm at least *partly*
to blame. I told her I'd pay for the trip as a graduation present...
if she committed to going to college. She's already made a list of
schools."

"What a generous uncle you are, Michael. In that case, the
World Almanac and Encyclopedia DVD set, which includes a hard
bound Reference Guide is my recommendation. And my personal
favorite. It has all kinds of neat stuff for kids of all ages. It's

interactive and she'll have a chance to virtually visit all the places she wants to go in about, what, six years."

"Sounds good, I'll take that."

"Wonderful! Good choice. She'll enjoy it immensely. Let me get you a new set, these are my desk copies." She strolled off to a side room to get his gift.

Michael watched her and he instantly became aroused. The yearning in his groin came at the most inappropriate of times. "It's been too long old boy," he muttered to himself. He struggled with all his might to stop the growing bulge in his pants, involuntarily betraying his desire for this lovely woman. He made a valiant effort to ignore the activity in his pants.

Rita came back and put the DVD set in a colorful bag emblazoned with the museum's log. "Here you go."

"Ms. Haley, I don't want to sound too forward, and I really did come down here just to pick up my free gift. Can I take you to lunch?" he asked. "I'm not asking you for a date or anything, but I want to thank you for all your help in some way. I know a great little Italian deli, two blocks away that serves a delicious pizza. You can tell me more about the museum's volunteer programs. It's time for me to get more involved in the community again. Actually, it's long overdue. I think I know what I want to do, but I could use your advice to help me decide. What do you say?"

Rita paused a moment before she gave him an answer. She searched his eyes for a tell—for a hint of concealed motives behind in his request. She didn't see anything unusual. He seemed genuine. Besides, she figured, someone like this, with monetary resources to spare, probably had wealthy friends that might donate to the museum as well. It occurred to Rita that she may have hit on a gold mine.

The delay caused Michael a great deal of consternation. "Oh no! She's going to turn me down," Michael fretted.

"Really...this isn't a date or anything," he assured her. Just something to show my appreciation for all your help and to get some advice...no gimmicks...no strings. Just lunch."

"Oh shit, I've blown any chance I had completely out of the water," he somberly thought.

Rita had turned down many requests for dates recently. She was doggedly determined not to open her heart to anyone other than Keith. She thought about the lunch invitation a bit longer. She *was* hungry and it *was* time for her lunch break. She even knew the deli he mentioned. They *did* serve a delicious pizza. As far as she could tell, Michael seemed to be an honest man. Professional. Didn't seem like he was out to jump her bones. He genuinely seemed to be interested in some friendly conversation and advice over lunch. She reminded herself that not many members, or guests, ever thanked her for her help. "It feels good to be appreciated," she thought.

She finally broke the silence. "That is very kind of you, but..."

"Oh no! Here it comes." Michael didn't interrupt her, his breath held in anticipation. He waited patiently for her answer—good or bad—while he stared into her hazel eyes and forced himself to remain outwardly calm.

"...first I need to grab my purse and tell my colleagues that I'm going to lunch, then I'll be right back."

Michael didn't exhale until Rita walked back to the side room and then he did so slowly and quietly because he was certain she was still within aural range. He could hear Rita telling someone she was going to lunch. His heartbeat was so loud he felt certain she could hear it. As she bent down to pick up her purse from behind her desk, he ogled her round posterior.

46

A Modest Proposal

It was a beautiful warm day in the Windy City. The delicatessen was just a short walk down Michigan Avenue. Along the way, they unintentionally weaved in and out of the lunchtime mass of humanity and tried to stay together, despite the unyielding crowd. Michael tried to start a conversation but the crowd separated them. Then Rita made an attempt and the crowd deflected them away from each other again. They gave up trying, laughed, and agreed to wait until they got to the deli to have a conversation. At a corner, they waited side-by-side for the light to change. Michael could smell the scent of her perfume waft through the countless odors of the city. He couldn't identify the scent. No matter. He thought she smelled as wonderful as she looked.

The little deli—favored by locals—bustled like a beehive. They chose a red and white checkered table near the back where it was a little less boisterous and gave them ample privacy. They ordered salads, personal pizzas, and drinks—she a diet cola, he an iced-tea. They stared at each other for a brief, awkward moment. Neither of them was sure where to start now that they had the chance to talk. Rita finally broke the silence. "So, Mr. Halloran, what do you want to know about the volunteer programs we have?" she asked.

"Well, as you know, I'm an architect by trade, and I read in this morning's newspapers that the museum is planning to add an annex to the north side of the complex."

"Yes, we are!" Rita exclaimed. "I am *so* excited about it. The board of directors finally decided to move forward with the project.

It will be the Children's Discovery wing," she said, resting her chin in her palm, elbow firmly on the table. "Why do you bring up that particular subject?"

"I read that the museum hadn't selected an architectural firm yet, and well, I'd like to offer my company's services. Pro bono. You know. For free."

"You're...kidding me?" she responded. A perplexed, intrigued look flashed across her pretty face. Her body snapped erect—alert. She moved her chair closer to him.

"No, I'm not kidding," he replied matter-of-factly. He was pleased by her response. "I've decided that my firm, Halloran and Associates, needs to give back more to the community than it has been, and I believe this project is in compliance with our community policy. Who would I talk to move forward on the new annex?"

Rita was speechless. It suddenly dawned on her and she made the connection of Michael's name with that of Halloran and Associates, one of the leading architectural firms in the country. She couldn't believe she was having lunch with the president of the company. "Crap! This conversation just went far beyond my pay grade," she thought.

"Ah...well, um, I guess you'll need to make a proposal and submit it to the board and see what they say. I mean, although I'm on the steering committee, I'm not authorized to make such a decision alone. That's quite a generous offer Mr. Halloran. Are you sure about this? It's likely to be expensive. We've already come to that conclusion."

"Please, call me Michael, and, yes Rita, I'm quite sure. It is ok if I call you Rita isn't it? Your enthusiasm has sparked something inside me that's been dormant for a long time Rita. Too long, so...I'm here to help in any way I can."

Their food arrived. They eagerly discussed the finer points of Chicago-style stuffed pizza before the conversation shifted back to business. Michael mentioned some of his hastily assembled thoughts for the new annex. Rita talked about some of the marketing and promotional ideas she had developed. They were collaborating already.

They pushed back their plates, looked at each other, and smiled. Silence engulfed their small island of privacy for a few more moments before she once again broke it. "I sure wasn't expecting *this* when I accepted your lunch invitation. I had no idea pizza could be a power lunch," Rita giggled. "I must tell you, Michael, now that I made the connection with your name and your firm, I'm kind of embarrassed. I should have known who you were. I think the board members will be absolutely thrilled by your generous proposal."

"It's my pleasure, Rita, and frankly, unless you're into architectural design, I don't know how you'd know who we are. I can tell you though, I prefer to stay out of the limelight. Don't like throwing my name around, unlike most of my competition," he said with a modest yet flirtatious smile.

Michael had volunteered his company's resources to the expansion of the museum. She was truly impressed. She decided that she liked Michael Halloran. "He's quite humble," she thought. "And generous. The kind of a guy, who has everything he could possibly want, yet has the desire to give back to his community, was more than willing to do his share, and didn't want any praise. He's a good man. That, and he's damn good looking too!"

Then it hit her—the similarities with Keith are uncanny. "I need to get back to the office," Rita nervously proclaimed, after glancing at her watch. "I'm so sorry but I only have an hour for lunch and my time is up."

Michael wanted to seize the moment. "Here's a thought. Permit me to walk back to the museum with you, and if any board members are in the office, maybe I can speak to one of them and see if I can get myself on the agenda for the next planning meeting. I'm ready to get this project going."

She beamed. "My goodness Michael Halloran, you *are* a man of action aren't you?"

47

The Meeting

They marched up the giant steps leading to the columns that marked the entrance to the fabled museum, through the massive doorway, through the main atrium, and finally into the administrative offices. As they strode through the halls next to the museum president's office Rita raised her hand, signaling Michael to stop. He responded automatically like a well-trained Australian sheep dog—stopped dead in his tracks.

Rita poked her head into the office, saw the president was there, and knocked on the door softly. "Excuse me Dr. Cutter, do you have a few minutes to talk with someone? I think you'll be very interested to hear what he has to say."

"Hi Rita!" A Cheshire Cat grin slowly appeared on Dr. Cutter's face. He glanced at the man standing with her. His first thought was, "If Rita addressed him as Dr. Cutter, and thought this sharply-dressed man would be worth taking some of his valuable time to speak to, it must be something worthwhile." "Why sure," Jake Cutter replied. He promptly turned his attention to Michael. "What can I do for you Mr., um...." He stood up from his desk and extended his hand—overly wide smile still intact.

"Halloran. Michael Halloran."

"Jack Cutter. My friends call me 'Jake'. Say, you're not the Michael Halloran of Halloran and Associates, are you?"

"Yes, that's me." Michael replied.

"It's a pleasure to meet you, Michael."

"Thank you, Jake. The pleasure is mine." Michael said. "I've admired your collection of artifacts and exhibits my whole life. Being a local boy, I've been here countless times over the years. In fact, I still come here often. This is a wonderful place, filled with all kinds of interesting and amazing things. The kind of place where the imagination of a boy any age can run wild. Mine certainly did, and still does. But Jake, it's not what you can do for me, it's what I might be able, and am prepared, to do for *you*."

"Please sit down. Rita, would you care to join us?"

"Thanks Jake, but no. I've got to get back to my monthly reports. The ones due on your desk by five o'clock," she reminded him. She flashed him a bright smile. "I know how cranky you get when you don't get your reports on time," she joked. With elegant composure, she politely turned to Michael. "Mr. Halloran, it was truly a pleasure meeting you and having lunch with you today. I hope to see you again soon." She turned to face Jake. "Those reports will be on your desk by five o'clock, scout's honor. Good day gentlemen, have a nice talk." She nodded to both of them. With that, she turned on her heels, slipped through the doorway and quietly closed the door to Jake's office behind her.

48

The Ring

The anticipation was agonizing. It was 7 o'clock. He should have received a web call by now. Jillian and Michael had not specified a time, but said they would call as soon as they could. Maybe Michael had chickened out—had gotten cold feet, and didn't go through with the plan—didn't go to meet Rita. Maybe he couldn't get away from work. Maybe. Maybe. Maybe.

"*Shit*," Keith said aloud. "He could have at least called me and said something happened. Or didn't." As far as Keith was concerned, it was ok if the plan was delayed another day because of unforeseen circumstances—he could deal with that. It was not knowing what did or did not happen that was driving him crazy. He had to know that his plan was working. He could feel his body losing strength as each minute passed. He realized that he might not have enough time to see his plan to fruition. He *had* to keep pushing all the players in the right direction.

At 7:20 his webcam beeped. It startled Keith. The ringing sound brought him back to the here and now. His heart raced. He answered the call before it rang the third time. Michael and Jillian appeared onscreen.

"Michael! Thank God you called. Tell me everything!"

⟹●⟸

After he heard the good news from Michael, Keith calmed down a bit and decided that things were actually progressing nicely.

It was time to divulge the final puzzle piece. It was a lunatic's idea. One to be shared with only those he trusted completely. He *had* to trust Michael. Michael was his last hope.

"I have a ring," Keith said.

"I'm sorry," Michael responded, puzzled. "I don't think I heard you. Did you just say you have a *ring?*"

"Yes. It's a very special ring. It's for Rita. You see, it was found on the very first expedition that Sammy and I made together, in some nasty waters off of the Azorean coast."

Keith continued the story. "It was three fold nasty. The first nasty, the currents there were unrelenting, strong enough to pull our anchor off the sea floor, and send our ship and equipment adrift. The sea that day was a bitch to dive in. As soon as we got to a spot we could work in, the currents jerked us several meters from where we were. Nasty number two, the reefs all around us jutted up here and there from the ocean floor, out of nowhere, waiting to tear us and our vessel to shreds in the blink of an eye. Then there's nasty number three, the sharks. The *real* reason we were there in the first place. Searching for treasure that might or might not be found was fine and dandy, but the ultimate objective of the expedition was to study and video the behavior of certain shark species, right next to one of those deadly reef outcroppings. Sharks sell, and Sammy and I liked to get close to the action. Perilously close," Keith smugly explained.

"While videoing the sharks and their goings on, I kept out of harm's way on the ocean floor, off camera, out of Sammy's way of a good shot. Cruising the bottom I spotted something that looked strangely out of place. As I swam closer to get a better look, the object took shape. I brushed away the sand and saw that the object was a metal strap...around a ship's chest. A bona fide treasure chest!"

Keith gleefully embellished this long ago memory. "Lo' and behold, we'd accidentally stumbled on a real treasure on our maiden adventure. A shipwreck! The ship belonged to the King of Spain, no less. And it had quite a lot of treasure on board when it sank. According to maritime law, in international waters, the fabled edict of finders keepers applies. So, technically, and legally, we owned the whole enchilada. The value of the treasure was astronomical. It allowed Sammy and I to do a lot more dives, adventures, exhibitions, as well as fund some noble community programs. Sure, since then we've both made more money than we ever thought imaginable, but finding that treasure was special. We photographed and catalogued everything, and afterward, although we owned it, in good faith we shipped everything to Spain to be stored properly and for display in a future exhibition. With one exception. This ring." Keith held the ring closer to his webcam.

Michael and Jillian didn't blink or move a muscle. This was like listening to a real-life fairy tale.

"As for this beauty, I can't think of a better person in the world who deserves to wear it. I don't know how you're going to give it to her. That's up to you. I'm not saying you should ask Rita to marry you, just give her the ring. But...she must *never* know it came from me. She needs to think it came from you and you alone. Sammy, my business partner and friend, who technically owns half of it, and who knows I have possession of it, knows all about this plan. Sammy knows how I feel about Rita, knows about you and what we're trying to accomplish. In case you don't go through with it, he's got your contact information so he can get it back. I'm not saying you are going to run off with it. Though I'm sure it will be tempting once you hold it in your hand."

The magnificent ring splayed brilliant rainbow prisms, even visible by Michael and Jillian, who gawked at the ring on their computer monitor. The ring was enormous. It comprised a crystal-clear, flawless, 12-carat, emerald-cut diamond as the center stone. It was surrounded by diamond baguettes that flowed from the center. At the corners were yellow diamond marquise droplets.

The ring's magnificence stunned Jillian. Not the kind of person to utter expletives in professional situations, she couldn't contain her amazement. "Fuck me! Look at the *size* of that thing!" Then she quickly realized how that sounded. She blushed and apologized for her outburst. "I am so sorry, but that has to be the most gorgeous piece of jewelry I've ever seen! Was it…was it really made for a queen? You wouldn't be pulling my leg, would you?"

Keith's face contorted slightly. If his facial muscles could react to his brains commands, there would be a big smile on his disfigured face. "No, I wouldn't, Jillian. I'm not pulling your leg. It *really* was made for a queen."

49

Keith let the call go to his answering machine. He didn't want to talk to anyone other than Michael, or maybe Jillian. All he could do was hope it was one of them. He suddenly heard Michael's voice emanate from the speaker. "Hi Keith, it's Michael. Just checking in. Call me back when you can."

Keith picked up the receiver. "Hi Michael. Sorry I didn't answer before you started to leave a message. The media keeps calling and those blood-sucking bastards are the last people on earth I want to talk to. I was really starting to worry if you were going to call or what."

"I'm sorry Keith. I got tied up on the phone with my project in Beijing. I know it's late for you."

"Can we cut to the quick here? What happened today? You were going to talk to your friends at Vittorio to see what happened with Simon, and you were going to fill me in on what you have planned for the ring, remember?"

Keith was getting grumpier by the day. Michael could not imagine how Keith must be feeling. "Good news on the Simon front. I had my friend offer him a job on a freighter bound for Hong Kong. Simon snatched up the opportunity. *That* problem will soon be on a slow boat to China. Literally. There's no reason to worry any more about him, at least for a while. Now the ring is a different story. That problem is not totally solved yet."

"What do mean it's not totally solved yet? It's simple. Give her the ring. What am I missing?"

"Keith, it's not *that* simple. That ring has been on the cover of National Geographic for Christ's sake! When she wears it, someone, somewhere, will recognize it. And I don't want to be in a position to have to explain how I got it. I mean, she knows I'm not poor, but a ring like that is worth far more than I can afford. And I'm having a difficult time thinking up a proper reveal without it looking like I'm buying her love. Or *sex* for that matter."

So, here's what I'm thinking. I'll arrange to have all of the jewels removed from the ring and made into an ensemble for her. I'll ask an old friend of the family, who happens to be a master gemologist and jewelry designer, to handle it. I have no doubt that he'll absolutely flip his lid when he sets his eyes on this baby. But like I said, he's an old family friend who I completely trust. I'll have him to set the stones in a ring, two earrings, and a necklace. This way, I won't have to give it to her all in one shot. She'll still be wearing everything in the ring. I'll even have the gold melted down for all the settings. What do you think? A reasonable solution, wouldn't you say?"

Keith agreed. The ring *was* a little over the top.

50

Vladimir Petrovsky, the ship's commanding officer, shook Simon's shoulder, and was greeted by an unwanted, unwelcome whiff of the stench emanating from the reeking lad's pores. In perfect English, albeit with a moderate Ukrainian accent, he sternly addressed the newcomer, "Cathcart, get your sorry ass up! You're on duty in thirty minutes. Get a move on!"

Groggy from the the previous night's bootleg rum, which was still at work damaging his brain cells, Simon rubbed his half-closed eyes and tried to recall where he was. The last thing he remembered was losing over $500 to some of the other crewmembers in a strange—to him—card game called Pai Gow. "What the hell kind of poker is that," he asked the amused crew. He later regretted his decision to play since he was comically and systematically fleeced. He suspected they had been cheating him and figured it was customary for the ship's crew to gang up on the new guy, but he had no proof. If he was honest with himself, he would have to admit he was terrible at cards.

"Ok! Ok! I'm up! Fuck, I'll be there in a minute. Can I at least take a shower?"

"Judging by your stench, a shower is the first thing you should do. After that, grab some coffee down in the galley, and report to your duty station. *Don't* be late, Cathcart!" Vladimir shouted.

Vladimir had no sympathy for Simon whatsoever. He had seen this kind of lazy newcomer too many times. He walked away, shaking his head in disgust. He knew the captain only hired this kid as a favor to someone important. *He* never would have hired him. Vladimir wished he could abandon Simon in Hong Kong, but much to his chagrin, his wish would likely be unfulfilled.

Simon groaned as he rolled out of his bunk, set his feet on the wet floor, and did his level best to counter his weight against the steady, rhythmic rocking of the vessel. He grasped the bunks for support as he made his way topside. "If only I could get my head to stop spinning. I need to go back down and sleep this off. This job was *supposed* be a piece of cake," he moaned. He immediately formed a contemptible plan—he would find a place to hide and enjoy the ride to Hong Kong. He thought it would be a good idea if he saved his energy for his forthcoming encounters with some of the Hong Kong prostitutes. "Yeah. Hong Kong. Some of the best whore houses in the world. I'm gonna' visit all of 'em. I haven't had any pussy in months. Better not play any more Pai Gow."

51

Not only had Rita secured a $50,000 donation for the museum but the man who made the donation also offered to design the new annex for no charge. "Damn, I do good work. I'm on a roll," she thought. A self-satisfied grin appeared on her face.

Rita returned to Jake's office to turn in her reports. With a bit more pep in her step than usual, she turned the corner and knocked on the museum president's door. "Come in," Jake called out. Rita swung open the door to Jake's expansive office, where he and four of the board members were having a conversation with Michael Halloran—the generous benefactor. Gathered around Jake's conference table, they intently stared at several hand-drawn diagrams of the museum grounds that covered the expensive table.

Rita was accustomed to seeing various board members in Jake's office, nothing new or interesting about that. However, she was *not* expecting Michael to be here. Expensive pinstriped suit jacket folded neatly on the chair, shirt sleeves rolled up, his arm gesticulated a wide arch over one of the diagrams that depicted the new annex. Michael spoke to the group as he pointed and sketched frenetically. Then he paused. "See here...the natural curvature of the hill will blend into the new structure. Fifty percent of the building will be covered by grass and flora, with the other fifty percent covered with a special solar-paneled see-through glass. We're doing some pretty groundbreaking stuff in architectural design these days," he said rather arrogantly.

Michael was on his game and he was visibly excited about the project. The whites of his eyes dominated his ocular cavities as he tried to help everyone in Jake's office envision his concept. "The integrated technologies used in the annex will actually become part of the exhibits, you see?" he boasted. "If you want to, uh, I mean...I'm so caught up in the potential here. When Rita first explained what you were trying to achieve with the new annex...it all just...clicked. I could see the whole thing in my mind as clear as the pools at Buckingham Fountain. What I'm trying, but failing to say is, it's *Rita* you can thank for all this," he said. His arms spread out over the diagrams atop Jake's expensive conference table.

In unison, everyone in the room turned to look at Rita, as if a puppet master controlled their movements. Each of the board members took great delight in hearing that it was *their* Rita who was responsible for the plans for the new annex. "Hi Rita," they greeted her. Betty Forsyth, the chairperson of the board, in her tailor-made, navy blue suit, oxford blouse, silver hair faultlessly coifed, addressed Rita directly. "Rita, please join the discussion, we were just talking about you."

52

A New Job

In quiet disbelief, Rita turned several shades of red while looking at every one in Jake's office. "Did Michael just tell them that *I* was somehow responsible for his plans for the new annex?" she asked herself. She was still dumbfounded by seeing Michael in Jake's office again so soon. "Did Betty just say they'd been *talking* about me? What were they talking about? Did Betty just invite me to join their conversation? I must be dreaming. I don't belong here. But, to reject an offer from the chairperson of the board would be stupid," she quickly decided as she snapped back to reality. "Yes, ma'am," she responded courteously. "Where would you like me to sit?"

"Anywhere you like. Come take a look at Michael's designs. They're amazing. But you already know that, don't you," Betty smiled.

"We've got a seat for you right here Rita," said Clyde Richter. The museum's Vice President graciously pulled out one of the luxurious boardroom chairs.

Betty spoke again, halting the flow of the murmurs that had begun to crop up. "Everyone, I guess this is as good a time as any to tell Rita the plans we have for *her*. What do you think?"

Rita's ears started ringing. "Did Betty just say they had *plans* for her?" she pondered. "Oh no, not more work!" Between managing her staff, taking care of members and visitors, and her paperwork, she felt she already had a full workload. "What now?" she thought.

195

She reluctantly took a seat in the plush chair, unsure of what to do next or what to expect.

"Relax Rita," Alex Coriopolis, the museum's Treasurer, grinned. "What everyone is talking about is this. You know Sam Williams is retiring next month, don't you?"

———⟫●⟪———

Sam Williams was the Director of Marketing and Promotions for the museum—Rita's boss. She had heard the rumors about Sam's imminent retirement, but she thought they were just that: rumors. Rita was not normally the type of person who believe water cooler talk. "Maybe I should be a little less skeptical in the future," she thought.

———⟫●⟪———

"Well," Alex continued, "the board has discussed it, and we all agreed. We would like you to take Sam's place. Sam thinks it's a great idea. In fact, he made the recommendation himself. He's impressed with what you've accomplished in such a short time and believes you'd make the perfect replacement for him."

She felt she was dreaming—she had to be. Certain she would wake up in her bed and laugh at the craziness, she pinched herself, but the voices calling her name were real. She was *not* dreaming.

Betty interrupted Alex quickly, "Rita, listen. No one here has more knowledge and passion to move our expansion projects forward than you." Betty smiled the way a proud mother would when one of her children had done something wonderful. "Your performance and devotion have been exemplary, and we all truly believe there isn't a single person in the entire organization who wouldn't follow you to the ends of the earth. We wouldn't think of trusting anyone from the outside to take over for Sam. And, frankly, that isn't even an option. Even Michael agrees."

"Michael!" she thought. Her expression telegraphed the fact that she was stunned by the announcement of her promotion. So much had happened so quickly. She couldn't wrap her brain around the recent events. "Just a few days ago he called me to purchase a membership. Then he donated $50,000 to the museum. He's here presenting his designs for the new annex to the board, which his company is going to design for free. *And,* he'd apparently voiced his agreement of the board's decision that *she* replace Sam as the museum's Director of Marketing and Promotions!"

"What was going on?" she wondered.

53

It was 6 o'clock when the meeting in the boardroom of the Museum of Science and Industry finally ended. And that was only because everyone started talking about food. One by one they exited, but not before shaking Rita's hand and congratulating her on her promotion. After everyone had left but Michael and Rita, he turned to her, placed his hands on her shoulders, and spoke triumphantly. "What an afternoon! I'm elated. I can't wait to get to the office tomorrow and tell the gang what I got us into. They'll probably applaud me and want to kill me at the same time. I can guarantee you there will be no shortage of volunteers for this project even though they're already overworked. This project is going to be great fun! Rita, I've got some ideas I want to run past you. Things I want to present to the board at the next meeting. Expand on some of the points of our earlier conversation. You're going to be in charge of marketing this project, so we might as well start this working relationship off on the right foot. Do you want to talk...over dinner?" he asked, changing his tone subtly.

Rita was exhausted. But she *was* hungry and the day's unexpected events still had her mind reeling. Her initial thoughts were that it would be nice to have a distraction rather than go back home, switch on the TV, have a frozen dinner, and inevitably fall asleep on the sofa. Besides, there was no one there waiting for her. Keith had left her a voicemail earlier in the day to say that he had undergone physical therapy and that he she should not expect a call from him that evening. She could tell by the tone of his voice that he was deeply depressed. He usually didn't call on treatment days or the day after, due to the way he felt after his body had been pumped full of chemicals. She knew that treatment days left him bereft of passion, strength, and the desire to communicate with anyone—even her. She had what most people would consider a great day. She had received a significant promotion unanimously bestowed upon her by the entire board and was now on the steering committee of the most ambitious expansion ever undertaken by the Museum of Science and Industry. "Nothing should ruin a day like today," she thought. She cocked her head, turned to Michael, and said, "Sure, why not?"

54

Michael, always the gentleman, asked Rita to decide where they would dine. He liked being chivalrous and considered Rita to be worthy of such behavior. Moreover, he wanted confirmation that Keith's anecdotes about her favorite places to eat were true. She serendipitously chose Lou's On Clark. She said that it had been one of her family's favorite places to go when she was young. Michael mentioned that he had known the owner, Lou Santorini, for over thirty years. The same thought occurred to both of them at the same moment: it is a small world.

Since his car was parked in the museum's parking lot, Michael offered to drive to the restaurant and drop her off at her home after dinner. Rita approved of his gallant offer. Despite the bustling ambiance of the Windy City, they were quiet during the drive. Traffic inched along. Horns honked at anyone who impeded progress on Lake Shore Drive.

⟫◆⟪

There was a small crowd of people in line when they arrived, so they decided to wait at the bar for a table. Michael ordered cocktails for both of them—a Grey Goose cosmopolitan for her, Maker's Mark on the rocks for him. Rita excitedly talked about her promotion and told him how nervous she was about having more responsibilities, while an accordionist played classic Italian songs in the background.

"You'll do fine," Michael assured her. "Everyone loves you there. Even I can see that."

30 minutes later, they were shown to their table—a private booth with all of the typical accoutrements of a fine Italian restaurant neatly in place. The live accordion music was replaced by beloved recordings of crooners Frank Sinatra and Dean Martin—arguably Italian modern classics. It was a very relaxed atmosphere.

Lou was in the process of making his customary rounds—visiting the occupants of each table in his restaurant—when he noticed his two newest guests. He ambled over to their table, face beaming, arms outstretched. "Rita Haley! My, my, my! Look at ya'! Isabella told me she'd heard that ya' moved back home to Chicago. You sure are a sight for these old eyes!" He shot a look of astonishment at Michael. "As for this fine gentleman here, I didn' know ya' knew each other." Then he quickly turned his attention back to Rita. "Michael doesn't know this, and I hope he never says a word, but I had a crush on his gorgeous mother the minute I laid eyes on her."

He looked at Michael again. "Your father brought her into this very restaurant. My mother and father had jus' opened the place. I was twenty years young then, was workin' the kitchen, waitin' tables, washin' dishes, ya' know, learnin' to run the place. I hadn' met Isabella yet, and this guy, your father, walks in with this very nice lookin' young lady. I mean heart jumpin' out of your chest gorgeous. I sat them down at that table right there. I remember like it was yesterday. I greeted them, and your father introduced himself and his date. I remember thinking, 'what a lucky bastard'. Then I met Isabella," Lou gave a deep belly laugh, "and I thought to myself, 'what a lucky bastard *I* am'. My Isabella. The only one for me. She oughta' be canonized, puttin' up with me for all these years. To think that was almos' 50 years ago. Oh, Michael, I forgot to ask you the other day, how's your family doin'? I haven' seen your folks or that lovely sister and niece of yours either in what seems like forever. I miss 'em. They're really great people."

Michael knew Lou was trying his best to appear to be blasé—making small talk—but he knew Lou was eager to find out if

Rita was his date or if this was just a business dinner. Michael also had little doubt that Lou would be whispering about the couple to Isabella inside a New York minute. Then, it just as quickly, Isabella would be on the phone with the neighborhood busybodies. He took comfort in the fact that his parents were in Europe, otherwise, Isabella would be on the phone with his mother before the appetizers arrived. And, even though his mother was on another continent at the moment, he would not be surprised if Isabella still managed to connect with her before their dinner was finished.

"They're doing great, Lou. The family is doing great. Mom's dragging dad all over Europe as we speak. If my memory serves me, they should be in Italy tonight, if you can believe that. I'm expecting a call from them in the morning. I'll tell them 'hi' for you. And don't worry Lou," Michael winked, "I won't tell dad or Isabella about your crush on mom. I've seen Isabella wield a rolling pin. I wouldn't want to see what she could do with that even to my worst enemy." Michael laughed.

Lou laughed too. A full body laugh—where every muscle is involved. His laugh was so boisterous Michael and Rita could feel the it. "The missus is back in the kitchen now. She jus' got back from Florida visitin' Cristina and the grandkids, spoiling the heck out of 'em, drivin' Cristina crazy. I love it. Bein' a grandparent is the best. The payback is so sweet. It's a delight to see our kids deal with the same issues we had wit' them when they were young. The apple doesn't fall far from the tree, huh Michael? Anyways, the rest of the family is doin' fantastic, we got nine grandkids now, everyone is healthy," he said and patted his belly. "Life is good."

Lou turned to Rita and quickly reverted into the harmless flirt that Rita always knew him to be. "Look at me, what a doofus I'm bein'. Where's my manners? I'm ignoring this fine looking lady joining you tonight." He reached out with bear-sized arms and gave Rita a hug that elicited a gasp from her. "I remember when your father and mother would bring you little Haley kids in here for our Saturday Night Family Specials. How the heck is *your* family? All good I hope."

"They're all doing great, Lou. Thanks for asking, you sweet old man. Dad is happily retired. He doesn't miss a single Cubs home game now. Us kids all chipped in and got him the season tickets he dearly coveted. I'll tell them I saw you and that you're doing great and asked about him. Oh, and I'll insist they swing by."

Lou looked inquisitively at Michael. Michael knew that *the* question Lou had been desperate to ask was coming. "So Michael, is this a business dinner or pleasure? C'mon throw an ol' dog a bone." He winked at Michael, knowing Rita could easily see it, and patted them both on their shoulders. "Pleasure. I hope." He winked again, this time in Rita's direction. "Anyways, I need to get back to work. If there's anything you two need, let me know. And, oh, yeah, the scaloppini is excellent tonight, I don' know what I did differen'. Maybe the missus put something extra in it. Or maybe it's jus' cause I'm hungry. I don' know. It's just really good tonight. Now listen you two, come back to the kitchen and say goodbye to Isabella before you take off. If you don', you-know-who will get upset, and *we* don't wan' that to happen." He gave another one of his tremendous belly laughs and strode away, barking orders as he barged through both of the two-way doors that led to the kitchen.

Eddie, alert as always, noticed that friend of Lou's was here again. He was seated at Table 14 with a *different* woman. "She's even hotter than the last one. He must be a helluva' guy," Eddie thought.

After he listened to Eddie describe the evening specials, Michael ordered for both of them. He then asked Eddie for a bottle of wine that paired nicely with their meals. He then looked at Rita. More silence. He liked Rita. A lot. What was there that was not likeable? She was attractive, fun loving, caring, eloquent. So many of her traits reminded him of Liz that it was scary. He wanted to find out more about her, from her perspective, and knew of no other way to do so then by asking questions. He wanted to avoid being perceived as a control freak and he knew that his questions would require tact and grace, especially if he wanted her to like him back. Maybe even love him back? Moreover, the last thing he wanted was for her to think that he was anxious to rip off her pants. That idea caused an impish smile to appear on his face.

Rita noticed his burgeoning smile. "Penny for your thoughts," she teased.

Michael sensed the impending tipping point in their relationship had arrived. With the exception of superficial chitchat, until now all their conversations had been about the new annex. He suddenly thought of Keith. And the plan. And felt a not-so-nice feeling in his stomach. The feeling made him uncomfortable and he felt a groundswell of guilt consume him. He felt disgusted by the way he had been manipulating Rita. Everything about the plan seemed suddenly very unethical. Unlike just a week ago when he was ready to battle any obstacle to find true love. Even deceit. He agreed to involve himself with the plan to find love again. He now knew the only true love for him was seated directly in front of him. He thought about all the things that had transpired to bring them together. And now it all seemed so unfair.

"I have to admit my mind was wandering there for a moment... sorry," he said. "Penny for my thoughts, huh? Ok, here goes. I have a confession to make, and don't want to sound like I've had ulterior motives all along, but I was thinking how much I wanted to know more about you Rita. You are liked and admired by everyone I know, and I'd like to find out firsthand why. I'd like very much to get to know you better, on a personal level." Warning signs and klaxon alarms resounded in his head. He nervously continued, "I hope I'm not being too forward or presumptive, and that you don't mind me you telling you this so early in our...relationship. I mean, we've only known each other for a couple of days. I hardly know anything about you, but I feel as if I've known you a long time. You're...you're very easy to be around." He smiled.

To lighten up the sudden tension he had created, Michael changed the subject. "Tell me about yourself, Rita. What do you do when you're not working diligently, beautifying your workplace, and finagling dollars from gullible citizens?" They laughed. His remark instantly made the uncomfortable situation less intimidating. Less awkward.

Rita told Michael the Reader's Digest version of her life. She told him about growing up in the city. One of six children, in a blue-collar family, not wealthy except in love, patience, and understanding. And acceptance. They were a diverse lot, an ever-expanding socio-ethnic blend. Most of her family still lived in the city, or the surrounding suburbs, and got together regularly for meals, holidays, and outings. They regularly filled each another's houses with screaming children, feisty elders, and much frivolity.

"Do you have a love interest?" Michael inquired, trying to sound nonchalant. He wondered if he should have asked her if she had a *lover,* and if she would think that word would be inconsistent with his demeanor. He wanted to know how she would respond, and more precisely how she really felt about Keith. He wanted to hear from her if their relationship was as real as Keith alleged. He felt culpable asking. He knew it might be painful for her to talk about—and for him to hear, if it was true.

"Rita, I don't mean to be forward. Damn, I'm terrible at this. And I'm not hitting on you, not that you're not hit-able. Oh, God, that was a dumb thing to say." He paused to gain his composure. "But I'm just curious, you know, for conversation sake. Man, am I screwing this up bad. What I'm trying to say is that I'm sure an attractive and highly personable woman like you has a significant other, and...." his voice trailed off.

Her smile faded. Her eyes dampened. His innocent question, his fumbled words—obviously rough in their deliverance—caused Rita to think of Keith fighting for his life, alone. She was unable to stop the tears from flowing.

"Damn it," Michael thought as he saw her eyes well up. "I really screwed this one up!" He felt like a heel carrying on this charade. "I've done this all wrong. What a mistake this is. What a mess I've put myself, and now her, into."

He kept silent—unsure of what to say next. He was not accustomed to making total strangers cry.

"I'm sorry," Rita said as she wiped her eyes with her napkin. "Yes, I have a partner. Boyfriend. Lover. Whatever you want to call him. He lives on the west coast, which is kind of a problem for a stable relationship, but that's not why I'm crying. I'm not the only person in a long distance relationship. I'm crying because he's got cancer, is going through treatments, and I'm not there to support him. Hell, I'm not sure if I'm ever going to be with him again. That's why I'm crying," she continued. She wiped her nose with a tissue. "I'm feeling a little embarrassed right now. I usually only get all weepy at the proper times, you know, funerals, weddings, births," she said. She tried to maintain her normally composed composure.

He instinctively knew this would happen. Everything Keith had told him about Rita was true. Her sudden emotional display proved the case yet again. He felt horrible, having inadvertently caused feelings of heartache, anguish, and guilt for someone she loved, who was dying. After all, he had gone through the same emotions himself in the past. Michael knew firsthand, that the sudden realization that your mate is leaving you to fend for yourself is the loneliest feeling in the world. The feelings of pain and sorrow of losing his beloved Elizabeth involuntarily erupted. He let the flow of his own tears roll down his cheeks. He couldn't shake from his memory her beauty, her devotion to him, and the time they shared together. "She would have cried right along with us," he thought. Michael and Liz had often cried together in times of sadness, and joy, wiping each other tears away with kisses.

Michael missed Liz more than he could ever say. His heart still ached for her, but at the same time, he needed to find love again. And he had felt an attraction to Rita right from the start. She *was* everything Keith had said she was—and more. He felt he could easily love this woman for the rest of his life. Rita was comfortable to be around—like well-worn slippers or a worn-out t-shirt. She fit. He was certain Elizabeth would approve.

Michael wanted to be there for Rita—be her friend on this emotional ride. Whether their relationship ultimately went beyond friendship would be up to her. He only knew that he wanted to be there for her. He was still trying to get past his own tragic grief with the help of friends, counselors, and therapists. He felt certain that he would not have made it through the emotional gauntlet of pain, sorrow, and guilt without their help and compassion. He knew some of the best psychoanalysts and therapists in the city. If or when that time came, he would introduce Rita to them. He felt it was the very least he could do. Michael wiped his cheeks, looked into her eyes, and let his tears continue to flow unchecked. He whispered to her, "I am *so* sorry."

He took a deep breath to stabilize himself and the predicament he had created. He felt the need to share his own grief with her—let her know he shared her pain. That he understood the suffering she was so clearly enduring. "I...I think I know how you feel Rita. I recently lost my wife to cancer." More tears flowed.

Rita stared at him for a moment. She suddenly realized that his tears were not only for her, but for himself, and another lost soul. He reminded her even more of Keith—unafraid of public displays of emotion, not thinking it unmanly to cry for happiness or grief, sharing in other people's pain or joy.

Michael reached his hands across the table—hers reached out to meet his. They clutched each other's hands and exchanged their feelings of despair as if connected by an emotional conduit. Michael knew that when emotions were running high, and discerning feelings prevailed, silent communication was more powerful and comforting than spoken words. Still holding each other's hands, they wept together as the accordion player resumed his playlist.

55

From Eddie's vantage point, it appeared they were having a very personal moment. He thought maybe Lou's friend was breaking up with this woman for the other one. He had in internal debate with himself as to whether or not he should interrupt an obviously sensitive moment to serve their meals. His reputation, and his desire to serve their meals while still hot, prevailed. He noisily interrupted their moment—and their tears—and put their meals in their respective places. He offered them freshly cracked pepper and grated cheese. "I'd better give them plenty of space for the remainder of the evening," he thought. Then just as quickly as he arrived, he was gone.

Reluctantly releasing each other's hands, they thanked Eddie, who was already out of earshot, and glanced at their meals. Neither felt very hungry. Their bloodshot eyes met. After a short time, with a new bond forged, they slowly, cautiously relaxed. A pantomimed happiness forced.

"I wasn't expecting this kind of evening," Michael broke the silence this time. He feebly attempted a smile as he wiped his tear-streaked face with his napkin. "Honestly Rita, I was not prepared to share so much of my personal life with you tonight. But just the mention of your significant other. All of my not so distant feelings of sadness, sorrow, unhappiness…loneliness, just sort of popped into my head. I couldn't stop them. Or my tears. Didn't want to. I just had to let you know that I…I understand. I want to be there for you, but I want it to be on your terms. We can talk more about this if you want. If not, we can put this behind us. Pretend what just happened never happened. Change the subject back to something more pleasant and finish our lovely meal in a better humor. We can...."

"No. No,...it's all right. Thank you. For...sharing," Rita responded quietly. In reality, she felt a bit embarrassed but like Michael, she didn't care. She patted her eyes, suddenly aware that her mascara must have bled down her cheek making her look like a melancholy clown. She opened her eyes wide and vocalized her thoughts. "Oh dear, I must look something of a freak. How's my mascara holding up? Do I look as hideous as I imagine I do?"

"No, you don't. Not at all. And it held up remarkably well."

Rita smiled. "Thank for being so kind. Ever since...ever since I found out, I keep thinking I've got it all under control. That I can maintain that control, but sometimes my...emotions just get the better of me. And I lose it. Sometimes it happens when I dwell on my...his misfortune. Sometimes it's over rather trivial things. I'm ok now. Thanks again. Tell me about her, Michael. What was your wife like?"

It was his turn for full disclosure now. He had prepared for this so he started at the beginning, knowing—hoping—she would benefit from his tragic past. "I met Elizabeth the week before we both graduated college. We met at a frat party. She was with some of her friends, I with some of mine. A close friend coerced me into going to the party. I'd made other plans but this guy was pretty relentless. Said he wouldn't take 'no' for an answer. We were getting our first beers from the tap, and there she was. Laughing. Dancing with her sorority sisters. It was love at first sight. After she stopped dancing, I somehow managed to muster enough courage to go over and start a conversation with her. My experience up to that point with the opposite sex was limited, to say the least. I was enthralled at her beauty. Her wit. Her...charm. She told me later, after we got married, the thing that won *her* over was that I said I could cook! There I was thinking that she thought I was *handsome*. And smart. And witty. To find out it was my ability to cook that sealed the deal was, well, more than a little bit humbling. But of course that was before I found out what a truly wonderful person she was. Then it made all the sense in the world."

Michael continued. "I wondered why I hadn't seen or noticed her during my years on campus. Wondered where she'd been hiding herself. How I could have missed her? We both came to the conclusion that we were destined for each other. Fate. We had a short, whirlwind romance straight out of a '50s movie. Got engaged and married in less than three months. Neither of us wanted children. We were content with each other. From the onset, we'd both immersed ourselves in work, charities, and our extended families. We had an amazing life together. Then out of nowhere, cancer paid us a visit. It didn't take long for it to take her from me."

Michael reached his hands across the table and gently held hers. "I still struggle about whether or not I'm glad it was quick. Although I'm still so heartbroken to have had her snatched away from me so fast. I...I would have hated for her to suffer any longer than she did." He flashed a feigned smile. "She has...had a wonderful family," he continued, "very loving. I still communicate and socialize with them frequently. They're part of my safety net. Real people. Salt of the earth."

Michael's face radiated when he spoke about Elizabeth. Yet Rita could see the pain of his loss as he described their lives together. She was both saddened and jealous. Felt sorrow for his loss, yet jealous that he had had a wonderful life with someone. The irony was not lost on Rita. It was the same kind of thing that happening to her at this very moment. "Poor, dear Keith," she thought. "Enough about me and my life," he finished. "Do you feel like talking about yours some more? I've been blathering on as usual and haven't touched my dinner. I'm glad to see you've at least made a big dent in yours."

Rita wiped her mouth politely, set her utensils on the plate and moved it to the edge of the table so the bus boy would know she was finished. She delicately placed her napkin back on her lap, and looked at Michael. "Good timing. I was famished. Ok, I think I'm ready to talk about Keith and I. "We met at the New England Aquarium in Boston. Out of the blue he invited me to lunch. I accepted, though at the time I figured it was just a friendly gesture on his part. We rapidly developed a wonderful repartee, being flirty, coy, and so on. At first, we were both overly concerned with maintaining businesslike decorum. Both of us were in high-profile positions and didn't want to jeopardize our reputations or job security. We found remarkable similarities in our likes and dislikes, such as the fact that we both hated...hate jerks." Michael surmised, correctly, that by 'jerks' Rita was referring to Simon. "That and we made each other laugh. That was...is important to us both. I'm sorry Michael. This is a very confusing time for me," she said softly.

"Like you and Elizabeth," she continued, "we hit it off right from the beginning. On our first real date he was quite the gentleman. Cavalier. Suave. Charming. A real man's man. He placed his hand gently on my back to guide me as we were going through a crowd at a concert that we attended. I remember that I deliberately yet softly pushed back into his hand and he responded by placing his arm around my waist. From then on, it was downhill...or should I say uphill, for both of us. Keith was diagnosed with cancer during a routine checkup. It all happened so fast. Like with Elizabeth. By the time his doctors at USC discovered it, Keith's cancer had spread to his vital organs. His doctors started various treatments right away. Some pretty aggressive stuff. He lives in California. A million miles away. All his doctors are there, 'the best money can buy' he says. The only thing I hope for now is the day that he finally returns to me. I think I know how you must have felt, Michael. Hopeless. Helpless. Knowing there was nothing you could do. That's exactly how I feel right now."

Michael had eaten all that he was going to eat. He felt a bit queasy as he listened to her talk about the man he was conspiring with to win her heart. "Reality is strange," he mused. Eddie swiftly removed his plate and disappeared again. They stared into each other's eyes. "Rita...." Michael began again, but stopped. Eddie arrived with their dessert and then flitted away without a word.

⇒➤●◄⇐

Eddie was eager for a big tip. It seemed to him that the couple had worked through their issues. Nonetheless, he didn't want to intrude on their privacy any more than was necessary. As far as he was concerned, he had been as respectful as possible, carefully and considerately attended to every detail of their dining experience. On his watch, every aspect was of great importance: salads must be served cold, ground pepper offered, breadcrumbs immediately cleaned up, used tableware quickly replaced, meals served hot, empty water glassed refilled. And the coup de grâce: serving one of Mrs. Santorini's scrumptious desserts. Eddied always provided five-star service.

———⇒►●◄⇐———

"Rita, I want to thank you for opening up to me," Michael began again after Eddie disappeared. "It's been quite an emotional day. For both of us. What do you say I take you home...I mean drop you off at home? Now that I dumped my entire life story on you and spent a full evening doing so, seems to me it's the least I can do."

"It's me that dumped *my* life story on *you*. My burden has been shared, and my belly is full. I feel better now, like a happy, bloated deer-tick. You're a *good* man Michael Halloran." She accepted his offer. Michael drove her to her apartment in Lincoln Park. He found and pulled into an ever-elusive, unoccupied parking spot in front of her building and turned the car off. "Thank you for a wonderful evening, Rita. It was special. Sorry I kept you out so late. I know you need to report to Jake first thing. Can I pick you up in the morning and take you to work? It would save you some time. You won't have to take the El or a bus. It's on my way so it's no problem, really."

"No worries, I'm fairly resilient with just a few hours of sleep as long as I don't make it a habit," she responded. "It *was* an emotional day, and I'm glad you were there for me. I accept your offer Mr. Halloran. You can pick me up promptly at seven-thirty. Don't be late! Jake can get cranky, and...." She leaned over the seat, gave him a long hug and a warm kiss on the cheek, her eyes beginning to water up again. "Thank you Michael, for a wonderful evening." Before the first teardrop fell, she quickly opened the passenger door, got out, shut the door behind her, and walked away. She didn't turn around, striding to her door quickly, and didn't hear the sound of Michael's car pull away until she safely entered her apartment.

Had Rita turned around she would have seen Michael, his eyes tear-filled also, staring longingly at her. Concerned for her safety, he was not going to leave until she closed the door behind her. He saw her lights come on, quickly glanced in the rear view mirror, and drove away.

56

ichael, in his daily briefings with Keith, didn't know where to start to describe the events of the previous day. He could not believe that they had actually happened. "Let me start at the beginning, it's easier for me to think chronologically." Michael then told Keith everything, from his clammy hands to the tear-filled goodbyes in front of Rita's apartment. Michael confided that he *liked* Rita. That she seemed to be a perfect match for him.

Although Keith was distraught at Rita's angst—knowing he was responsible for it—he was thrilled about Michael's news. He was happy to still be alive to see the plan come to life. Keith was awestruck when Michael told him that he had agreed to design the new annex for the museum for free. "Michael is truly a good and compassionate person. And Jillian! She is a Godsend," Keith thought.

"That is great news, Michael. I'm glad to hear things are moving along. I wish it were moving faster though. I've got to tell you…things for me are looking grim. I'm not going to make it very much longer, and I don't know how to help your blossoming romance move more quickly. Is it time for me to just let it run its natural course and hope for the best?"

Michael thought about what Keith had just said. Had an idea. Expressed it. "Why don't you come for a visit, tell Rita about your situation face-to-face. You do know Keith, she's still clinging to an optimistic, hopeful outcome and your eventual return to her. I think it's time to stop sugar coating things. She's stronger than you realize. Come on, tell her like it is. She deserves that."

After considering Michael's suggestion, Keith was unable to find a flaw in the logic, and agreed to visit Rita. "Of course you're right, Michael. I promise to make flight arrangements first thing in the morning. After I reveal the reality of my condition to Rita, it'll be up to you to win her heart. I know it's not going to be an easy task. Rita and I have...had something really special." He would tell Rita the next day of his plans for a visit. Besides, his treatments were useless and there really was no hope for him—he couldn't think of any reason not to go to Chicago.

57

ichael returned to Rita's apartment promptly at seven-thirty, double-parked his car, and set his emergency flashers on in case an inattentive driver passed by. He strolled deliberately to her porch and picked up the recently delivered copy of the Sun Times from the sidewalk—he had read his copy earlier over his first cup of coffee. After his emotional evening with Rita and then the exhaustive late-night discussion with Keith, he was unable to sleep soundly. He woke up every few hours haunted by images of Rita. And Liz. As he was about to knock on Rita's door, it opened, and she emerged with a weary smile on her face.

"Thank you," she said, as he handed her the newspaper. "I got up a little late, so I didn't get a chance to grab it. It took me longer than usual to put myself together," she quipped. She mimed the act of applying her makeup. "I cried myself to sleep. Between that and all the tears I shed during dinner, this morning I looked like a heavyweight boxer after twelve rounds." Michael chuckled at her analogy. "I know I look horrible," she laughed. "No one will want to sign-up or make a donation today with me looking like a female Quasimodo."

Michael thought she actually looked beautiful, although he knew their evening had been an enormous strain on her mentally, as it had been on him. "You look great," he said. He hoped to start the new day off on a less somber note. "Would you like a cup of tea? I picked you up some on the way over, the same kind you ordered last night, I hope that's ok."

"That's wonderful. Thank you. That's very thoughtful of you."

"My pleasure. It's from a local coffee shop right around the corner from my house. The family that runs the place is from India. The Singh's are great people," he said, smiling. And then blurted out, as if it was at all relevant, "I have one of their VIP cards."

They got into Michael's car, buckled up, and headed to the museum. A few moments of silence passed as each tried to determine who was going to be the first to speak—who would be the one to guide the conversation for the duration of their commute. There was only a hint of tension in the air. Neither one of them knew whether it was best to talk about business or to take the conversation back to a personal level. The consummate professional, Michael decided to bring up the day's business agenda. "Well, we certainly have a lot of work to get started on today don't we?"

Rita laughed. She was relieved that Michael had chosen not to talk about anything personal. She was not ready for that again so soon. "Have you told any of your staff yet?" she queried. The early morning sunrise breached the skyline, causing her to squint.

"As a matter of fact, I sent an email to the entire staff last night, but all they know is that there's an all-hands, mandatory meeting in an hour. I'm sure rumors are flying," he chuckled. "On your side of the equation, I would love to be a fly on the wall in Jake's office when he and Sam inform your staff about your promotion today. Congratulations, by the way. You really deserve it, Rita. Honest to God. Your hard work and dedication really paid off for everyone. Truly a win-win. I couldn't be happier for you. Just look how much you've inspired me in the short time I've known you. I can't imagine how much you've inspired those you've been around since you've been there."

Rita didn't know what to think about his comment. A very successful person, highly regarded in his industry and the community, yet here *he* was telling *her* that *she* inspired *him*. She had a tough time wrapping her brain around that. "What do you mean, I inspired you? How?"

Michael waited until he stopped at a light to reply so he could figure out how frame the perfect reply. "It's...it's your verve. Your mojo. Your *spirit*. It's not just me that feels it. Everyone I've met at the museum seems to genuinely want to help you with whatever you do. It's like, whatever you feel is worthy of your time, they feel the same. You motivate people naturally. Effortlessly. That's just one of your gifts. It is a very special gift. And if I may say so, you use it wisely."

Rita blushed. "I'm truly flattered, Michael. I guess I've never thought about it quite that way. I just try to always be myself. It's easier that way. I hope I'm not going to change now that so much is at stake with the decisions I'll have to make. That's what I'm most afraid of. That and whether I can actually handle all these new responsibilities. Not let everyone down," she said, overtones of uncertainty and doubt in her voice. "Sam has big shoes to fill. That's all I know," she concluded.

⟫●⟪

Keith had explained to Michael that Rita had a problem with self-esteem. He said that no matter the accolades, compliments, or praises bestowed upon Rita, she always felt confused when she received them. Keith also said she was very humble. He was right again.

"I'm *sure* the board members know what they're doing," he teased. He rolled his eyes—eyebrows raised for emphasis.

Rita gasped in mock disbelief, and exclaimed, "Was that an eye-roll I just saw?"

"Yes...yes it was," he laughed heartily, not unlike Lou.

Rita quickly pinched Michael's arm. "You nerd," she chided him. Still feeling giddy about her promotion, she started to laugh with him.

They spent the remainder of their commute talking about work-related issues, both still a bit nervous—and hesitant—to delve back into personal conversation. Michael dropped Rita off at the museum precisely at 8 o'clock.

58

"Hi Sweetheart. How are you? How've you been?" Keith asked. Although he was anxious to tell her of his plans to visit her the following week, he felt that could wait.

"Hello, my love. Frantic would be the best word to describe my last couple of days. I landed a really *big* donation for the museum from a very generous benefactor. It looks like we are going to get our new annex designed for free! That news has the entire staff and board all abuzz!" She deflected the discussion back at him. "How are *you*? How are your treatments going?"

It was time to tell her, although he was certain she was not ready to hear about his prognosis. Keith paused. In his mind's eye, he saw Rita, phone in hand, waiting for good news. He couldn't bring himself to do it—wasn't able to tell her why he was calling. To give her the bad news. He continued the lies. "The doctors have, um, stopped my treatments for now, and are in the process of determining what to do next. *Sooo,* I thought I might come out to see you before I head into whatever they decide to do. What do you think? Do you think you could put up with me for a couple of days?"

Silence. Keith knew she was excited. He could see her jump with joy more than 2,000 miles away.

59

Keith reclined in Zeke's chair and talked of his dreams and nightmares. Described them to Zeke in detail. "In one, I'm in the hall, standing outside Rita's bedroom, watching, as her silky smooth alabaster skin is being softly caressed by a striking, well-hung, dark-haired, young man. Their bodies are intertwined. His hands exploring her body. Teasing her. His lips passionately kissing her, all over her body. His is hard and ready. She's wet and willing. When she feels him slowly, passionately enter her, she cries out, urges, begs him for more, and when he wholly slides into her, she groans in primal satisfaction. Their pelvic thrusts intensify. Their skin exudes sweat from the animalistic physicality of it all. He completely satisfies her physical and emotional hunger. She grabs him, pulls him deep, wraps her legs around him, and as her juices flow, clasps her arms around his broad shoulders. They bring their lips together to complete the bond. Then it's over."

They breathe deeply in the afterglow, still coupled. I silently turn and walk away. I smile for her happiness."

End of dream."

After this disclosure, Keith laughed aloud. "Any other man would be angry, upset at the horrible, bullshit-hand fate had dealt him. But I'm not. Rita's happiness is my only concern now."

"Keith, it's common for moribund people to project their subconscious thoughts into their dreams. *You* are the virile man in the dream. It was *you* who satisfied her."

Although Keith wanted to doubt that hypothesis, he realized that it was probably true. He also knew it was probably something more than that—it was his core intellect sending a message to him that he was not going to survive to see the day he would be her virile lover again. He was arranging, consciously and sub-consciously, for a bright and happy life for Rita—via his replacement, Michael.

60

Michael's entire team displayed tremendous enthusiasm and dedication—more than he thought they would—to the new annex project. There were committees to form. Ideas to flesh out. Plans to be made and carried out. It didn't take long for their ideas to become reality. Halloran and Associates was a vibrant, bustling hive of activity.

Rita and Sarah sat across the table from two of Halloran and Associate's brightest architects: Correy Crawford and George Ramirez. They were discussing some of the details for the new annex—gawking over the complexity of the initial plans. Sarah wanted to get Rita alone to chat. "You know, if you want to get a peek at the latest design George came up with, I can show it to you. It's really cool. When you remove the shell of the mockup, you can see the new configuration," she whispered.

"Yes. I'd love to see it. But of course you knew that!"

"George? Oh great master of engineering marvels," Sarah teased, "would you please show us the latest trick you worked out with the folding walls. I'll go get the mockup. I'll need some help moving the pieces." Sarah turned to Rita. "Care to give me a hand Rita?"

"Sure." Rita replied. She sprung out of her chair. "I'd be glad to."

61

Sarah sat at her desk, warmed her hands with her coffee mug, and brainstormed with Michael on the new Los Angeles high-rise project. Michael sat across the desk from her, coffee mug cupped in both hands. He was amazed at her ingenious idea. He knew she would soon get restless working for Halloran and Associates and would want to break out on her own. He had no doubts that she was good enough. As soon as she honed her people skills, she would do really well running her own firm. That would be good for the industry—there was plenty of work to go around for exceptional architects.

"I was thinking...I know, I know, there I go again. I was thinking that we could use the same photo-voltaic glass for the museum's new annex that we used on the high-rise project. For that matter, we could use it on a lot of our projects. The efficiency of the PV thinfilm is over 25 percent now. It seems like a perfect fit, all the correct angles...plenty of surface area. I checked with engineering and all the specs pan out. We could generate enough electricity to power the whole building at 100 percent occupancy *and* throw juice back to the grid. It would be our second net-positive sustainable project. I'm excited. How about you?" she asked. She scanned Michael's face for a sign of approval. For confirmation that she was still of sound mind.

"It certainly looks like you've done your homework. The folks in engineering told me you'd been bending their ears," Michael remarked. He was well aware that his subtle insinuation wouldn't get past Sarah. He *wanted* to let her know that her idea had already been communicated back to him. "In fact, Tran says you hit it right on the mark. He said he had been toying with the same idea from the technical side…thought it could work."

Sarah became visibly upset, her mouth slightly agape. To let her know he had not been spying on her, he stopped her before she had a chance to respond. "Listen, Sarah. I'd just walked into the weekly engineering meeting. Tran and the rest of the team were talking. I asked them what they were discussing and Tran told me your great idea. It's that simple. By the way, they agreed unanimously that very few modifications to the electrical system would be required to accommodate the retrofit." Michael sensed Sarah was still not convinced that he was not spying on her—second-guessing her work. Her facial expression and mannerisms confirmed her lingering suspicion.

"That's *it* Sarah. I wasn't spying on you. Or micromanaging. It's a great idea, really. Let's run with it. I'll call the client and tell them the good news. It will add an unbelievable amount of value to the structure. I'll drive home the point that they'll *never* have electricity, gas, or water bills again. *Ever.* And I'll make sure they understand that they'll even accrue energy credits they can convert to revenue. Trust me Sarah, I'm on your side, remember?"

Sarah's emotions turned from anger to embarrassment. "I'm sorry, Michael. I guess I don't hide my emotions very well, boss. I thought you were pulling a fast one on me, you know, like James Bond. I know I've been asserting my authority around here quite a bit lately, and probably have ruffled a few feathers in doing so," she admitted, frowning. "I hope I haven't been too pushy. You know, I'm still working on my management, uh, people skills. It's just that I get so focused or amped up about a project or concept, that I think everyone else should have the same level of commitment to perfection that I do. I obviously have a little work to do on projecting that excitement with a little more…diplomacy. Ok, a *lot* more work. Honestly I don't know *how* Chuck does it, you know, put up with me. I'll be the first to admit I can be high maintenance sometimes. I'm so fortunate. I wish you had someone like him in your life." she said.

Michael's eyebrows raised noticeably.

"Uh, wait a second. That didn't come out quite right. What I meant to say is that you need someone who lets you be yourself, and still loves you, despite your shortcomings. Damn it there I go again. Michael, what I'm trying to say is, well, I'm no expert...not like...Jillian, but,...." She swiveled her chair around and stared at the panoramic view of the Chicago skyline, as if she was hoping for divine intervention. "I'm thinking that Rita might be *that* certain someone. I've been doing my own bit of James Bonding lately, and I really think Jillian is right. Rita might be *the* one."

Michael briefly considered telling Sarah about his dinner plans with Rita but decided it would be better to tell her after he and Keith's cat had escaped its bag and the bag had been crumpled up and tossed into the trash.

62

The last few days had been a series of meetings, briefings, and more meetings as Rita adjusted to her new position and her new responsibilities.

Everyone at the museum, from the staff, to the president to the board fully supported her in her new endeavors. There was a lot at stake for everyone. "Having an assistant sure helps," she thought. She reviewed the daily agenda with Carlita Simpkins.

Carlita had been Sam's executive assistant for years. Rita thought *she* knew everyone—but Carlita was extremely well connected. No one at the museum doubted this. There was not a single thing that happened in the museum that Carlita was not aware of. Not even a whisper or a sideways glance.

The rumor mill suggested that Carlita had eyes in the back of her head. "Like my third grade teacher, Ms. McDonald," Rita thought. Carlita's premonitions were never questioned or doubted—her sixth sense had proved to be correct time and time again.

Rita had gone to Carlita many times for guidance on how to approach Sam—or any of the other upper management of which she was now a part of—with a project or an idea. As far as Rita was concerned, Carlita's advice was as good as Warren Buffet's.

After Rita's promotion was announced, Carlita made a point to express her confidence. "Rita, you know I'm always here for you. As is everyone else. I've talked to all the people who matter, and they all concur. You are the best person to take over for Sam." Carlita added, speaking deliberately, for emphasis, "I am very glad to be working with you, especially now on an even grander scale. We've worked together very well in the past, and had a lot of success and fun in the process. The future holds even brighter possibilities for both of us."

Rita smiled and said, "Thank you, Carlita. Coming from you that means so much to me. Honestly."

63

Keith was eager for Michael and Rita's relationship to flourish. He called Michael at work—interrupting a meeting—and insisted that Michael ask Rita for a second date.

"Patience, Keith. Patience," Michael responded. "I want to move our relationship forward as much as you want me to, but I've been physically and mentally overwhelmed with the new annex project. More precisely, because of what *you* started," he snorted, tormenting his tormentor. "In fact, there is a steering committee meeting tomorrow afternoon with the city aldermen, and Rita will be there. I was planning on asking her out for dinner. I hope that this time it will be devoid of tears. Since she and I are both on the new annex committee, we will be spending a lot of time together as it is. But Keith, this romance, if that's what it's to be, is going to take some time. She's still very much in love with you. You mean the world to her. She's said so to me more than once. You're not going to be an easy guy to replace, Dr. Vintner. Rita thinks that you've got tests or treatments or something tomorrow, so she's not expecting a call from you. Otherwise, she'd rush home to get your call, rejecting most any call or request, from anyone, to be available for you. And just to remind you, her weekends are packed with family activities. You know that, don't you? All that aside, I promise you, I'm going to ask her out to dinner for tomorrow night, ok?"

"Damn it, Michael! There is no way you want to be with her as much as I want you to," Keith responded. "I'm running out of time, man. I'm desperate. I *need* to be assured she'll be taken care of after I die." Petulantly, unwittingly antagonistic, Keith interjected, "You're not making me feel any better by not trying to get another date with her, for fuck's sake!" He immediately realized what he had just said. He was so involved in his own problems, it didn't sink in that Michael had just said he planned to ask Rita for another date. Keith was embarrassed—his mind was deteriorating further with each moment's passing.

"So this is what having Alzheimer's is like," he thought. This type of behavior was happening more and more frequently. He would make a fuss, hurt someone's feelings, and end up feeling sorry for himself. He realized, with a great deal of despair, that he couldn't control this behavior. He *knew* he was being extremely unreasonable with Michael. But he couldn't control his emotions.

"Michael...I...I don't have *time* to wait. Don't you see?" Keith broke down. Started to sob without regard for humility. Michael could hear his gasps. His sniffles. Envisioned Keith's slumped, demoralized, and deteriorating body. He allowed Keith to open up and share his feelings. He understood Keith's feelings more than Keith knew. He vividly recalled Elizabeth's powerfully debilitating, spontaneous emotional outbursts. Michael let Keith release his pain. His fears. His grief.

"I'm afraid, Michael." he sniffled. "And not for me. Not for me at all! For Rita. Promise me you'll take care of her! Promise a dying man his last request," he pleaded.

And, as if shifting gears in his Porsche, he uttered softly, "Before I forget, tell me about your progress regarding the ring.

64

Hong Kong

Simon fled the ship the instant it was unloaded—his sea legs at long last contacted terra firma. He and a few of his shipmates found their way to a popular brothel. Simon had heard about it from one of the other sailors, Tai Fam—whose home base was Hong Kong. Tai told Simon that this was the best whorehouse in the Hong Kong—beautiful Asian women, some Russians, and some Caucasians too. He told Simon that any kind of pleasure desired could be had for the right price.

——⟩●⟨——

The ship was only going to be in port for a few days. Simon was determined to fully satisfy his needs while he was in Hong Kong. He and a fellow deckhand, Joey Saldane, contrived to get a couple of girls for the evening and share them. Joey thought he had special talents to share with the ladies and was anxious to do so. Simon was, at first, unable make up his mind which of the women to choose. Joey also had difficulty deciding which prostitute to pick. "So much pussy, so little time," he chuckled. After ten minutes of gawking and queries, Simon made up his mind—he wished Joey would also, post haste.

——⟩●⟨——

Simon and Joey purchased an Around the World Special—three ethnically different women. Joey decided to treat his new friend Simon to something extra—he paid two of the women to spend the night with them.

———>•<———

The prostitutes had offered Simon a little opium to calm him down—he was an edgy customer. He took the pipe eagerly—figured 'when in Rome'.

———>•<———

Simon woke to the sound of water running in the unsanitary bathroom. He was having a difficult time remembering parts of the night. "What was her name again?" The young woman he had slept with was washing her face. Joey, passed out on the bed across the room, was curled up next to one of the prostitutes.

"Oh yeah! Julie! She said her name was Julie. Right! If her name is Julie, then my name is Kim Jong Un." Julie had imbibed a large amount of opium with Simon before, during, and after sex. "Why not?" Julie—which *was* her real name—thought. "The gui lo paid for it."

She felt logy and tired, and was ready to call it quits. It was almost 8 A.M. The clock had 'struck midnight'. All she wanted to do was go home, take a long hot shower, wash body fluids off and out of her orifices, and try to get some sleep before she went back to the brothel again. She had done her job—pleased and spent the night with the 'sordid, dirty foreigner devils'. She didn't sleep during the night, however, she chased the dragon enough to numb the pain and put herself into a semi-comatose state so she could tolerate the stench of the two men. During sex, Simon was rough with her. Had hurt her. She wondered if all Americans were sadists and assumed that to be the case. Julie knew that her pimp was going to be angry because Simon had bruised her arms and legs. Julie knew he would charge extra for damaging his goods. After all, no one would want to pay for an obviously bruised whore. She slipped on a sheer, flimsy piece of fabric that was ostensibly a dress, and started for the door.

Simon's slow-arriving awakening was accompanied by a residual buzz from the beer and the opium he consumed. "Damn I'm hungry! These Asian bitches sure knew how to take it out of a guy." From what Simon remembered of the night before, Julie gave him a great blowjob. He was still horny and decided he wanted another one before he left to get some food and sober up. "Hey, *Julie!*" he shouted. "Before you go, I want another blowjob. Whataya say? For old time's sake," he joked.

Julie wanted to get out of there, but, given the chance to make more money, she agreed. "Sure lover boy. That'll be $100. My shift ended at eight o'clock," Julie replied. "He should know the rules. It was pay to play, all the way," she giggled to herself.

"Bullshit!" Simon roared. "I paid for an all-nighter! Get over here and give me head, bitch, or I'll come over there and *make* you do it."

Julie decided it was time to get out of there. "Fuck this clown." She thought. Luckily, she was close enough to the door to escape. At least she thought she was. As she twisted the doorknob, Simon lunged, grabbed her, and spun her around.

Simon screamed at Julie, "Listen bitch, you'll do as you're told or I'll beat the shit out of you! Ming bai ma." Simon backhanded Julie across her face. She recoiled from his blow and screamed at him in Cantonese.

The door swung open, and hit the wall with a bang. The noise woke Joey. He mumbled, "What the...?" Fury arrived in the form of two of the brothel's strongmen. Both nearly identical: five-feet tall, one hundred and thirty-pounds. The twin bouncers sized-up the situation from the doorway: two johns, obviously strung out and drunk. One of them was roughing up Julie, and had been, based on her noticeable bruises. The other john struggled to get off the bed.

Simon scoffed at the site of the small bouncers. He figured he could easily take them both out by himself. He was certain he didn't need Joey's help. Then he could get on with the business at hand—he was determined to get another blow job.

Joey started to laugh at the bizarre scene, but stopped laughing when he saw the glint of machetes materialize, and deftly handled by the two bouncers.

"Listen you little shit stains you're not stopping me from getting what I got coming to me!" Simon spat.

Chaos ensued. One of the bouncers attacked Simon. Simon was startled by the speed and agility of his attacker. As the bouncer swung his blade in an effort to remove Simon's head, Simon grabbed him and flung him against the wall. As the bouncer hit the wall he fell on his own blade and impaled himself.

Both of the prostitutes screamed and fled out the door. Joey jumped off the bed and stumbled, still under the influence of the alcohol and drugs he had consumed. He rubbed his eyes, trying to focus on the unfolding scenario. In that brief moment, the other bouncer reached him before he could react. One slice was all it took. Joey instantly dropped to the floor—blood pulsed from his twitching body. Moments later his spasmodic convulsions came to a sudden halt.

Simon screamed at him. "You fucking asshole!" He tackled the lone bouncer. Entwined, they knocked over a nightstand with several large candlesticks that illuminated the room. The candles flopped to the floor igniting the bed sheets, which ignited the bed, which set the dingy little hotel room ablaze. The bouncer was motionless on the floor, inches away from the growing inferno.

Simon was in a state of shock. Not only had Joey been carved up and bled to death, Simon had just killed one of the bouncers. Maybe both of them—accidently, of course. Nevertheless, he did not want, nor could afford to be associated with this scene. Incarceration in a foreign prison held no appeal to him. He had to get out of there fast.

"But how?" Then it hit him. Simon rifled through Joey's pea coat, found Joey's ID and swapped it with his. He crawled across the room beneath the billowing smoke, found the door, and raced out of the room. Simon figured the fire would render Joey unidentifiable, at least enough so that the authorities might not be able to make a positive ID. They looked enough like each other that Simon believed the ruse would work long enough to enable him get out of Hong Kong. He felt bad for Joey. He liked him.

Simon escaped from the brothel and fled into the Hong Kong morning rush. The narrow streets were already filled with dozens of people yelling 'fire' in several languages. As Simon turned the corner and headed away from the crowd, he realized he was lucky that he didn't see Julie or any of the other girls from the brothel before he escaped.

———◦———

Sal Vittorio called Michael immediately upon hearing of Simon's demise. "I got a call from my ship's captain. They're presently docked in Hong Kong. Simon, along with some fellow deckhands, got off the ship and headed straight for the red-light district. My captain got a call from the Hong Kong Police Department. They said Simon and another deckhand were engaged in a confrontation at a brothel early this morning Hong Kong time, and Simon got himself cut up with a machete and burned to a crisp along with two bouncers. I don't know how, but his wallet and ID were found, no money of course. The prostitutes probably grabbed it off him before he blackened. The police are searching for the other deckhand. Regardless, you don't have to worry about Simon any more. He took *himself* out of the equation. I'll have a representative from the company deliver his body, back pay, and our condolences to his next of kin. We have insurance for such things." Then Sal somberly clucked, "Tsk tsk. It must be difficult being the mother of such an idiot."

Tired of talking about Simon, Sal got down to new business. "About the 'Star' do you still need her? Are we on?"

"Yes. We are. Thanks Sal, I owe you, big time. For everything."

———◦———

"Frannie, Frannie!" Rita shouted into the phone. "You won't believe what I just heard! Sit down. This is gonna blow your mind."

"What's going on?"

"So I get a call this morning from my lawyer at eight o'clock. He tells me Simon got killed! In Hong Kong! At a whorehouse, no less! The Hong Kong police department's statement says he was killed by a machete during an altercation. Then his body was scorched in a fire!"

"I knew he was a filthy pig!" Frannie responded with unconcealed glee. "Can you believe that? Getting hacked up by a whore's bouncer and then getting fried...in Hong Kong. Serves the dirt bag right. I'll probably spend extra time in purgatory for my ill thoughts, but as far as I'm concerned, he got what was comin' to him. The person I feel sorry for is Mrs. Cathcart. Her son was nothin' but trouble."

65

"Keith, you're not telling me something, what's going on?" Rita asked desperately. The other end of the line was silent. "Tell me!" she implored. When she got no response from Keith, she began to cry. "I'm losing you, aren't I?"

Keith finally spoke, still not able to tell Rita the truth. "I'm sorry. I feel like a bus hit me. And you know I don't feel like talking when I feel this way." Keith felt terrible. Manipulating Rita. Stubbornly keeping her in the dark about his prognosis. What he and Michael had been doing behind her back. But he couldn't break the news to her. Break her heart. "I've got several treatments tomorrow, so I'll be pretty tired. Plan on me not calling. I'll give you a call in a couple of days, when I'm better company. I wish I was my old self again, we'd be celebrating, dancing in the streets, living the good life," he sighed. "Good night sweetheart. Sweet dreams. I love you madly, truly...deeply."

66

Something Old, Something New

Kathleen Higgins, one of Rita's co-workers, and new best friend, was preoccupied with Rob Brezny's weekly horoscope during their lunch break, when she suddenly looked up. "Sugar, what's your sign? Leo, isn't it?"

"Yes, Leo," Rita confirmed, distracted her last conversation with Keith. She knew him very well. Knew he wasn't one for sharing grief or bad news. She also knew he was being less than truthful with her to protect her—shield her from his own strife. But his chivalrous attempts had the opposite effect on Rita. The unspoken words, the gaps, the lies rang louder than the truth.

Kathleen read the day's prediction for Leo. "Ooooweee, look what Mr. Brezny says. 'The Mystic Astrology Wizard' says: Close one of your eyes. Tap your forehead three times with the palm of your left hand. Think of a sexy image. Lick your lips and whisper the words Love Whisperer. Insert your middle finger in the Delight-o-Meter slot. Keep your finger there until the Passion Lamp turns on. Flash. Flash. Flash. Thank you. Your evaluation appears below. It says: Your libido has been a bit off-course, semi-absorbed in unfruitful or irrelevant distractions. But now it's realigning itself with the central dream themes of your life. Prepare to experience a truer juiciness'."

That is *hot*!" Kathleen squealed. "What do you have going on that I don't know about?" she asked. "Is Mr. Halloran becoming something of an item for you? I sure see you two together a lot lately."

"*Nothing* is going on," Rita curtly replied. "It's strictly business between Michael and me."

"That's too bad, sugar, he's a hunk! Real dreamy. If I had a chance to hop in the sack with him, I would in a heartbeat. Besides, he likes you. I can tell by the way he looks at you in our meetings. The look of desire. Oh, I had better stop that kind of talk right now otherwise I'll get myself all worked up. I'm already feeling moist just thinking about his sculpted body, all shiny with sweat. Come on sugar, when was the last time you got a little? Huh? You have that look about you that says you haven't got any in a long time."

"*Shut up*, Kathleen!" Rita barked. "There is *nothing* going on between us. He knows I have Keith in my life and respects that."

"You may be right about that. He sure is an honorable kind of guy, but that doesn't mean he don't have urges like anyone else," Kathleen quickly added with gapped-tooth smile. "You're a fine looking woman Rita. Who wouldn't want to get jiggy with ya'?" Then Kathleen got serious. "Sugar, Keith is not going to make it through all this crap he's going through. You know it, and I know it. He's gone through all those treatments and ain't nothin' working. Not to sound cruel, but Little Sister, you need to start watching out for and taking care of yourself. And Big Sister Kathleen recommends a funky good time with a big hunky man to rectify that situation. Um hmm. I surely do."

"Honestly, Kathleen," Rita sighed, "my sex life is none of your business."

"Sugar, it *is* my business. Why? Because you're my best friend, and *as* your best friend, I see a beautiful woman wasting away right before my eyes, saving herself for someone who will never be there for her. And I see a very handsome man, waiting for you very patiently to come to that same conclusion. He's just being shy about it because he knows about Keith. Michael and you are meant for each other. I see it, everyone else sees it, but you haven't. Not yet you haven't. Or won't. Wake up girl, go for it. You know Keith's situation isn't looking good, bless his heart. But, sugar, your real knight in shining armor is right in front of you and you want to walk away from him? Most of us get maybe...*maybe...* one chance at love. You're getting two. Take that chance! All I'm sayin' sugar, is the last thing on earth Keith wants is for you to be unhappy and unfulfilled. He has always wanted the best for you. Can't you see that?"

"That's enough, Kathleen. This conversation is over." Rita picked up her dishes and placed them in the cafeteria's depository, and walked away without saying anything further to Kathleen.

Kathleen shook her head then stared at the remainder of food on her plate. "That girl just doesn't get it," she said to herself. "Poor Rita Haley. She has it all and doesn't even know it."

67

R ita—back at her desk—had mixed emotions. She busied herself with the new annex project, putting the final touches on the marketing plan that she would present at the board meeting in the afternoon.

"Getting in a relationship right now would only complicate things," she thought. "I'm spinning too many plates as it is. Ah, damn it all to hell, Kathleen is right! I know Keith's chances of recovery are not good, even if he hasn't told me. But I have to give him...us...hope, something to live for."

Her tear ducts started to activate just as Kathleen walked up and placed a hand on her shoulder. It startled her. "I'm sorry, sugar, I didn't mean to upset you earlier. It's just that I care for you. I thought you and I were friends."

Kathleen grabbed the box of tissue on Rita's desk and held it out it to her in a gesture of compassion. "Here sugar, have a tissue. That one is looking ragged."

"I'm sorry for snapping at you Kathleen. You *are* a true friend... and I know you care. It's hard for me to accept the fact that Keith is dying and he's not going to be in my life forever. Life sucks."

"There, there, little one. Acceptance is a big step in the healing process. Get rid of that thing called denial, and move on. Things will work themselves out. They always do."

68

Moving On

Rita took Kathleen's advice and allowed her relationship with Michael to blossom—slowly. No one could deny, Rita included, that there was a certain something between them, and it would only require a little more of that certain something to lift their relationship to the next level.

As she exited the museum's boardroom after a working lunch, Michael noticed he was safely out of eavesdropping range of the others. He turned to Rita and dropped a bomb. "Will you be my date Saturday night? The venue is quite posh. Please say 'yes'. I can't think of anyone else I'd rather take with me. If your answer is 'yes', wear something that will knock my socks off. It's a black tie affair. I'll be wearing a tux."

"Just where would we be going?" Rita asked curiously.

"Someplace special. I'm not telling you where, I'm keeping *that* a secret, but I will tell you that you won't be disappointed. I promise."

"O...k," she said with a touch of hesitancy. "Knock your socks off, huh?"

Michael couldn't hide his pleasure. His face beamed. "Great! I'll take that as a 'yes' and pick you up at 6 o'clock."

69

To New Adventures

Rita thought Michael seemed uptight. He had barely said a word on the way to where they were going. He steered the car down Lake Shore Drive and turned off onto East Grand Avenue toward the Navy Pier parking lot. Rita instantly thought Michael was taking her to one of her favorite places, Riva on the Pier. But she quickly realized she was wrong as he pulled into the parking lot next to the long docks. Michael got out of the car and went around to her side and opened the passenger door. Offering her his arm, she grabbed his bicep, smiled, and Michael proudly escorted her down one of the docks toward a large, obviously expensive yacht.

"We're going on a dinner cruise! How fun! I've never been on the lake at night." Rita told him how much she loved being on Lake Michigan. She held Michael's arm tight as they walked along the dock.

"You guessed it! We're going on a dinner cruise. Rita, there are many things I want to share with you tonight. I want it to be special. And this seemed like the perfect place for our first real date. I hope you like it. Let's get on board, shall we?" Michael guided Rita up the gangway. When they stepped onboard they were greeted by a distinguished gentleman—sharply dressed in a finely tailored white suit with maritime-themed anchor-and-rope brass buttons. He reminded Rita of Marcello Mastroianni.

The Mastroianni look-alike bowed to Rita. "You must be Rita Haley. Welcome to my ship, 'The Star of Helena'. My name is

Salvatore Vittorio, your host for the evening. Please, call me Sal, only my crew calls me 'Captain'.

The two men gave each other the Dragnet look of approval—they nodded their heads in unison. Then a huge smile broke out across Michael's face and he reached out to give his old friend Sal a hug. Sal responded by clutching Michael and enthusiastically patted him on the back. "Michael! It's so good to see you again. Now that you've arrived, we'll cast off right away. My good friend, since I'm driving tonight, could you please show Rita around 'The Star'? I'd appreciate it. You know your way around her as well as anyone." Sal turned to Rita. "Rita, Franco, your chef, will be serving an exquisite meal tonight, specially created for the two of you. Rico will be your attendant for the evening, so if you need anything at all, don't hesitate to ask Rico. Champagne will be brought to you shortly. Enjoy the evening and the cruise." Sal turned toward the city and spread his arms as wide as possible. "It's quite a splendid night to see the Chicago skyline."

Rita looked around and then back at Michael. Other than Sal and the crew, she hadn't seen any other people onboard. Maybe the party had already started in one of the staterooms. It occurred to her that they might be the only ones onboard other than the crew. "Michael Halloran, tell me what's going on here."

"Rita, Sal and I go way back. We met when I was on a business trip in Bermuda. Halloran and Associates has designed the interiors for the Vittorio fleet for decades. Our fathers were... are old friends. Sal and I have since taken over our father's firms, strengthening our relationship personally and professionally. Sal's good people, Rita. He comes from a long line of ocean dwellers. Back when scuba diving began to gain popularity, Sal's father, Benito...'Benny'...worked with Jacques Cousteau! Jacques and Benny were close friends. When Jacques needed a new research vessel, since the Vittorio family had connections, Jacques asked for Benny's professional assistance in acquiring a suitable boat. Bennie had a friend who owned an old Royal Navy minesweeper. Jacques loved it and bought it on the spot."

Michael caught himself rambling—but was powerless to stop. "That old minesweeper ultimately became the world renowned 'Calypso'. He said it was perfect for his needs. It served him very well until it sank in '96. Not long after it sank Mrs. Cousteau bankrolled its recovery and restored it as an eco-friendly 'green ship'. Anyway, Sal has helped me develop a different view of the world. 'The Star' is just one in a fleet of six, each one cruising around different parts of the world. Remarkable isn't it? 'The Star' is here in Chicago for a tune up and I asked Sal if I could borrow her for the evening," he said as a wide smile spread across his face.

Rita was impressed. This was a different level of existence. One just like *Keith's*.

"Come on! Let me show you around the ship and introduce you to the crew, especially Franco. I can't wait to see what he is going to cook up tonight, he is a magnificent chef." Michael gave Rita a tour of the incredible ship: the powerful engines, the luxurious staterooms, the immaculate galley. Michael deliberately finished the tour with a visit of the command room, then out onto an overlook that doubled as a sundeck. It was there that their table was set, fine linens, china, hand cut crystal—service suitable for a king.

Sal, after barking out an order in Italian, walked out to meet them. "Rita, how do you like her? She's a beauty isn't she? Michael does good work, yes?" Before she could reply with the obvious answer, Sal interjected. "I'll leave you two alone. After all, I have a ship to run. Enjoy. *Ciao!*"

Rico was waiting with crystal flutes and a bottle of chilled Champagne. He poured some into each of the flutes and then wrapped the bottle in a fine-linen cloth—emblazoned with what Rita presumed was the shipping company's crest. Rico then placed the bottle in the sterling-silver ice bucket near their table. "Your appetizers will be here promptly," Rico said, in perfect English. He promptly bowed slightly, turned, and left them to enjoy the incredible view and the warm Midwestern evening.

Michael, flute in hand, raised it and faced Rita. "To new adventures."

———◦◦◦———

Michael parked his car in front of Rita's apartment, extracted himself and went around to let Rita out. As they stood there under a moonlit sky, Michael hoped for a kiss. So far, the evening was everything he had wanted it to be. Good weather. Great food. Wonderful ambience. Delightful company. He hoped Rita had enjoyed it as much as he had.

Rita startled him. "Michael, I know you want to kiss me. Maybe even spend the night with me. But I'm...I'm not ready. For now, I need to stay...friends. Thank you for a delightful, memorable evening Michael Halloran. You're a wonderful man."

70

Frannie was ready to crawl into bed with Howard after putting their kids to bed. One of them was infected with the latest bug going around their school and required extra time and care to fall asleep. She could tell by the number that flashed on the caller ID that it was Rita calling. Frannie answered the call, "This had better be *real* good. It's way past my bedtime. I was about to snuggle up to my man and start counting sheep."

"Sis, you won't believe what happened tonight! Michael took me out on his friend's yacht. Oh my God Frannie! You should have seen the size of this thing! It must have been two hundred feet long! We had dinner prepared by the ship's chef. Michael knows the whole crew, and...oh Frannie, I'm so confused, I think I've fallen in love with another man!"

"Whoa, whoa, whoa! Slow down Rita. Start from the beginning." Frannie realized very suddenly that her plan to get a good night's sleep was quickly evaporating. "Relatives—you don't choose them and you love them regardless." She thought as she sat down on her sofa and took control of the conversation. "Rita, you've been telling me you've been going out to business lunches with this Michael person. That he's a nice guy. So what changed all of a sudden?"

"I couldn't believe it, but this afternoon he asked me out for a date! We cruised around the lake in this beautiful yacht, up and down the lakefront. What breathtaking views of the city. How beautiful it looks with all the lights, the Navy Pier with the Ferris wheel. The Willis Tower. The Hancock Center. The Aon Tower. The whole skyline. It was like a dream! We had a truly splendid evening."

Then Rita changed the subject. "Frannie, he wants to sleep with me."

"Hold on a minute," Frannie interjected. "What did I just hear you say? You slept with him?"

"No!" Rita replied. "I said he *wants* to sleep with me. At least I'm pretty sure he does. I can't bring myself to do it, though. I can't give up hope for Keith."

71

Michael meticulously reviewed the scale model of the museum's new annex with his team. They were in total agreement: it looked fantastic. The landscape surrounding the annex would gently, almost imperceptibly become one with the structure, creating the illusion that it emerged from the Earth. This was the exact effect they had envisioned just a few short weeks ago.

"You people are *good*," he proclaimed. He removed the roof of the model to expose the inner chambers. "What do you think Sarah," he continued. "Should we remove this wall to expose this chamber to additional ambient light, or do we keep it as is and, maybe pull back the covered roof portion to allow more light in that way?" He seemed to be posing the question to himself rather than Sarah and the rest of the team. "I'm inclined to just take the wall out, or at least drop it down halfway so more light comes in. I do love the way the existing rooflines flow. Sarah, pull up the design on the computer so we can see what it looks like in that configuration."

Sarah brought up the design on the large flat-screen display on the wall and demonstrated how Michael's idea would happen in real-time. The response drew 'ooohs' and 'aaahs' from everyone, including Michael. "That's it! Let's make those changes to the interior and we're good to go. Guys...and gals...you have outdone yourselves again." He was as proud as he had ever been. His team had designed what would be the city's newest landmark structure.

He was so proud he almost cried. "I can't wait to show it to the museum's board of directors. I'm certain they will be very, *very* pleased."

Everyone in the expansive conference room glanced around at each other—the unmistakable look of smug satisfaction affixed on their faces. The entire team agreed the board would indeed be thrilled with their design. However, they knew the real cause of Michael's excitement: he was anxious to show the model to Rita. They all had seen Rita and Michael working closely together for weeks and had seen their bond evolve into something beyond professionalism. They were all happy for their boss. Happy that he was finally breaking down the wall created after the tragic loss of his wife Elizabeth.

Sarah abruptly broke the momentary sound of silence. "Well then, that's an easy enough change to deal with," she said, taking the reins of the meeting. She manipulated the CAD system deftly. "Alright. The changes have been made." She turned her attention to George. "George, I sent you the new specs, take that wall down per the new design and that should do it."

"It'll be ready tomorrow," George retorted.

Sarah leaned over to get very close to Michael. "It's up to you now, boss. Time to work your magic on the board members. Not that it's going to be that tough of a sell, you silver tongued devil."

72

"Keith? It's Michael," he said into his office speakerphone. "When are you coming to Chicago?" Michael was certain it wouldn't be possible for him to take his relationship with Rita to the next level unless Keith held up his side of the bargain. With all of her thoughts and free time devoted to worrying about her doomed lover, any chance of romance between Rita and Michael was similarly doomed.

Michael insisted that Keith stick to the plan. After all, it was Keith's idea to drag him into it. Michael felt that Keith could be a little more accommodating. Sick, dying. No matter. "She's still *hooked* on you man. There isn't anything else I can do right now until you tell her your real condition. She has too much hope for your return to health to think about having a relationship beyond friendship."

So, I ask again, *when are you coming to Chicago?*"

73

George enthusiastically—albeit somewhat unconsciously—gnawed on an large, barbeque sauce-slathered, beef rib that Michael had just pulled off the grill. George felt like he was in rib heaven and likened himself to Fred Flintstone. Ever since Elizabeth had passed, George had been a frequent guest at Michael's home, always finding some reason—excuse—to stop by and raid the refrigerator.

George was a confirmed bachelor. He preferred to lead a mostly solitary life. A simple life with very few personal connections. He had been Halloran and Associates' chief model maker for longer than Michael could remember—arguably one of the world's best.

One of George's weaknesses was good food. Trampling the stereotype of a lifelong bachelor, George had an extremely sophisticated palate. He enjoyed a well-cooked meal as much as anyone could, and it was no small deal to George that Michael was a master in the kitchen and with the grill.

Earlier, while they hovered over a new model for one of their clients, he asked if Michael had any plans for the evening. Michael, caught off-guard by the out-of-the-blue inquiry, replied that he was whipping up a batch of ribs. George, forthwith, invited himself—offered to bring Michael's favorite imported beer. A few hours later, half the beers were gone as were two racks of ribs. The two longtime colleagues were completely satiated as they relaxed in gustatory bliss.

"You know, Michael, I was thinking you should sell Halloran and Associates to me and open a restaurant. Seriously. You've missed your true calling. Damn, you make good barbeque. Smokey, sweet, with a kick of hot. Fall-off-the-bone juicy meat! You know, you really could give those other guys a run for their money." He smacked his still sauce-covered lips in satisfaction.

Since it was just the guys, George made what he felt was an apropos segue. "Hey, speaking of smoky, sweet, and hot, when was the last time you got some sweet and hot? I didn't know that when someone got widowed they were supposed to commit to a life of celibacy. If that's the case, there's one more good reason I'll never get married. *I* couldn't do it, though. The whole celibacy thing. There is no *way* I could go even a month without some kind of action, if you know what I mean. Nudge nudge, wink wink."

George slurped up the last of the coleslaw Michael had prepared. "Tasty. But seriously, Michael. When *was* the last time you got laid?"

"I'm trying, George. Believe me, I'm trying."

74

Blue

Keith, resting on Rita's couch bundled up in thick wool blankets, complained about the chill in the room. Rita's love and patience were being tested. Of course, she was thrilled that Keith came to see her and felt certain his presence meant he was getting better, but the news that his doctors decided to halt his chemotherapy and radiation treatments left her dumbfounded.

He told Rita that his visit to Chicago had upset his doctors. They feared his exposure to so many people on the plane and in the airports presented an unnecessary risk of contracting a germ or virus that would unnecessarily worsen his condition. Even something as harmless as the common cold. But he and Rita decided that if he felt good enough and had the desire to make the journey, he should do it.

This visit had turned out differently than either he or Rita had expected. They realized right away that the flight out had adversely affected Keith's health and spirits. A short walk to the car would quickly deplete his energy. They tried taking a walk together along the lakeshore but he frequently needed to stop and catch his breath. Too frequently, Rita felt. After that, he just didn't feel like going outside at all, even for a stuffed-pizza dinner at his favorite restaurant—just three blocks away.

Rita knew what was happening. He was literally dying right before her eyes. It hurt her to see him suffer. She tried everything she could think of to make him happy. She desperately wished she could get the old Keith back. She thought that sex might make him feel better—motivate him and provide a psychological boost to his psyche. She put on his favorite lingerie, sauntered saucily into her bedroom, did her best Sherazade moves, and tried to arouse him with suggestive talk. Keith genuinely seemed to appreciate her effort, but instead of arousal in his expression, in his eyes, she saw only pain and despair. Teardrops trickled slowly down his cheeks as he sheepishly admitted that he was unable to get an erection. In an effort to show his appreciation, he offered to please her orally.

She cuddled up next to him. "It's going to be all right, sweetheart. Don't you worry. You've always been able to keep me happy with these," she said, touching his lips. "It will come back. Trust me," she whispered in his ear.

After a few brief kisses, and very little fondling—which was quite unlike the rousing foreplay they both normally enjoyed—he kissed his way past her stomach and headed farther south. Something was wrong. He seemed completely detached from the moment. He began kissing her moist vagina and licked her clitoris for a few moments, then abruptly stopped. He looked up at her and shook his head. "I'm sorry. I…just don't have it in me anymore, Rita." Tears began to form again—one trickled down his gaunt face. Utterly dejected—and humiliated—he kissed her on the cheek, curled up in the fetal position, and turned his back on her. "It's so cold in here," he said as he pulled the blankets and comforter over himself. "I'm so sorry. Good night," he mumbled.

He could hear her sobbing but he didn't turn to comfort her. "I shouldn't have come here. This is going to be a long weekend," he thought.

Rita would have been completely satisfied with just some cuddling. Touching. Caressing. Some passionate kissing. But what she couldn't accept was the way Keith literally and figuratively turned his back on her. Shut her out of his life. That he had a lot more going on in his mind than he let on, was obvious to Rita, but she was unable to prod it out of him. He simply clammed up. He selfishly—deliberately, she felt—kept his feelings and what he knew of his health to himself. Rita wondered which was worse, knowing the love of her life was gravely ill or him rejecting her in every way. She felt frustrated and helpless. And alone. Even so, she truly wanted and tried to be selfless, compassionate, and understanding. But, she was in a frenzy of despair and he was challenging her character and resolve.

She contemplated the harsh reality: he was no longer the old Keith. Then she cried herself to sleep.

In the morning, Keith was still in a dour mood on her couch. Still smothered in blankets. Still whined about being too cold. He complained about everything. It seemed Rita could not do anything right. He didn't want to eat anything she prepared. The coffee she made for him was too weak. Nothing she did pleased him. Nothing she said changed his mood in the slightest. Nothing was going right. Indeed everything was going *very* wrong.

Just as she felt that things could not get any worse, she realized that Kathleen was going to come by and drop off some paperwork that needed her approval before Monday. That realization had little time to sink in when the doorbell rang, followed by three quick knocks on the door. "Great timing!" Rita groaned.

The door opened with a grand sweep, and there stood Kathleen. Her shiny black hair pulled back, her skin-tight, metallic-blue tube top and stretch pants clung to her body like Saran Wrap. Her clothing made her look even bigger than she really was. Her enormous cleavage and voluminous rear-end were literally on the verge of bursting out. Her extremely long fingernails were painted in every color of the rainbow. "She is quite a vision," Rita thought. It took every ounce of her diminished patience to stifle a laugh. Then she admitted to herself that she was actually grateful for the comic relief.

"Hi Rita, it's me," Kathleen announced as she barged in the condo. "I would have waited for you to answer the door, but it's *cold* out there and I didn't wear my coat. The door was unlocked, so I figured, what the hell. You know Rita you really should lock that thing. Even though you live in a nice 'hood and all. You never know sugar. You have to be careful these days."

Keith shot an angry scowl at Rita. He had repeatedly told Rita how much he worried over her safety, even with Simon out of the picture, and it angered him that she was so careless. Rita noticed Keith's expression and her cheeks flushed with embarrassment—not only for herself, but for Keith as well. She quickly diverted attention to Kathleen.

Kathleen saw Keith covered in blankets on the couch. "Whoops! I am *so* sorry you guys! I hope I didn't interrupt anything. Hi Keith. I forgot you were gonna' be in town this weekend. Otherwise, you know, I would have waited to come in…after knocking. Rita did tell me. Oh damn, do I feel pretty foolish right now. I'll drop off this stuff and be on my way. Here you go, sugar."

Kathleen handed the stack of papers to Rita, headed toward the door, opened it, and gave Rita a quick glance—a hangdog smile on her round face. "I'm really sorry you guys. Take care, Keith. See you later, Rita!"

She quietly and quickly removed herself from Rita's apartment. "What a stupid thing to do. Barge in on them like that," she bullied herself. "Lordy, lordy, it was tense in there. I wonder what the hell was going on."

75

From the moment Keith stepped off the plane at Chicago's O'Hare International Airport, the trip had been one catastrophe after another. Keith concluded he wasn't going to tell Rita the doctors' final analysis: he had very little time left, there were no more treatments, there were no last ditch efforts to stave off the inevitable. So, as far as he was concerned, he really had nothing to say to her. Yes, he had been reclusive. Showed no joy in being with her. Moped on the couch the entire time he was there. Expressed no affection. But what else was he to do?

She made plans for them to go to a play. He nixed it. She tempted him with dinner at his favorite pizza joint. He scratched that. She pampered him with affection. He rejected it. She wanted to have sex. He cast off her advances.

As Keith left her at the airport's departure curb, he held her briefly and gave her a peck on the cheek. "I love you," he said dispassionately. And then he lumbered slowly into the terminal.

He reminisced about the weekend's events and determined that he had been a selfish, insensitive bastard.

76

Kathleen could not *not* see it. Rita's usual, infectious bounce was gone. A disingenuous, strained grin had taken the place of her normally infectious, delightful smile. The sparkle was missing from her eyes. They no longer twinkled. It didn't take Kathleen long to place the blame for Rita's pensiveness exactly where it belonged: on Keith.

Although Rita was often depressed after Keith's treatment days, her current disposition was distinctly different. Usually by midweek, interacting with everyone and the day-to-day bustle at the museum would bring her back into true form. Not this time. This time, Rita tried to forcefully divorce herself from her personal problems, but it was not working. She was uncharacteristically curt with everyone. It was all so very *unlike* Rita.

Well-intentioned Kathleen wanted to let Rita know that everyone was well aware that something was wrong, but she avoided confronting Rita until the end of the day. She bit her tongue as she watched Rita have a meltdown in plain sight of members and visitors.

It had been an extremely busy day at the museum, but even that had not helped lift Rita's spirits. As Kathleen and Rita tallied up the day's receipts, Kathleen was not able to hold it in a moment longer. She spoke up abruptly, "Ok sugar, I'd eat worms to hear what's goin' on between you and Keith. For two days now, I've avoided askin'. I'm tellin' you, it's been hard as hell. You've been aloof and testy with members, visitors, and everyone here in the office. Someone has to say something, and that someone is me. What's wrong, Rita? It's about Keith, right? It has to be. How did your weekend go? How's he doing? I'm *so* embarrassed that I burst in on you guys. I remembered that you said he was coming to see you, but I forgot it was last weekend. Come on, tell big sista' Kathleen what's goin' on with you. I know no one else has told you this, but you've looked like shit the last coupl'a days. And you've been...a bitch. We've all noticed. Did you really think we wouldn't have?

"The old Rita gone missing in action? Yes, it's not just me. I'm the one who got picked to ask the questions. Believe me, I didn't want to. But seriously, we all *know* that something is *wrong* with you, and just want to know if there is anything we can do to help. I'm sorry for prying, and you don't have to tell me anything right now. But we care 'bout you sugar. Each and every one of us."

Rita stared at Kathleen. She felt awkward. Uneasy. "I don't know what to say, Kathleen. I'm angry with Keith for shutting me out. Not communicating with me, not touching me like he normally does. I keep asking myself, 'why'? 'Why is he kicking me out of his life?' He knows I love him. Is there something terrible happening to him that he doesn't want me to know about? All I'm left to do is to connect the dots on my own, which leads me to thinking the worst, and that's driving me crazy."

Suddenly, the obvious answer became obvious. She buried her face in her hands and wept. "I...I guess I just answered my own question, Kathleen." She sobbed, not caring that tears, mixed with her mascara, were now streaming down her creamy white cheeks.

Kathleen gently wrapped her arms around Rita. She encouraged Rita to let it all out. She knew a good cry was God's tincture for a disconsolate soul.

77

"Hi darling," Rita spoke into the phone. She knew it would be Keith—felt it had his ring to it.

"Hi Sweetheart. How was work today?" Keith asked, trying to sound upbeat. He had to fake it because his day had been particularly bad caused by his afternoon session with his physical therapist. His doctors insisted that he maintain a rigorous physical regimen while he still had mobility and energy.

Right from the start of his physical therapy sessions, Keith decided to give his therapist the nickname 'Attila'. He likened her to the infamous conqueror of Asia. It had come down to that or Nurse Ratched. Either choice was entirely appropriate. Suzie 'Attila' Sheehan, CPT, cheerfully bullied Keith, sadistically maneuvered and manipulated his emaciated body, forced him to do exercises she was certain he would dismiss unless she was present. She made it her top priority that he do the strenuous, painful exercises on her watch. After his sessions, he usually told Attila that he felt like he had been run through a meat grinder or otherwise let her know that his therapy made him exhausted and feel ill. She customarily thanked him for the compliment, with an undeniably evil smile on her face. She enjoyed her work immensely.

Lately, with everything that had transpired, Rita had difficulty deciphering her feelings—she couldn't decide if she was angry with Keith or worried sick about him. With the exception of a courtesy call to let her know he had made it back to California safely, Keith had not called for a week since his weekend visit to Chicago. And he had not responded to her repeated voicemail messages. She was extremely distraught and worried that something had happened to him.

She recalled how she had tried everything in her power to make their weekend memorable, but Keith quashed all of her attempts. He looked terrible and told her that he felt the way he looked. She could not get over that way he pushed her away—rejected her. She let him know she didn't like being treated that way by him. He was no longer the old Keith. The one she had fallen in love with that day in Boston, which now seemed so very long ago.

⎯⎯⎯◦◦◦⎯⎯⎯

"How did Attila treat you today?" she asked. She intended to let Keith control their conversation, since she truly didn't know what to say to him. She struggled with reality. Their relationship had never been strained—constrained—before. They had never had an argument, quarrel, or even the slightest tiff.

"Yeah, she beat me up pretty good today," he growled.

"How about your nutritionist, what did she have to say?"

"She wasn't a happy camper."

"Why?"

"I've lost more weight."

"How much?"

"Five more pounds."

"So you weigh how much now?"

"A hundred and thirty-five pounds."

She paused, wiped a teardrop away, and continued, "What's going on Keith? Tell me damn it!"

Keith was unable to tell Rita to her face—had literally his back on her over the weekend—but he *could* tell her on the phone. That way he would not be able to see her cry. He hated to make her cry unless it was for joy. But he didn't have any of that salve to spread today. "I didn't know how to tell you when I was there... but, um, the doctors...the doctors don't give me very long," he said somberly. Then he just let the truth stream out. "I've already made the plans for my cremation. Gotten a great hospice to arrange everything. They're the best. They've taken care of me way beyond my expectations. I'm not the easiest patient to deal with," he said with a forced chuckle. "Actually, as *you* know, I'm a real pain in the ass." He waited in silence for her reaction. He knew what to expect and deserved whatever came out of the receiver.

"Keith...why didn't you *tell* me?" she demanded, her emotions red lined. "Damn you for not respecting my feelings! Treating me like a child! You didn't think I could handle it? Is that *right*?" She instantly felt remorse. Her anger quickly evaporated with his revelation that he would no longer be a part of her life. And that he was going to die.

"I'm so sorry, my love," she continued. "I can't imagine what it's like to be in your place, but can't you understand how *I* feel? Being left out. Ignored. Having to figure this out by myself? I had already put two and two together, but you never confirmed it... until now," she sobbed. Rita was devastated, but regardless, she felt she had to probe. "Don't the doctors have *any* good news, any treatments that will help? *Anything*?" Rita was now grasping at the very same straws he had just a few short months before.

As he listened to her, he relived that agony all over again. But this time it was worse. "No, they don't. We just didn't catch it in time. I apologize for not telling you sooner. I...I didn't have the balls to tell you. I've turned into a real chicken shit. I'm such a loser that I didn't have the nerve to tell you goodbye to your face. I know it's hard for you to understand, but I don't want to see you again. My family doesn't even know how bad things are, so don't feel like you're being singled out. I want to die in solitude. I've built a wall around my emotions and want every brick to stat intact. All that's left is darkness and I don't feel like sharing that. This is the worst thing I've ever had to do in my life Rita, but...this is the end of our relationship. The end of me."

Rita refused to believe Keith would leave her this way. "I want to come out and be with you," she pleaded. "I can be there right away, I have vacation time. It's no problem." She *had* to see him again now that her fears had become reality. She frantically searched for rationalization. Surely, he needed her there. No one wanted to die alone.

"No Rita! I want to die *alone*. It's something I believe a person should do in their own way. I don't want you here. It sounds harsh. It is harsh. But it's the way I feel about my death. It's personal for me. I hope that you can respect that."

Rita bit back. "Respect? What about respect for my feelings. Don't my feelings count too?"

"I love you with all my heart, but I'm sorry Rita, this is goodbye." He hung up the phone and cried. "Fucking cancer."

78

Hope

The final mockup of the proposed annex was in the museum's conference room. Everyone who gathered around was amazed. The mockup flowed from the terrain's natural contours and spanned into the cavernous atrium where the museum's new exhibits would be housed.

———>•<———

The Museum of Science and Industry had a longstanding reputation as an avant-garde institution, but the new annex project was going to put it at the forefront of the world's architectural structures.

The annex would be the first building in Chicago to exceed the U.S. Green Building Council's LEED Platinum rating, ranking it as one of the most eco-friendly structures on the planet. It was an achievement from which all other buildings would now be rightfully gauged. It would be completely self-sustaining. All of the energy- and water-system requirements for the vast expanse—automated exhibits, electrical-, pneumatic-, hydraulic-, and HVAC-systems—would self-powered by a cutting-edge photo-voltaic solar-energy system embedded into the building's windows. Every drop of water consumed and used, would be from reprocessed rainwater. In the event of overload conditions, all of these systems would be powered by a rechargeable silicon-based lithium-ion battery dubbed the 'Bloom Box'. The new annex truly was a modern marvel.

———⟫●⟪———

Betty Forsyth, astonished by the presentation, wrapped up her speech. "Mr. Halloran, and team, you have really outdone yourselves. The fact that you've completed this incredible design in such a short period of time is astounding. I commend each and every one of you for your efforts. Frankly, I don't see any issues that should delay a vote on this project. Make that a formal comment, Carol," she said to her administrative assistant, who was recording the meeting minutes. "Do I have a second for the motion to accept the design?"

"Seconded," Alex chimed in.

"Do we need to do this by secret ballot?" Betty asked.

Heads shook side to side.

"All right then, all in favor of adopting the Halloran and Associates design for the new annex, say aye."

It was unanimous.

"Good, it's settled then."

With no additional new business, the meeting adjourned.

79

Sarah, George, Michael, Betty, Correy, Rita, and Eddie were waiting for the elevator to hurl them fifty stories below to the mass of humanity assembled onto the streets of Chicago.

"Why don't you all come over to my house for a celebration? I'm cooking," Michael asked.

Everyone, except Rita, hastily agreed. Michael noticed the lack of response from Rita. He hoped she would accept his invitation. His desire to win Rita's heart grew stronger. Not because of his pact with Keith, but rather for his wish to be a part of her life. He had fallen in love. Again. Something he didn't think possible. Life with Elizabeth had meant everything. His recovery had been difficult, but over the last couple of months, had felt the icy tomb of his heart begin to melt away.

When the elevator door opened, it was half-full—just enough room in the car for five people. Michael went into managerial mode. "Hey guys, I've got to stop off at the market and pick up some things, but you all go over to the house. Sarah, you have the security combination. Grab a couple of bottles of Dom' and a couple of bottles of wine out of the cellar that will go with surf and turf. You know what everyone likes. George, Correy, help yourself to whatever's in the bar, you know where everything is. I'll get a cab for you all after dinner. Betty, call your husband and tell him to come over if he can break away. Eddie, call your wife and tell her I'm cooking tonight, have her get a babysitter for the kids, on me, and tell her to get over there. Pronto." The unwitting participants of

Michael's last-minute scheme enthusiastically boarded the elevator, and left Michael and Rita alone.

"That went well," Michael said matter-of-factly.

"I'd say so," Rita shot back. She had a strange feeling that his comment was directed at himself. "You do put on a good show," she said, getting back to business. "To think that the building can really transform itself with all those maneuvers, it seems almost *human*, or at least robotic...which I suppose it is. All the exhibits with ample facilities for anything our heart's desire. It's just remarkable."

"Without my team, none of this would have been possible, I'm not *that* talented," he chuckled. "Their combined talent and individual creativity consistently astounds me. Not only are they quite competent at what they do, but when they get hooked on a project and you tell them to let their creative juices flow, they go...bananas. All I do is put the plans into motion and everyone else does all the work. You heard them, they only use me as the mouthpiece," he joked and then laughed.

She joined him. "It's true, you are a smooth operator."

Michael got right to the point. "I noticed you didn't agree to join us. You *are* coming over aren't you?" he asked with a hint of pleading and desperation in his voice. "Come on, let me make you dinner. It's a night to celebrate. I really love to unwind and talk over the day's events while cooking. I don't know if I told you, but I'm something of a homebody. I like to attend social functions, but I'm really a very private guy. I prefer to be at home. That probably surprises you, seeing me in public, outgoing person that I am, but my home is my castle. And I can relax there."

Rita couldn't think of a reason to say 'no'. It *was* a special day for Michael—for all of them. This occasion *should* be celebrated. "Besides," she thought, "he deserves it."

The elevator door opened. The car was empty.

"Everyone else seemed to be enthusiastic about your dinner invitation," Rita said, as he held the doors for her.

"Oh yeah, they've all been to my place before, many times, raiding my liquor cabinet, wine cellar, and refrigerator with gusto.

Nothing makes me happier than to see people enjoy my cooking and my home. Oh, speaking of that, I'd better pick up another bottle of Glen Livet, George's favorite. I haven't had a large group over in a while. Normally I'm pretty stocked up with the essentials. *So*...are you coming over?" he asked, feeling a *long* forgotten urge.

"Hell, why not?" she thought. "It's just a party with a new set of friends." After making him wait just a bit longer, she replied. "Sure. How do I get there?"

Determined to ensure a favorable outcome, he said, "You're going with me! It would take you too long to get there by public transportation or taxi."

80

The rest of the week raced by with no word from Rita. She had not returned his calls or voicemails. It seemed very unlike her. Michael began to worry that maybe he had pushed their relationship a little too far—a little too fast.

He completed his daily debriefing with Keith, but this time there was no news. Both men were frustrated at the pace—or lack of—Michael's progress. Neither of them were able to figure out what was going on in Rita's mind.

It was obvious to Michael that Keith might be dead at any moment. Once again, he asked Keith to reconsider his plan to be alone to the end, and to reminded him that Rita's feelings were important—that she desperately wanted to go to LA to be with him until the end. Keith rejected the idea, but Michael wouldn't take no for an answer. Not this time. He took advantage of Keith's lack of energy and resolve, and browbeat him into submission.

"Damn it, Keith, she needs to have closure! Stop being so fucking selfish!"

"You're right Michael. You're the second person to express that same sentiment today. The first was my mother. Not quite in those words, but the same sentiment. Now there's a particularly scary and delightful thought. You and my mother in agreement. You two should meet someday. You would get along great with my parents. You have a lot in common with them. Maybe one day. Ok. I know I've been insensitive, even selfish. I'll call Rita and ask her if she still wants to come here. It should be soon. Very soon."

81

Saying Goodbye

When Keith called to say that he had changed his mind, Rita was immediately thrilled. Then just as quickly, saddened. She knew how the trip would end. Keith apologized again for being selfish and asked for her forgiveness. Rita with a curiously flat intonation informed him that she would be on the next available plane bound for LAX.

When she arrived at Keith's hospital room, she found him asleep—attached to a myriad of tubes and wires. He was as white as the sterile sheets he laid on, his veins eerily visible through his nearly translucent skin.

Ralph and Wanda were there. Rita briskly, but warmly greeted them, then immediately took one of Keith's ice-cold hands in hers. "I love you," she whispered.

He opened his eyes. She leaned down and gently kissed him on the lips. Her lips warm, moist. His cold. He forced a smile. "I love you too," he whispered back. Keith turned to his parents. He asked flatly, "Mom, dad, can I have a little time with Rita please?"

"Of course son, we'll see you in the morning," Wanda replied.

Turning her eyes towards Ralph, then back to Keith, she grinned. "Besides, I need to feed your father. I can tell his blood sugar is getting low."

Rita released Keith's hands as his parents approached him. Wanda was first. She bent down to her son, caressed his barren head softly, they very same way she did when he was a young boy and had a head full of hair. She cradled his face with her hands. "I love you," she said, remaining stoic even though her tear ducts were starting to involuntarily activate.

Ralph didn't hurry Wanda. He didn't think his son would make it through the night. This wasn't Ralph's first rodeo. He knew death's march and he was not going to stop Wanda from being with one of her boys as he lay moribund. When she was done, she would let him know.

Wanda kissed her son knowing it was to be the last. It was not Wanda's first rodeo either. It was not supposed to be like this. What do you say to your son knowing it will be the last time he will hear your voice? "I love you, Keith. Sleep well. See you in the morning."

Wanda gave Ralph a teary-eyed glance—the sign he patiently waited for. It was his turn. Ralph duplicated Wanda's act of caressing Keith's bald head, held his face, and kissed his forehead. "Get some rest, son. See you tomorrow. Love you."

Ralph looked at Rita, tears welling in his eyes. Rita wanted everyone's attention. "Keith, may I have a word with your parents before they leave?"

"Sure," Keith croaked.

After receiving an obvious non-verbal cue, Ralph and Wanda followed Rita into the hallway. Once there, Wanda wiped a tear from her cheek and sniffed. "We're so glad Keith called you. So glad you came while there's still time. I told him it wasn't fair to shut all of us out, even if we can't do a damn thing. That he mustn't do that to the people who care about him. That it was a selfish, unforgivable act. After I scolded him, I cried, seeing my baby like that. I tried to stop but couldn't. Maybe I wouldn't have reacted that way if I would have seen him sooner, saw his regression as it was happening. I don't know. But I know he hates to see me cry."

Wanda clutched Rita's and Ralph's hands and brought them all together as one. "Rita, you are family. Don't ever forget that. Ralph and I know how important you are to Keith. Don't be confused or hurt by how poorly he's treated you lately. He loves you. All he ever did was gush over every little thing you did. He never did that with anyone else. Really." She wiped another tear from her cheek. "How long are you going to be in town?" she asked, lips quivering.

"I have some vacation time. Thought I'd spend it here, where he needs me, where I belong," her voice trailed away uneasily. "I already checked into a hotel just a few blocks away." Rita was barely able to keep the fabric of her emotions from completely unraveling. Tried to be a rock. She could breakdown later.

"Dear child. You do realize he won't be here that long. The doctors say it's going to happen very soon. Ralph and I have spent the last few days here and we can tell they're right. They were nice enough to let us have a couple of cots for his room, but they're hard and uncomfortable. Ralph's back has been acting up something fierce. We need to get some real rest, but we'll back first thing in the morning. We'll see you then, Rita. Goodbye sweetie."

Wanda concluded the solemn gathering by bringing the three of them together again in a group hug, kissed Rita on the cheek. "We love you, Rita. We *do*. And if you like you can stay with us instead of all alone in that hotel room. Don't hesitate to call. You have our number. You're *always* more than welcome in our home." Ralph and Wanda turned and walked down the too-bright corridor, Ralph held Wanda close. Her arm around his waist. It was difficult to tell who was comforting whom.

Rita returned to Keith's bed. He opened his eyes once again. "I'm so sorry...for shutting you out. I was so scared and unable to deal with the situation myself. That I couldn't understand that someone else...could deal with it better than I could," he muttered in an uninflected monotone voice. His breath was short. Sentences broken. "I finally came to...my wits...and determined that I had to...had to tell you something...before I...go." Keith was very frail now. Completely spent from thinking. Speaking. But he had something important to tell her. Before it was too late. "Rita. My darling, sweet Rita...you need to find someone to take...my...my place. You *need* someone in your life." He coughed. "You're so very special." Keith sobbed. The obtrusive, ominous tubes that surrounded Keith jiggled and twisted with his convulsions.

Rita crawled into his sterile bed and snuggled against Keith's cold body. The warmth of her hers transferred to his, albeit quite imperceptibly to him. Her touch instantly calmed his spasms. Soothed him. Comforted him.

"Oh how much I've missed your embrace. What a fool I've been," he whispered.

"Keith, I need to tell you a something as well. My life...changed that day you came into the New England Aquarium. You taught me how to trust again after my marriage to Simon failed. I learned what loving someone truly means, and how wonderful it feels to be loved in return. Please know that *my* life has been better for having had *you* in it. I love you Keith. I always will."

Tears flowed down Keith's face as his breathing slowed. "I love you so much. I'll always be with you," his voice barely audible.

Keith faded off to a morphine-induced sleep. His pain numbed. His body relaxed. Quietly, anonymously, discretely, Keith shrugged off his mortal coil.

Rita, curled up next to him, envisioned the wonderful memories they had shared at the very moment Keith passed from this life into the next. She heard—felt—his last breath.

His internal organs were in final descent and his fibrillations abruptly ceased. His life sign monitors wailed. An ominous indication that another life had gone. Nurses rushed into the room. After a few minutes, the doctors pronounced him dead.

Rita took a last look at Keith, left the hospital, and went back to her hotel.

—————⟫●⟪—————

Rita sat in the darkness of her hotel room—drapes shut. Used tissues littered the floor next to the bed. She needed to talk to someone. She was falling. She dialed the phone. It rang three times. She heard the other end pick up.

"Michael, can you come to California? I need you."

82

A New Beginning

Keith's lawyer arranged to meet Rita for lunch at Lou's On Clark where he told her of her inheritance. She looked at him as if he was speaking an ancient, dead language. It took several minutes for her to comprehend the magnitude of her sudden affluence. It took several more minutes for her to wrap her mind around the number of zeroes she could now write on a check.

—————◆————

The naysayers said it would be impossible to build it on schedule—there were too many obstacles. But their negativity was no match for the tenacity, dedication, and drive of the annex project's team members.

From the start, everything moved at breakneck speed. The plans for the new annex had been submitted to the City of Chicago for approval—where normally they would have been mired in bureaucracy for months, just for the permits for water, power, and sewage alone. However, the new annex needed no additional services from the city. The annex would be completely self-sustaining.

The Building Commission had never seen plans like these before. The new annex would be net- and service-neutral and integrated into the museum's main systems—it would actually *reduce* the consumption of electricity, water, and other services for the entire museum. In fact, the museum had been a beacon of energy efficiency and reduced/reused water consumption for years, largely due to no-flow urinals, low-flow toilet and water faucet sensors, and ultra-efficient electric hand dryers. But those were just the part that the public saw—there were many other such processes deployed by the museum to 'walk the green walk'. The museum's forward thinking adaptations lead the community by example. After all, community outreach and involvement was a key component of the museum's mission statement.

Rita delegated a team to put pressure on the local politicos in order to cut through the red tape and allow the museum to lead the way, unhindered, to a greener future.

The construction crews were ready, and ground would be broken in weeks, not months. The shell could be erected before winter arrived and the interior ready for public display by the Memorial Day weekend.

It was a lofty objective—but wasn't the only incredible feat of engineering that the museum had concocted and accomplished. As far as the board and staff of the museum were concerned, challenges and questions were to be met head on. It was not in their collective nature to shy away from challenges, even those that seemed impossible.

Rita's 'green' media blitzkrieg exposed the weaknesses of the city's bureaucracy. It addressed such forward thinking ideas as reusing gray water for toilets and the use of microbial fuel cells on human waste to create biofuel. Her marketing campaign, which was specifically designed to educate and inform the public—to reach out to the entire Chicagoland area. It was time to get everyone involved and on the same page to make the new annex a reality.

Saturating the airwaves, radio and video, her campaign received airtime on every hip-hop, country-and-western, rock-and-roll, heavy-metal, classical, techno-pop, and news radio station within one-hundred miles of Chicago. She arranged interviews for Jake Cutter on the TV: WLS, WBBM, WGN, WFLD. The print media—The Tribune, The Sun-Times, The Red Eye, The Onion—were not exempt from her info-barrage.

The press conference took place on the magnificent concrete stairs of the Chicago Museum of Science and Industry. After the media outlets witnessed Halloran and Associates' presentation of the new annex, cameras whirred, pens skirted across notepads, and fingers genuflected on smart phones and tablets. A local pundit known for throwing the proverbial monkey wrench into the mix— the gotcha question—asked about the costs for the annex and the potential ramifications of these costs on the city's already thinly stretched budget. It was always about the money.

Jake Cutter confidently fielded the troublemaker's inquiry. Jake's ruddy, weathered face broadened, accentuating his well-etched wrinkles. "Ladies and gentleman, that *is* the question, isn't it. 'How much will this amazing addition cost?'. The answer is $150,000,000." Murmurs ensued. "But, the *bigger* question is, 'what will it cost the museum, its patrons, and the public in the long run?'. The answer to that question, ladies and gentlemen, is…" he paused for effect, "not one damn cent!" Jake let the words hang in the air for several moments. His flair for the dramatic had achieved the desired outcome. Puzzlement and incredulity spread across the faces of everyone in the gallery. They were all trying to figure out if what they *thought* they heard was what they actually *had* heard.

"Good." he continued, captive audience at hand. "By the way you're all staring at me right now, I can tell you were paying attention. The fact is that the Museum of Science and Industry received an anonymous donation for $200,000,000 to fund this expansion from here into perpetuity. The donation will cover the initial construction costs, and the extra $50,000,000 will be used to fund lifetime maintenance and future expansion of a new ecological-based research laboratory, which will be built and operated in conjunction with every university in the great state of Illinois."

"This," he turned to face the museum, arms spread out like Moses parting the Red Sea, "is a *gift*."

Rita and Michael stood to the left of Jake, his hand in hers. Rita affectionately squeezed Michael's hand as word of the donation spread through the large crowd.

Rita was in Jake's office as he railed about how the bureaucrats had stalled the approval of the funding. How they repeatedly brought up the terrible state of the economy as an excuse not to approve the expenditures.

Carlita interrupted the meeting—a lawyer was in the atrium and requested a meeting with Jake. Carlita told Jake that the lawyer insisted he was there on urgent business of the utmost importance. She handed Jake the lawyer's business card. While Carlita waited for her instructions, Jake read the business card aloud for Rita to hear. "James Miller, Attorney at Jenner and Block. Hmmm, I know those guys, big firm headquartered right here in Chicago. Let's see what he has to say. Send him in Carlita."

When James Miller came into the room, Rita got up to excuse herself, but Jake insisted that she stay. "How important can what Mr. Miller have to say that you shouldn't hear it firsthand? Sit. Stay."

Jake gestured for the well-dressed attorney to have a seat at his expansive conference table. "What can I do for you, Mr. Miller?" Jake asked, with more than a hint of curiosity in his voice. Jake hated interruptions. He was anxious to find out exactly why this attorney was here, and wondered what he could possibly have to say that was so important he couldn't make an appointment like everyone else.

When James Miller, still in his first year of practice at the prestigious Jenner and Block law firm, received this assignment, he was delighted. How he had been chosen was anyone's guess. Rookies didn't normally get a chance to deal with such important duties.

James, wearing the requisite Brooks Brothers suit, was as calm on the inside as he appeared to be on the outside. He frequently bragged to his colleagues that 'Confidence' was his middle name. "Mr. Cutter, I have some great news for the museum. On behalf of an anonymous donor, it is my pleasure to give this check to the Museum of Science and Industry." He slid some papers across the table—a cashier's check and two addendums. Jake looked at the check then at the sheets of paper. His raised eyebrows indicated confusion. James continued, "The two documents describe in detail how the money is to be utilized, and also serves as proof that I've faithfully performed my duty in transferring possession of the check to you. Please sign both documents. I'll do the same and keep one of them for our records."

Jake looked at Rita, then back at James. "Is this for real?" he asked.

"Yes, Mr. Cutter. I can assure you it is *very* real," James grinned.

Jake looked back at Rita. "You're not going to believe this," he said and slid the check across the expensive table to her.

She knew she had to play it cool—no one knew, yet, of her newfound wealth. The only story the media had was that hundreds of millions of dollars were being funneled into various charities, all managed by S and K Enterprises' co-founder Sammy Tagaki. She reached over, held the check close to her face, and pretended to scan it. Of course, she didn't have to—she knew precisely the amount listed on the check, but she needed to play out the charade convincingly.

"Well, this should certainly speed things along," she deadpanned. Her eyes twinkled.

———————

Rita had planned to make the donation for some time, but she was waiting for a favorable moment. Keith's lawyer in L.A. explained to her that the best way throw the media off track would be to have a firm in Chicago deliver the cashier's check along with the fiduciary stipulations.

Irrespective of her good fortune, she planned to lead a normal life. She would take care of her mom and dad, just like Keith had done for his parents. Their house was free and clear, but they *were* getting up there in years. Her family wouldn't need anything from anyone ever again.

She decided to continue to live in her tiny apartment. She would not splurge on anything lavish—that was not her style. She didn't need a car, so there was no need to buy one. She asked Michael to set up a meeting with Sal Vittorio for investment advice.

———⟶●⟵———

The donation put a halt to the bickering among the city's leaders—the plans for the annex were fast-tracked.

The excavation completed, eco-friendly concrete slab poured, recycled steel and lumber assembled, and infrastructure in place, all of the mechanisms were tested and retested, construction finally commenced. Project coordination was imperative. Morning and night the workers—electricians, masons, engineers, laborers, and thousands of volunteers—toiled, shedding gallons of sweat-equity. The crews were oblivious to the passage of time, and were relentless in their objective: to complete the new annex on time and on budget. They were determined to prove it could be done—that they were the ones that could get it done.

The naysayers lost the battle of the budget concerns, but took some measure of satisfaction in the notion that it would be impossible to complete the annex on schedule. All doubts were quashed when the board members formally announced that the new annex would be completed *ahead* of schedule. They proudly proclaimed that the project would be completed *under* budget and that most of the new exhibits were already being installed.

———⟶●⟵———

At the new annex opening ceremony preparation meeting, Rita suggested that they not only display the exhibits during the opening ceremony, but also show how they work, behind the scenes. A once in a lifetime viewing experience.

83

New Wrinkles

When Simon removed Joey's wallet off his charred corpse, he knew a few key facts about his deckhand friend: he was an only child, he was from the Chicagoland area, both his parents were dead, he had no one waiting for him back home.

What Simon didn't know was that Joey's pea coat pocket had over $5,000, an American Express Platinum card, and his passport. There were only two problems now: how to get out of Hong Kong, how to get back to the United States to assume Joey's identity.

He also knew that he was now a fugitive, as Simon *or* Joey. And he knew that the Hong Kong P.D. would be after him, if for nothing more than as a material witness. So, Simon holed up in a seedy hotel in Kowloon. He paid for the room with cash and waited for the storm to pass. He spoke no useful Chinese and knew he couldn't just hop on a plane—HKPD would probably stop him before he could board. Somehow, he had to get back to the States on a ship. "But how?"

Simon assumed that his face was on posters placed around the docks and passed around Hong Kong. But, he was tired and bored of waiting for time to pass in his hotel room, and being in Kowloon made him feel claustrophobic. He thought about heading over to Macau and trying his luck in one of the casinos. But quickly nixed that idea after he recalled his luck with Pai Gow. He finally decided to go down to the docks, incognito, and find out if indeed he was an infamous man. It had been almost two months since the deadly incident. He hoped that the case had already been forgotten—was old news.

Simon skulked around the harbor trying to come up with a plan to hitch a ride on a ship bound for the U.S. He was feeling thirsty and spotted a bar, and thought he might find someone inside who spoke English. An American, Canadian, or a Brit would be perfect. Even a local bartender would do, since so many foreigners came and went from the port, many of the restaurant and bar workers would undoubtedly speak a little English.

As he meandered through the crowded bar, he saw some men, who sounded Canadian, sitting around a table covered with empty beer mugs. He ordered a shot and a beer, and took a seat at a table close enough to the Canadians' table to hear their conversation. A humungous man who was talking over the din mentioned that they were going to be returning to Nova Scotia in two days. Another one of the men complained about the lack of workers to load the cargo. He was irritated that this would cause a delay in their departure and talked about how much it cost the shipping company each day they remained in Kowloon Bay.

Simon casually pulled his chair over to their table. "Hi," he said. "Can I buy you guys a round?"

<hr />

"A *week*?" Michael bellowed. "That's all the time I've got to get the ring to California? A *week*? You couldn't have told me sooner?" Michael asked. "Surely, I can have a little more time, Sammy."

Sammy knew this news was not going to elicit a warm response from Michael. He had no other choice. "No Michael, I couldn't and you can't. I got the call less than thirty minutes ago. It took me that long to find your number."

Michael couldn't believe what he was hearing. He hoped this was a prank. The timing couldn't have been worse. The opening ceremony for the new annex would begin in less than three hours.

He had to pick up Rita in two hours and he had four hours of work left to do.

"All right, Sammy. I'm sorry for snapping at you. I know you're just the messenger."

84

A New Start

The opening ceremony of the museum's new annex was a must-go-to and be-seen-at affair. Everyone who was *anyone* was there: dignitaries, politicians, celebrities. The museum's board members and staff proudly did their part as ambassadors of good will and ensured everyone in attendance had the time of their lives. '*Ooohs*' and '*aaahs*' permeated through the halls. The attendees mulled about and drank Champagne. Astounded by the new annex, everyone gleefully celebrated and admired the exhibits.

Michael and Rita held hands and stared out at the crowd. They sipped Champagne and wondered what was going to happen next.